BILL THE BIKER

An Odyssey

by

J.R. Waterbear

First publication: March 2016

2nd Edition: June 2026

“In the beginning was darkness. Then Bill moved, and his shadow no longer blocked the light.”

—from the Book of Bill

CHAPTER ONE

Room J, Alpaca Motel, Ball, California, July 31st, 2010

He was a man of few words, and those words were usually "Fuck you." He had a chipped front tooth and when he smiled small children and dogs ran away. When he laughed, he displayed all seven of the lovingly-maintained teeth that he brushed at least once a week.

He was named Bill. No one had called him William since he was nine years old. The only person he had allowed to call him William was his crusty maternal grandfather, and then only after a boot to the face.

The saddest day of his life was when Grandpa was mangled by a harvester. What Adolf Butcher was doing in a Pennsylvania wheat field was a mystery, since he lived in Brooklyn.

The farmer said his last words were: "Keep that goddamn thing away from me." He was forty-six. The only part of Grandpa to survive was his kicking boot. Bill kept it in his saddlebag.

Bill had a dream that someday he would be at a ball and slip it on the foot of a beautiful woman. Several attempts at ZZ Top concerts, however, had ended in pain and embarrassment for all concerned.

His longest relationship was his current one - two days and three nights, so far, with Nellie Florentino. She was a value-sized female whose mountainous thighs spread deliciously across the saddle of his Harley. She said exercise was for pussies and called a belly laugh "internal jogging."

The boot hadn't fit but he kept thinking one day her foot might shrink. Besides, he'd woken up chained to the bed during the Ballmeister motorcycle rally and decided to just go with it.

Now, however, he was having second thoughts as she twisted the barrel of the antique Colt Peacemaker in his cavernous nostril.

"Honey, I have to pee. Can we discuss this later?" he snuffled.

Her tangled, fire engine-red hair fell across her furrowed brow like the pelt of an enraged yak.

"Where were you last night?" she asked. Her gritted teeth looked a bit like a harvester, Bill thought.

"What the hell?" he said. "I was here, with you. In bed."

"You lying sack of ... LIES!" she screamed and cocked the trigger.

"Honest to God, Sweetie. We did it twice."

She did not look convinced.

"We broke the bed," he said desperately.

There was a rustling under the sheets, then the click of the Colt's hammer being gently released. The barrel slid out of his nose.

"Oh yeah," she said. "That's a bed slat poking up, isn't it? No wonder I was getting splinters. My memory sucks today. That damned Freddy must have cut my snow with rat poison again."

"Yeah, you gotta find a new supplier."

"Naw, I'm quittin'"

Nellie shoved the gun, barrel-first, between her Everest-sized breasts, where it nestled like a hobo cooping between two haystacks.

"Snowball, I really gotta pee," Bill said. "Bad."

And at that vulnerable moment, his beloved of two days unleashed a bladder-crushing spasm of internal jogging. It got ugly after that.

The sound of shattering glass woke Bill a second time. He scraped funk from his eyes and glanced at the window. It was still there. Came from another room, then, he thought. Somebody was always getting thrown through something at Ballmeister. They did a good business in scars.

He stretched, his hairy arms and legs extending beyond the bed, which was now listing on one side, and listened to the familiar sounds of carnage in the street.

Nellie came in from the bathroom, holding a towel. She had managed to bathe without awakening him. Everything was pink and clean and wobbly. She reminded Bill of a truck-sized cherry snow cone – lickable. She didn't smell like a woman, though. The odor of cheap hotel soap had replaced the smell of her womanhood. Luckily, some had rubbed off on him.

"Hey, lover," she said. "You wanna eat?"

"Again?" He slapped the bed.

She laughed. Everything on her moved invitingly, like a mountain in a sexy earthquake.

"I like a man who's insatiable," she said. "But we've gotta fuel that beautiful engine."

That was true. Bill hadn't realized how hungry he was. On Ballmeister trips, he usually was only partially sentient.

"You are wise beyond your years," Bill said, admiringly. "Let's fuck. Then eat."

Nellie grinned. "It ain't either-or. You ever had a round-the-world with pizza?"

Bill's scrotum did something confused but joyous.

"I am open to all possibilities for education," he said. "But they don't have room service."

"Oh," Nellie said, and made a huffy face. "Well, then, I guess we gotta leave the boudoir. I'll get dressed while you shower and brush your teeth."

"While I *what?*" Bill said, bolt upright. Two days, and already she was trying to change him.

"Only if you want. Sweetie." Nellie raised her arms, lifting her breasts high, and began to towel her mass of hair, which flipped tantalizingly across her shoulders and face. Then she turned her back to him, bent far over and began to dry her ankles.

Bill swallowed hard.

"Hell," he said in a choked voice. "It's only water."

They shared two dozen eggs at Tony's, along with five waffles, ten pieces of French toast, a quart of orange juice and an untold amount of coffee. It was an uncomfortable meal, and not just because of the gastric results. Bill found himself silently contemplating Nellie's breasts but his eyes kept straying to her face. Her cheeks glistened with rouge and syrup. He wasn't used to making eye contact with women. Normally he stared at the tops of their heads.

Bill focused uncomfortably on his plate. He dimly remembered that you were supposed to talk to chicks during the daytime but he really had no idea what to say.

Nellie kept her eyes mostly on her plate but sometimes she would glance up shyly at Bill, and her fork would miss her mouth.

If she giggles, I'm hitting the door, Bill thought. He wished they were back in the bedroom where he didn't have to talk. Talking to a woman was harder than blind cage fighting. It was easy when your dick carried on the conversation.

After a strained silence, Nellie put down her fork, smiled brightly and said: "I can read food."

Bill looked up.

"You read food?"

"Yes, I do."

"Uh, what do you read it? And why? It ain't alive."

"No, you silly man. I read the leftovers on your plate, the way some people read tea leaves or palms. It's a language, like Elvish."

"Or Pig Latin," Bill said.

Nellie rolled her eyes.

Bill looked at his plate. It was licked clean. Did that mean he had no future, or that nobody knew what was coming?

Nellie caught his glance. "You are a hard man to read," she said. "Let's use mine." She picked up her fork and began to point things out.

"Now, you see this swirly line?"

"The ketchup?"

"No, the syrup. It starts clockwise but then it changes course." She traced it delicately with her fork.

"That's where you lifted the waffle," Bill said.

"Yes, but it was fate guiding my hand. Everything is cosmically connected. Every tiny thing we do reveals the true path of our destiny, if you know how to look at it."

Bill frowned. "Destiny and me are not on speaking terms."

"I know; you're a free man with free will, a knight of the open road. But lover, it's still a road. Let's see what my fate holds." She peered closely. "The syrup line represents the sweetness of life. It breaks here, by the toast crumbs, but then it continues and even gets a little wider. That means there's some hard times ahead but it will be all right in the end."

"What hard times?"

Nellie looked amused and exasperated. "Well, I can't read everything. The cosmos is too complicated and there'd be no surprises if I could. This is just the general outline."

"But you're going to have trouble?"

"Looks that way."

Bill frowned. Then he reached out. His spatula-sized thumb caught a golden drip of syrup that was clinging to the end of her chin. He held it over her plate. The drop fell, healing the break in the syrup line.

"Fixed it," Bill said. He pointed to the end of a leftover sausage. "You gonna eat all that fate?"

Nellie's belly laugh filled the diner. It also made her breasts heave like whales in a tsunami. Bill looked on appreciatively.

The guys have got to see this, he thought proudly.

“I want you meet my club,” he said.

“Meet how?” she said, tossing her head back like a startled horse.

“How do you want to meet them?” Bill asked in confusion.

“With my clothes on.”

“I meant that.”

“You'd better.”

It was a slow, wobbly ride through town. The main drag, Lycra Boulevard, was a solid wall of sweaty bodies and blaring music. Bikes jammed the curbs in gleaming chrome rows, their owners sprawling over them or one another. On one corner workers from the local DuPont factory were tossing samples of drip-dry wife beater shirts to an enthusiastic mob.

The air was scented with spilled beer and exhaust. People good-naturedly traded dope, jokes and punches outside of the bars. The sun beat Bill and Nellie with planks of light as the Harley rolled past stalls selling everything from boots to pit bulls. At a corner, a crowd was busy tearing down a bong stand that had unwisely put Justin Bieber on the speakers.

Bill passed a forlorn bandstand with “Wet T-shirt Contest” written on a banner. That had been crossed out and the banner hung with a cardboard sign that said: Closed Due to Drought" and underneath: "No-T-Shirt Contest. 6 p.m."

"I'd win," Nellie said casually.

An outdoor tattoo parlor blared Steppenwolf's "Keep Your Motor Runnin'" and Nellie pointed with approval as a drooling dragon took shape on a sun-freckled back.

"I want one with purple wings and pink eyes," Nellie said. "What do you think?"

"It would have to heal," Bill said. "You couldn't lie on your back for the rest of the rally."

"I've got no problem with doggy-style," she said and pinched his ear.

They passed a roped-off side street that rang with hammer blows and sizzled with welding sparks.

Owners watched with critical eyes as their bikes were customized and repaired. On another roped-off side street, a body lay on a table surrounded by people in masks who were doing something with knives. A sign read: "Appendectomies, $200 cash. Ask about Rally hernia specials."

"Need any work?" Nellie asked.

"I'm good."

Bill parked in front of a building whose sidewalk was littered with broken glass and whose swinging doors were spattered with blood. A sign said "Friendly's Saloon."

Bill helped Nellie down and they went inside.

Bill took a huge sniff of the urine-scented air. It was home. Wrapping his bazooka-sized arm around Nellie's waist, or as much as he could reach, he barged through the doors and confronted a row of leather- and denim-covered asses that formed a flabby human barrier against the bar. The light was dim and smoky and the waitress, a grandma in a minidress, was slinging beers at tables in dark corners. The ambient noise consisted mainly of grunts and farts. It sounded like water buffalos congregating in the Serengeti.

Bill began to say, "Morning, cocksuckers," but glanced at Nellie and decided that was indelicate in the presence of a lady. "Morning, gentlemen."

The sea of backs flashed as a wave of bodies swiveled to face him.

"Who are you talking to, cocksucker?" said Little Weenie, who smiled and then winced because his nose was newly broken. He had a gash on his forehead that was still bleeding a little. Without pause, Bill released Nellie, took two long strides, grabbed Weenie by the ears and slammed his head on the bar, twice.

"Morning, pee wee. As you may not have noticed, there is a lady present. I'll request that you moderate your language to something more appropriate. You stupid fuck."

Weenie looked up, his eyes moving in random directions.

"I do apologize. I didn't realize you were ladied up. We missed you."

Bill released the ears one at a time.

"Looks like you had some trouble," Bill said. "Who'd you rumble with?"

"Nah, nobody," Tiny said. "Weenie got drunk and got hit by the saloon doors." Weenie looked embarrassed.

The door swung open, accompanied by the smell of gasoline and Hatchet body spray. Only one man in the gang took such care with his personal hygiene.

"Jesus Christ," Nellie said. "It smells like a rutting goat."

Bill said, "Reggie can afford the finest. He's our leader and has a trust fund in addition to natural pheromones."

Reggie stepped through, stopped, examined the sole of one motorcycle boot, scraped it against the door sill, and moved in, the other boot making sticky sounds on the floor. He tossed his shoulder-length black hair, took out a tiny brush from the pocket of his leathers and ran it over the five hairs on his upper lip. He looked up at Nellie's looming presence, blinked, looked at Bill, smiled.

He flipped his hair again as he returned his gaze to Nellie.

"You are an imposing female," he said. "Gentlemen, asses up!"

A dozen bikers stood. There was a shuffling of boots.

"May I enquire," Reggie paused and gave his dazzling smile, showing a set of full but yellow teeth. "What brings you to our enclave?"

Bill turned around and said, "This is Nellie."

Reggie looked from one to the other. He gave a final stroke with his brush and put it back in his pocket.

"So I assume you are a rally couple."

Bill gave Nellie a swat on the ass.

Reggie declared, "Be it known that Bill claims this woman for his own."

Heads bobbed. Nellie felt like Snow White meeting the seven dwarves. At six-foot-one, she was taller than most of them.

"Now," Reggie said. "To business. We're leaving early."

"What?" Bleary eyes would have given Reggie piercing glances if their owners had been able to focus.

"We got another day of carousing," Little Weenie said sulkily. "Tonight is the Used Motor Oil Wrestling finals. The Tallahassee Grease Queen's gonna compete!"

"That's her stage name," Bill told Nellie.

"I sure hope so," Nellie said.

The bar erupted in protests but Reggie held up his hands and waited until the noise died down. He smoothed his mustache.

"I don't want to leave, either. But I just heard some bad news. The Pink Slashers are in town."

"Oh shit," somebody said. There was a round of groans.

Little Weenie went pale. Tiny slumped on his stool like a molting pigeon.

"Who are the Pink Slashers?" Nellie asked.

"Lesbian bike gang," Bill said quietly. "We fought them last year. There's still bad blood."

"You fought a bunch of lesbians?" Nellie asked. "Why?"

"Reggie tried to French kiss the leader," Bill said.

"He didn't realize she was gay?"

"She had a tattoo that said 'Butch' but Reggie thought it was her old boyfriend," Bill said.

"They don't fight fair," somebody whined. "They use body parts we don't got!"

"And they swing a mean tire chain, too," Little Weenie admitted, tenderly touching his nose.

"I know we could take them this year," Reggie said. "Heck, we can take any gang that ever rode a hog..."

"Except the Hells Angels," Tiny said.

"True dat," someone said.

"Or the Vagos."

"Or the Mongols."

"We could take the Prairie Dogs."

"I dunno. Those little teeth are sharp..."

"Shut up!" Reggie squeaked. "We could certainly take the Slashers this year if they just fought like dudes and Bill would join in. But as Knights of the Road, we cannot sucker-punch chicks. Whom we don't know personally, I mean.

"So," Reggie continued. He put his hands on his hips and said perkily: "All agreed, then, that we blow this popsicle stand and head home?"

There was a sulky round of agreement from the crowd.

So," Reggie said again, and then gave a soprano bellow: "Get your gear. We RIDE!"

Bill turned to Nellie, looked her up and down. It took time; she had a lot of up and down. Bill found himself swallowing hard. But it was time he hit the road to freedom. Reggie once again had saved him from entrapment. Like a gentleman, he held out a meaty paw to shake her hand.

"Well, it's been fun," he said. "Next year, huh?"

Nellie looked at Bill for what might be the last time. He was the first man in a long time who'd made her feel like a real woman. He'd lifted her like a feather. She cast a languorous glance over his mountainous chest, forested with goatish hairs. She felt her loins opening like a desert flower. She reached up and gently pulled a spare rib from his beard. The sweet sauce dripped on her tongue and over her smacking lips like the generous essence of love.

Bill followed the progress of her tongue as she licked the last of the drippings. Her mouth was ringed with barbecue sauce. He shuddered with desire.

"Well," he said slowly, eyeing Nellie. "I got to go back to the hotel and get my things."

"I'll go with you," Nellie said.

"Be back in ten," Reggie said.

Twenty minutes later, Bill and Nellie departed the hotel, leaving the hotel maid a pile of crumpled bills and her nastiest cleaning job of the day.

Bill rode up to the gang, Nellie perched on and overflowing the bitch seat. He killed the engine.

"She's coming," he announced.

Little Weenie looked at Tiny, who looked at Baldy, who tugged at his earring and frowned and yanked his beard as if to make sure he wasn't dreaming. Then all eyes turned to Reggie, who instinctively reached for his comb but then decided it wasn't the moment. He puffed out his pigeon chest in a leaderly pose.

"Bill," he said, fighting down the squeak in his voice. "A word, please."

Bill stepped off his bike and moved in to tower over Reggie.

"Goddamnit, Bill," Reggie said in an urgent whisper. "You know we don't take chicks and kids with us. This ain't a goddamn kiddygarden family camping trip to fucking Chuck E. Cheese. We are not a damn pussy posse. So give her some tongue and let's move. She's just a rally hookup."

He reached up and gave Bill a comradely slap on the shoulder - actually the elbow, which was a high as he could reach - and smiled his dazzling leadership smile, glad for once he'd completed that management course at Hoboken Junior College.

Bill lowered his head like a twelve year-old caught with his hand in his pants. But under his brows, he looked imploringly back at Nellie.

To Nellie, Bill looked like a trapped bear and her womanly heart was wrenched.

"Son of a bitch," she thought. "Men. Bigger don't make brighter."

She turned instantly and walked off, disappearing into the bar.

Bill watched her go with a lump in his throat like a half-digested caribou, and one nearly as largely in his pants that faded quickly. Reggie, crossed his arms in triumph, then gestured everyone to the bikes.

Bill straightened up, took a deep breath. It should have smelled like freedom. He thumped himself down on the Harley's sun-warmed leather seat, reached up to the handlebars and kicked the huge engine to life.

The pack's motors thrummed all around him. Slowly they lined up and prepared to hit the highway. Reggie's chrome helmet blazed in the unforgiving sun like a very tiny beacon. They had just started to move when Nellie emerged from the swinging doors of the bar.

"Wait up," she bellowed, matching the thunder of fourteen well-tuned leg pipes.

Heads turned.

She was hauling an enormous ice chest.

"You heroes look thirsty," she said in a voice like a Viking princess. "Here."

She put down the chest, threw it open, pulled out a Bud long neck, bit the cap off the brown bottle and handed it to Bill. Then she reached in, grabbed another bottle and slung it underhand at Reggie's head. The bottle arced straight and true twenty feet. Reggie threw up a hand to protect himself and it slapped magically into his gloved palm. He raised the bottle and the engines throttled down to a purr. Nellie tossed six more with machine-gun speed and precision. Each found its mark.

"Holy shit," Little Weenie said.

"That's nothing," Nellie said. "I can do it at 80 miles an hour."

"You can do that on the road?" said Tiny with thirsty lust in his eye. He looked around. "You mean we wouldn't have to stop every twenty minutes to beer up?"

"You can hold a lot in these puppies," Nellie said, puffing out her chest and slapping the cooler.

"But it's illegal to drink and drive," One Thumb said. He was their safety officer on illegal fireworks runs.

Nellie launched a bottle at his head. It connected and he fell like a stunned ox, snapping off a horn of his helmet. Two bikers looked at her with sudden fear in their eyes, then they helped One Thumb stagger up.

"That's right," she said to the pack. "It's illegal. You'd all be outlaws."

There was a sudden hush.

"Outlaws," somebody said reverently.

Reggie held up a hand again. It happened to be the one with the beer in it. He looked at it, popped the cap on his belt buckle and took a deep swallow. The cold gold rolled down his throat. He paused for what seemed like an eternity. A shaft of light reflected from his bottle and painted his face in a shining glow, turning his tiny mustache to bronze.

"Well, if you really can do that," he said slowly, and then deliberately sent a telling look to Bill in the rear. "You can ride with Bill."

A cheer went up. Bill blushed. Nellie blushed.

"But go refill that beer chest first," he said.

A few minutes later, they were off.

Bill took his usual place at the back of the pack. The sound of Joe Satriani's "Big Bad Moon" drifted back from a speaker taped to one of Reggie's handlebars. Reggie had salvaged it from the wreckage of his mother's Mercedes. She'd crashed it after losing a cocktail-fueled bidding war for an antique armoire at Sotheby's.

"It wasn't a real suicide attempt," Reggie often said. "It was a cry for help."

Reggie had hooked up a CD player but when he put a disc in, it wouldn't come out. So "Big Bad Moon" was the club's theme song until he got around to replacing it. So far, it had been two years.

"Where's the other speaker?" Nellie asked Bill.

"New Jersey."

"Why?"

"Won't say. When you ask, he just starts twitching. So we stopped askin'."

The group rolled out of town and past low hills and fields reeking of garlic. Bill felt the sun on his face and was happy. When he was on the road, he was free. The roar of the engines and the wind, the rolling play of the landscape was better than any drug - like Ecstasy with gas fumes. Yoga but with bugs in your teeth. On the road, with nothing for a hundred miles but his pack in front and iron between his legs, Bill felt right-sized in the world.

Except that Nellie's chest kept digging into his back. Also her boobs. He couldn't get into the zone. Whenever anybody signaled for a beer, he had to speed up, and she'd throw one and he'd have to jerk the ape hangars to compensate for her weight shift. Then he could drop back but she'd lean forward and he could feel her warm cheek against his ear. And when she did that, his jeans got uncomfortable.

Bill swore to God he'd never had to deal with so much woman so near for so long. It really fucked up his chi. The demon of self-awareness was riding his back. It was the worst ride he'd ever had.

Eighty miles west of Barstow, they pulled over for a pee break at a jerky stand. Bill remembered getting bit there by the petting zoo goat. The goats were no longer there but the shelves were freshly stocked with homemade goat jerky.

Nellie remained on the bike.

"Don't you have to go?" Bill asked.

"No, I'm good," she said.

"After three hours on a bike?" Bill asked, perplexed. "Is that normal for chicks?"

"Honey, I'll go just to please you," she said sweetly. "You better go pee. Those other guys look uncomfortable. That Little Weenie probably can't hold more than a pint."

Reggie stepped off his bike and adjusted his chaps at the crotch. Everyone else got off, too. They started to shuffle into a circle toward the back of the stand, then looked sheepishly over to Nellie.

"Uh, there's a bathroom inside," Reggie called.

"We usually just do a group pee by the road," Bill explained.

"How gentlemanly," Nellie said. "You have no idea how scratchy it can be to squat in manzanita."

Bill spent the next forty miles trying to get that image out of his head.

The green Central Valley burned away to high desert, the farm fields replaced with scrub and piñon pine. They stopped at a burrito stand for lunch. Vultures cackled and shat overhead, using their helmets as targets. Bill thought about the empty, lyrical beauty of nothingness as he combed chili fries out of his beard.

"I like to watch you eat," Nellie said as they sat at a picnic table. "You use both hands. And sometimes your feet. You're dedicated."

"I do live in the moment," Bill agreed. "You kinda have to. That's physics."

"You're not what I expected," Nellie said suddenly. "I kinda like that, too."

Bill rubbed his neck, leaving a trail of grease. He wasn't comfortable with compliments. It meant somebody was about to reach for your wallet or your crotch. Of course, he wouldn't much mind that with Nellie...

He pulled back his thoughts. "What did you expect?" he asked, and gulped from his plastic cup of beer.

"Well, at first, I thought you didn't even like chicks."

Bill choked and spat a yellow stream that had cost him three dollars. “What the hell? Why?"

“Well, you know, because of your patch." She tapped the logo on the back of his vest.

"What do you mean?" Bill asked.

Nellie opened her mouth, then thought better of it.

"Never mind,” she said.

The conversation was cut short as Reggie came stomping back and crumpled his yellow burrito wrapper in his fist.

“Let’s go gents. I want to get a headwind going before the beans kick in.”

Nellie said sarcastically, “Oh, I guess we better hurry. Don’t want to lose some dudes by sitting too long.”

“We did have a few blow up,” Bill said.

They rolled down into the Mojave Desert. Choking on dust as the pack sped down Highway 58, Bill thought with pride of the club's founding days: The beer-soaked arguments about what to name the pack, the patch design contest, and the brilliant name that Reggie's ex-wife thought up. He looked lovingly at the back of his leader's jacket. It showed a rear view of a burly biker rammed on a stylized banana-shaped seat that stood proudly erect between his buttocks; a macho design if ever there was one. And above that, in huge Gothic letters, the club initials. They had fought pitched battles over the name. They all wanted something like Hell’s Angels or Rusty Reapers. It had to be devils or Satan or demons or something. Living somewhere evil, like Hell or Canarsie. Or Chaos.

"No, not Chaos," Reggie’s then-wife, Tammy, had said, under the inspiration of a pint of Jack Daniels. "Kaos! With a K!"

"Fuckin' A, that's cool!" Bill had shouted.

"Yeah, Kool with a K!" Reggie said.

And so were born the Princes Reigning in Kaos.

Sometimes, as the PRIKs roared down the road, small children in minivans pointed and laughed.

For the first time, Bill thought about that. He had thought the children were cheering them. Nellie caused a lot of confusion. He was confused about that. He was confused about why he should be confused. What he wasn’t confused about was that he needed more beer. Anything involving bodily fluids was never confusing. Bill thought back to high school chemistry. That wall chart with the chemical symbols in little boxes, hadn't that had a B in there somewhere? Of course. Beer was the prime element.

"S must have been for Schlitz," he said. Mb was More Beer. He shook his head. Too much science. He'd known every element by name once but nobody at school liked a seven-foot-tall genius. He got tired of being called "Monster Nerd," so he forgot it all.

Which was harder than learning it.

Mom had approved, though, when he stopped pointing at things and shouting out stuff like: "Aluminum! Symbol Al! Average mass 26.982 grams per mole!"

"Dear God, son, I have a hangover!" his mom had said. "Zip it or I'll turn you into meatloaf. Atomic fucking symbol F *for shut the fuck up!*"

That reminded him. He had to make his monthly call to Mom. Bill didn't have a cellphone. If you couldn't shout, shake hands or spit at somebody, why in hell would you want to stay in touch? Except for Mom.

A tear came to his eye. He wiped the bug out of it and felt better. He patted his arm where he'd written "Mom" in Magic Marker. He'd thought about getting a tattoo but he had a thing about needles.

At the next gas stop, he left Nellie filling the beer cooler and borrowed Reggie's phone. Bill stepped into the restroom for privacy, evicting a drunk, a toddler and a distraught squirrel. He came out of the restroom looking worried.

Nellie saw him rubbing his arm and put down the cooler.

"What's wrong?" she asked. "It's your left arm so I know you didn't cramp up jerkin' off."

"I'm ambidextrous," Bill said. "But it ain't that. It's my Momma."

Nellie gave him a puzzled and then a horrified look.

"Ewww!" she said.

"No, no, no," Bill said hastily, and pushed up his sleeve to show the Magic Marker tattoo.

"I call her every month. I just called her now. And I got this feeling...." He shook his head.

"Is she sick?" Nellie asked.

"I don't know. But it's weird."

"Why?"

"She said she was fine."

"So?"

"Mom always says she's dyin' when I call. Something's wrong. Maybe she really is dyin.'"

Nellie gave Bill a quick kiss, reached down and picked up the chest. "Then we gotta go to her. She won't last forever."

Bill started. "Go there? In person?"

"Well, duh." Nellie looked suspicious. "Is there a reason you don't want to actually set eyes on your momma?"

"Hell, yes," Bill said.

"Me, too," Nellie said. "But sometimes you just have to butch up and be offspring-like."

Bill looked suddenly shy which was hard to do when you had eyebrows so craggy that they could shelter a herd of bighorn sheep.

"Look," Bill said. "I am concerned. But I don't want to force you to go. Mom ain't always pleasant to strangers..."

"Stranger?" Nellie's eyes flashed suddenly. If she'd been a desert, there'd be lightning on her horizon. Bill thought he could smell ozone and was suddenly aware that he'd made an error in judgment. Kind of like the one Lucifer made when he told God to go fuck Himself. His testicles tried to find an express elevator to his esophagus.

Nellie, again, had confused things.

"Did you know aluminum has an atomic number of thirteen?" he blurted desperately.

"What?"

"Nothing," Bill said. "What I mean is ... what I meant was...."

"You meant you're not ready to introduce me to your folks?" Nellie said sweetly.

"Uh, yeah?"

"Because you want her to look her best, right? Not any problem with me?" The sweetness had a hard edge, and a brittle smile to go with it. Like telepathy, Bill heard the sentence continue in his head. It said: "You wouldn't be that stupid, would you, lover?"

"*And it weighs 26.982 grams per mole*," he thought.

"No," he said out loud, then "Yes."

"Yes?" Nellie said frigidly and Bill realized he'd answered the stuff she hadn't actually said.

Nellie heaved the cooler onto one hip, which cocked fetchingly. "I understand you might be a little hesitant for me to meet her," she said soothingly. "Because you're not sure whether you want to stay with me and it's a big step."

Bill let out a sigh of relief. "You get that?" he said. "And you're not upset?"

"I understand," she said. "But I am upset." Without pausing, she kneed him in the groin.

"Oops," Nellie said.

After he finished rolling in the dirt, she bent down and hugged him. "Oh, baby, I'm sorry. I get emotional sometimes. It's good we've made up, though. So, let's go see your momma. If she's dying, we'd better get there fast. Don't want her ghost haunting us."

As Bill, struggled to his feet, he saw the entire gang goggling. Some wore grimaces of sympathetic pain. Little Weenie and Reggie unconsciously barricaded their crotches with their hands.

"I hope she gives 'em back," Little Weenie whispered.

"And this is why we don't let chicks ride," Reggie said under his breath.

"Reggie," Bill said, respectfully. "My momma needs me."

"We heard. Catch up with us after you do what you gotta do. You need gas money?"

"I'm good."

"Carrying that beer might slow you down," Reggie said, eyeing the cooler.

Nellie shoved it at him.

"Bye, amigos," Bill said, wincing as he mounted and kicked the bike to life. "I'll see you at the junkyard."

Waving a hand, Nellie said, “Gentlemen.”

They roared off.

Little Weenie scratched his bald head. “She’s really gonna meet his momma?”

Reggie looked at the vanishing rooster tail of dust from Bill’s bike, and said, “Fifty bucks says that chick throws the first punch.”

Nobody took the bet.

CHAPTER TWO

Joe's American Syrup & Fries Diner, New Jersey Turnpike, July 31, 1981

The high summer moon shone over the diner, painting its shabby walls silvery white. The air was lilac-scented from the neighboring Lux soap factory.

Wu Tsien Cho - Joe to his customers - had his back to the beauty. He grunted and felt a twinge in his back as he scrubbed black char from the grill with a wire brush. The perfumed air was clobbered by the smells of old fat and bleach and the reek of old drains. The turnpike noise was a muted but continual roar and mutter. Cho felt the nausea of exhaustion mixed with too many cups of acid coffee. There was grit beneath his eyelids. It always reminded him of the way he'd felt at sixteen, when he finally reached shore after days on a leaking, overcrowded boat fleeing Vietnam. Now he was in America, but she hadn't been paved with cigarettes and chocolate, let alone gold. He had already wiped down the counter, cleaned the plates, restocked the napkin dispensers. When he awoke after a few hours of blackness it would all start again. There was no moon in his world. Just his diner and himself to run it.

Somebody tapped on the front door.

It was after ten o'clock. He ignored it.

They kept tapping, hard little raps on the glass next to the big red cardboard CLOSED sign.

Cho threw down the brush irritably and turned, making shooing gestures with his hands, sheathed in yellow rubber gloves, like a conductor.

"We're closed!" He said, stalked to the door, pointed at the sign with angry jabs - and stopped short.

Standing in the door light stood a man and a girl. He was lanky, dressed in leather and a T-shirt and had a Fu Manchu mustache. The girl was ....

Cho dropped his hands.

Her long auburn hair, streaked with light, fell to her shoulders and in bangs over her forehead. Her face was small, her nose pert, her eyes large and green. She was slim, almost coltish, with narrow hips blossoming in a pair of tight jeans. Her slender, pale shoulders were bare in a sleeveless leather vest. Her expression was innocent, open, but her clothing was a parody of street-tough. She was trying hard to be hard. Like him - once.

She pressed her forehead against the glass and mouthed silently: "Please."

Cho thought he hadn't seen anyone like that in a long time. Someone so obviously out of place on the turnpike.

He fingered the door key in his pocket, pulled it out, unlocked the door.

The couple squeezed inside past him, accompanied a blast of lilac.

"Thanks," she said.

Up close, she was taller than Cho.

"Thanks, man," the man said. He wore fingerless leather gloves. "We are starving. Been on the road all day."

"What do you want?" Cho asked.

"Anything," the girl said. "A cold sandwich."

Cho looked at the girl again. The grill was still hot and they did look famished.

"Two cheeseburgers," Cho said. "Cokes. No coffee, sorry."

"That would be heaven," the girl said.

The man grunted, slapped his palms together. They sat down at the round red stools.

Cho went to the freezer, grabbed a couple of half-pound patties and some cheese slices and retrieved the buns. He turned the grill fans back on, slid the burgers onto the metal. They sizzled and flared. He buttered the buns and set them on the grill. The aroma of cooking meat filled the room. He thought about how that must smell to hungry people, who didn't have it in their nostrils all day long. He smiled to himself.

In a few minutes, Cho grabbed two plates from under the counter and set out two perfect cheeseburgers. He set out the two Cokes, the cups glistening with condensation.

They reached for the plates and dug in. He pretended to be busy cleaning glasses but kept glancing at them. The man ate methodically, not taking off the gloves. The girl sipped the Coke first, licked her lips with pleasure. She reached delicately for the burger, held it with her fingertips and nipped at it. But she finished first, making little noises of pleasure at every bite.

They ate without speaking until every crumb was gone, and the Cokes had been slurped empty.

The girl sighed as she leaned back on the stool. The man wiped his mouth with the back of his hand as he pushed the plate away.

"Goddamn," he said. "Goddamn."

"Uh huh," she agreed. She stuck one finger in her mouth and sucked noisily. "Oh my God, you're an artist, a burger artist."

Cho's heart warmed. He almost managed a smile.

The man stood up, burped, reached for his back pocket.

"What do we owe you?" he asked.

Cho felt jolted as if from a pleasant dream. He had to think for a moment.

"Three dollars," Cho said.

The man dug into his pocket, frowned, and came out holding a long chain.

"Oh, shit," he said. "Where the hell's my wallet?"

The girl rolled her eyes. "What the hell, Patrick. I told you that beat-up thing needed replacing."

"Shit, the grommet must have torn right loose. I had fifty bucks in there! Goddamnit!"

Cho looked at them, his heart sinking. Another scam.

"You owe me three dollars," he said.

The man turned to the girl. "You got anything, honey?"

She turned away from Cho and put a hand down her blouse. She came out with sixty cents in change and a tampon.

"That's it," she said. She looked embarrassed. Her cheeks colored.

Cho looked disgusted.

"It's okay," he said dismissively. "Just go then. On the house." His exhaustion had come back, and there was the grill to clean all over again.

"No," the man said firmly. "We gotta pay you. I never cheated an American working man. Even a chink."

He looked over at the woman questioningly.

She said, "I got this."

"I love you, sweetheart. Don't take long."

The man strolled to the door, which was still unlocked, swung through it and stood with his back to it in the moonlight, lighting a Camel.

The girl moved closer to Cho, looked him frankly in the eyes.

"How about a trade?" she asked.

Cho looked at her in confusion. She smiled, tossed her head. Her auburn hair flew across her face and then swirled around her lithe body like the mane of a wild horse. She parted her lips in a smile. Her teeth were small and white. She took a step toward the counter. Cho backed up. She took another step. Cho retreated again, moved through the open side space. Then he was backed up to the grill. The hot metal ticked and its heat rolled over his back.

She followed him, stopped a heartbeat away, leaned in. Her heat was fiercer than the grill's. She was an inch taller than he was. Her smell was intoxicating. *Too grown up for a little girl,* he thought again. His hands, still in their rubber gloves, were folded behind his back. He felt exposed.

The girl reached down and undid the top button of her hip-hugger jeans. Then another.

Cho swallowed. He felt like a bird mesmerized by a tiger. Red lips, green eyes.

She smiled, licked her lips, undid the last button. She peeled the skin-tight jeans below her hips and stood there, her smooth belly curving into...paradise.

Cho blinked, closed his eyes, swallowed. Parts of him shook; others rose.

"You don't have to..." he began.

"Shhh," she commanded. She put her cheek next to his and said: "I'm going to rock your world in seven minutes."

Cho, pressing a bag of ice to his scorched ass, watched the girl on the back of the motorcycle vanish into the night. He fancied she looked back just once. The grill would be sacred to him now, because she'd backed him up against it in their passion.

He opened his singed fingers, and looked at the jewel she'd left him: a single rhinestone that had fallen into the fryer oil. He'd lifted it from the shimmering gold. He would keep it next to his heart forever.

His heart was as light as his grilled ass was dark.

Cho thought to himself, with gratitude: *This is a gift from America.*

Of course she couldn't stay because she had to make other hearts happy. But from that day on, Cho realized the goddess of fortune was with him. He took out a massive loan, built and struggled. He decided to risk expansion - to dare to greatness - to be worthy of *her*.

And a quarter-century later, he had the largest truck stop in the world.

"Wait," his nephew said, interrupting the story. "Are you telling me you built an empire for a *whore*?"

Norman Wuu stared down at his uncle in the hospital bed.

"You shut your mouth." The old man's face ancient eyes glared.

"But, uncle, it was seven minutes."

"I have everything because of her."

"Uncle, you promised me the diner."

Uncle Cho looked at him with the wrinkled face and glaring eyes of a snapping turtle.

"I never promised you," he said peevishly. "I told you I would take care of you if you took care of yourself. Now you must be the help to *her* that you have been to me. Don't feel offended, nephew. This is the greatest honor I can bestow on you."

"No, uncle, the greatest honor would be the fucking diner!"

"Stop shouting! She was the reason that I built the diner. I did it for her, and now that I have finally found her, it is my dying wish that she have it."

"Oh, Jesus Christ!" Then Wuu calmed himself and leaned over the bed, smiling slyly. "Of course, I want to carry out your wishes, uncle."

"I know, nephew. That is why I want you to keep working for her. I suggested that in the will."

"You changed the will?" Wuu said icily.

"Yes. Last Thursday. Filed it with my attorney."

"Oh fucking hell!" Wuu said.

The door opened and a doctor came in. "Let go of the catheter, Mr. Wuu, and step outside. Now, please."

Wuu rose stiffly and stalked after him.

When they were in the corridor outside the room, the doctor turned to him angrily.

"You can *not* be shouting in a critical care ward. You scared your uncle, the other patients, and, frankly, me," he said.

"I'm sorry, it's a personal matter," Wuu said. "Chinese thing. You wouldn't understand Doctor ...," he stared at the nametag. "...Fong."

The doctor jerked his head. "Visiting hours are over, Mr. Wuu, and if you insist on this kind of behavior, I'll make sure you don't return."

Wuu said urgently: "He wants to give the diner to a whore!"

"I don't really understand what you mean," the doctor said. "But that man needs his rest."

"He's dying," Wuu said matter-of-factly. "What's he resting up for?"

"Please go now or I'll call security."

"Wait, tell me something," Wuu said. "He's senile, right?"

"Senile?"

"Yeah. Alzheimer's, stroke, whatever?"

"No, he shows no mental deficits. His body may be dying but he's one of the sharpest seniors I've ever met."

"So you wouldn't be willing to sign a form or something saying he's crazy as a loon?"

The doctor's face turned to stone.

"You need to leave now, Mr. Wuu, or I will call security."

"All right," Wuu said. Then he leaned in and said quietly. "But could you please leave him a message for me?"

"We'll see. What is it?"

"Tell him that his favorite nephew says..." and Wuu flushed red as a Chinese lantern. "That I will see his soul roast in hell before I give up that diner."

CHAPTER THREE

Bitter Pancho Springs, outskirts of Phoenix, Arizona, July 31, 2010

Bill and Nellie rolled into a neighborhood that looked like someone had decided to redecorate in post-Apocalypse. The few straggly trees looked sand-blasted, the streets were more dirt than asphalt and the homes were either paint-peeling shacks or rust-bleeding mobile homes. Bill stopped outside a small frame house with a sagging porch fronted by a brown lawn. Parked in the driveway was a shiny black Mercedes.

Bill frowned and killed the engine.

"That ain't right," he told Nellie.

"What isn't right?" she asked.

"That car." He pointed. "It ain't up on blocks. And Momma never would have put a stolen car right out front like that."

"Maybe she's got visitors?" Nellie suggested.

"That phone call," Bill reminded her. "Hey, you're a witch, right?"

"I'm a what?" Nellie asked shrilly.

"No, I said *witch*," he said hastily. "You read food and shit. I don't suppose you have a Spidey-sense or something?"

"You mean, can I sense danger?"

"Yup."

"Nope. But I do have eyes and I can see a big shadow behind the window shade and unless your momma is six feet tall, it's not her."

"She's five-four," Bill said absently. "In all directions."

"Maybe he's a doctor or something," Nellie said.

"No, Momma never held with doctors. And besides..." he pointed to the license plate on the Mercedes. It was a vanity plate from Illinois that read: "CHIMUSL."

They both spent a moment trying to decipher it.

"Oh," Nellie said at last. "Chicago Muscle!"

"Makes no sense," Bill said. "For a doctor or even a chiropractor. Wait here."

He got off the bike, strode up the driveway to the porch. He reached up above the overhang, fished around, and pulled down something. It was a rusty crowbar.

"Still here," he said with satisfaction, and thumped it on the door.

It was answered by a neckless man wearing a Chicago Bulls T-shirt and sweat pants tucked into black socks.

Bill hit him in the groin with the crowbar.

"Sorry, doc," he said.

The man screamed, turned white and fell to the floor, retching. Bill ducked and stepped over him into the living room.

"Momma!" he shouted. "I'm home! Are you okay?"

"Billy!" her voice came from the back bedroom. "You're screwed now, asshole!"

"That's really hurtful, ma'am," someone said, in a voice that sounded like a bull elephant that had grown up on the Southside. Then the man called out, "Frankie! You okay out there?"

Frankie was still retching in the doorway.

The floor shook as the other man lumbered in from the bedroom. He was even larger than Frankie, his buzz-cut head only inches from the ceiling. He wore a Hawaiian shirt decorated with hula girls and the ugliest pair of cargo shorts Bill had ever seen. The legs protruding from them looked like dinosaur drumsticks. He was wearing open-toed sandals. He gaped at Frankie's supine form. He had two bottom buck teeth like a rabbit.

Bill smiled.

"How's Momma?" he asked.

"Is that how you greet your mom's guests?" the man said. "Rude is rude, dude."

Without warning, he swung a massive fist at Bill's head. Bill ducked. The blow grazed the top of his head. Bill slammed the crowbar onto the man's naked toes.

The man shrieked and hopped up and down, holding his foot like a character in a bad cartoon. His head thumped the ceiling with each hop. Bill stepped forward and grabbed him by the throat.

"Momma," he yelled. "Should I kill these guys or not?"

"Not, please," the man croaked.

"Momma?" Bill shouted again.

"I'm thinking," Momma said from the bedroom.

"What's going on?" Nellie asked, stepping daintily through the door and over the collapsed Frankie, who was now doubled up with his hands between his legs, moaning softly.

"Dunno," Bill said.

The man he held was gripping Bill's wrist with both hands. His eyes bulged slightly and he seemed to be turning ever-so-slightly blue.

"No," Momma said. "They're just a pair of dumbasses. Stash them outside and come and give your momma a hug."

With one hand, Bill threw the man on top of Frankie.

"Stay," he said.

"*Gaaack*," the man said.

Bill took that for a yes. He and Nellie walked into the bedroom.

It smelled of anchovies and garlic and the peculiar smell of a room where old people have been living without opening the windows for far too long.

Momma was propped up on pillows in a bed littered with pizza boxes. She wore a purple nightgown that clashed with the wallpaper, which was yellowing and full of large butterflies. She was watching a game show on an old TV set propped on a bureau. Her nearly toothless face lit up as Bill and Nellie entered the room. She put down the remote and reached out her arms.

"Billy! Billy Lime!" she said. Bill bent nearly in half to embrace her with a hug that made bones creak.

"It's been nearly a year," she scolded. "Freedom ain't another word for pissing on your Momma."

"I almost didn't recognize the street," Bill said. "They're really fixing it up."

"Yeah," Momma said. "They're talkin' about repaving and putting in streetlights. Somebody bought Mrs. Cartwright's trailer a couple months ago for near on two thousand dollars."

"No shit!"

"Yep. If this place gets anymore gentrified, I'm gonna have to move. What's this?"

Momma's faded green eyes squinted through enormous, smudged spectacles.

"Dear God, why did you bring an elephant?" she asked.

Nellie turned bright red.

"I don't care if you are dying, old woman," she said through gritted teeth. "I will bust your teeth in. I will shove my Doc Martins right up your fat ass."

"I like her." Mom wheezed. "Reminds me of me." She patted the bed. "I'm Lynette."

"Nellie," Nellie said.

"Pretty name." Momma patted the bed again. "Come and sit down. I think the bed'll hold."

"We've broken our share," Nellie said, looking at Bill. Bill blushed. Momma laughed.

"Ain't we all, Sweetie," Momma said.

They were interrupted by groans from the living room.

"Momma, who the hell are these guys?" Bill asked.

"No idea, son," Momma said. "They just showed up a day or two ago. Said they had to keep me here for three days. They bought me pizza, so I thought, what the hell. Company's company. But they wouldn't let me go. Lucky you called me when you they were on a pee break. Those two do everything together."

"But you're not dyin'?" Bill asked.

"Hell, no," Momma said. "They treated me pretty good - better than most men, anyway. But they were starting to get on my nerves. Peed everywhere like dogs. I kept telling 'em the pooper's out back but they're city boys, I guess. Didn't get the concept. I won't be washing any dishes in that kitchen sink anytime soon, I can tell you."

"I'm gonna go talk to them," Bill said.

He walked back into the living room. Frankie had managed to sit up. He leaned weakly against the door. The other man was standing, favoring one foot.

"I didn't move much," he swore as Bill entered.

"Yeah," Bill said. "So what's the deal with you goons?"

"Just a job," the man said. "Somebody paid us to keep your mom here for a few days. Didn't explain why. We didn't hurt her. Ask her."

"Bulls didn't suck last season," Bill said. "Not great though."

The man brightened. "You a fan?" he asked.

"I ride a lot," Bill said. "Watch a lot of games in bars."

"I'm Tony," the man said, and hesitantly stuck out a hand. "We didn't mean any harm to your mother, hand on my heart and swear to Jesus."

"Noted," Bill said. "But you don't know who sent you?"

"Well, we got a telephone number. We call it twice a day and report. A guy picked up once but he didn't say anything. Weird-sounding."

Bill grunted and raised the crowbar he still carried. "Keep staying," he said.

Tony nodded, vigorously.

Momma and Nellie were laughing as Bill reentered the room. Nellie had a big stack of mail on her lap.

"Oh, yes," Momma said. "We had this itty-bitty blowup pool out back. When I was having one of my headaches and I didn't feel like cooking, I'd put him in that and throw sardines at him. He'd pretend to be a seal." She chuckled. "Good times."

"Momma, those guys don't know anything," Bill said. "We can call the cops, let 'em go, or try to find out what this is all about."

"It all sounds like work to me," Momma said. "If they promise I'm safe, I say we just let 'em be."

"Although," she added slowly. "They do have a pretty nice car..."

"Momma, we are not parting out their car," Bill said. "The judge said you're going to jail next time."

Momma sulked.

"Hey," Nellie said, holding up a large manila envelope. "This looks legal."

"What are you doing?" Bill asked.

"Momma asked me to sort some mail," Nellie said. "She didn't get around to it." She looked at the envelope postmark.

"Lynette, this one is nearly a year old!"

"Yeah," Momma said. "Looked official. I don't like to open those. Usually subpoenas. Either that or they're fake ones that look all official and only have a dead bumblebee inside."

"This is from a lawyer in New Jersey," Nellie said.

"New Jersey?" Momma said. "I wonder if that's the man who's been leaving phone messages for me. Sounded like a scam. You can open it."

Nellie slit the envelope with her thumbnail and pulled out a triple-folded document. She looked it over.

"Holy hobbit on a stick," Nellie swore. "It says..." she read part of it again. "Lynette, did you ever know a man named Wu Tsien Cho?"

Momma let out a whinnying laugh that would have embarrassed any respectable horse.

"Honey, I don't even like Chinese food. Throw that sucker in the trash."

Momma rummaged through a discarded pizza box and dug out a gooey strip of cheese and an orphaned piece of pepperoni. Halfway to her mouth, she stopped.

"Wait," she said.

Nellie looked up from the letter and wrinkled her nose at the stale food pinched between Momma's fingers.

"No! I do not believe it!" Momma said and laughed again. "It can't be! But maybe... Honey," Momma said slowly, looking at Nellie. "Is that lawyer man sayin' anything about... a will?

Nellie said, "How did you..."

"That's what the caller kept sayin'. Thought it was a damn charity trying to take my money. What did orphans ever do for me?"

Nellie began, "This does mention a will."

Momma broke out into a chortle and the food flew as she clapped her hands together.

"It can't be!" Momma said again.

"What can't be?" Nellie asked, delicately lifting a piece of pepperoni from her between her breasts.

"Two cheeseburgers," Momma said, and winked behind her glasses.

"You *still* hungry?" Bill asked.

"No, son. I'm talking about a pit stop on the road of my wasted youth. I wasn't always a homebody, Billy."

"You never were a..." Bill began.

"Shut up, son, I'm reminiscing," Momma said. "I was a looker in those days. And I was looking for lots. Love, freedom, adventure. I was a wild minx. And one night, well, I sort of gave away the store. For a couple of cheeseburgers. To a Chinese-type guy at a diner... in New Jersey."

"Those were different days," she explained to Nellie. "It was the Spirit of the Sixties."

"Uh huh," Nellie said. "I love the Sixties. All that freedom. And unicorns. And whoring," She smiled at Momma.

"You're a bitch, but I still like you, honey," Momma said. "Anyway, I clean forgot about that. It was just a few minutes in my hectic life."

"Well," Nellie said. "If it is the same Cho, he went on to build a pretty big operation. This letter says it's not only the largest truck stop and diner in the world, but they plan to franchise a bunch of diners everywhere. And Mr. Cho has died and left it all...to you."

Momma went silent for a moment.

"Seven minutes," Momma said with wonder, "I knew that little guy for all of seven minutes. And he up and leaves *me*... "

She put a finger to her mouth in a curiously girlish gesture. Her faded eyes filled with tears.

"Momma, you okay?" Bill looked at Nellie. "Should we call a real doctor?"

"Shhh," Nellie said gently.

"I'm okay," Momma said, wiping away a tear and leaving an anchovy streak. "It's just, I didn't even know his name, and he remembers me and then he does this. Either he was crazy or he was the sweetest man I ever knew." She stopped, looked wistful and said, "But I never did know him, did I? What the hell did he see in me?"

She looked at Bill and then at Nellie as if they might have answers.

"He saw what I saw, Momma," Bill said, his eyes shining.

"Shut the hell up, son. It wasn't filial. It was carnal. I must have been the best piece of ass he ever had." She looked thoughtful. "Oh, that's sad. Still, I must say, I was a hottie, though."

She looked at Nellie, "Read the rest of it."

Nellie glanced down at the paper. "It says the will deeds the truck stop-slash-diner to you or whomever you designate as the recipient on condition that you prove your claim and identity."

"How do we do that?" Momma asked.

"This is weird stuff," Nellie said. "It says you or your designated representative has to appear in court with a document to prove your connection to this Cho."

"What kind of document?" Bill asked.

Nellie shook her head. "A half a Christmas card." She looked up in confusion. "What the...?"

Momma sat up so suddenly that her belly wobbled, knocking over the pizza boxes.

"Go on," she said.

Nellie ran a finger down the rest of the letter, pursing her lips in concentration.

"Well," she said finally. "You or the designated so-and-so have to appear with the document in the Bergen County Surrogate's Court and there's a deadline." She raised her eyebrows. "Oh shit! Shit! Shit! Shit!"

"Outside," momma said. "Just like I told those two city fools in the living room."

"Mrs. Butcher," Nellie said. "If you'd have just opened the damned letter a little sooner..."

"I told you, I didn't trust it," Momma said defensively. "Don't tell me I missed the deadline."

"No but nearly," Nellie said angrily. "You've got three days, ma'am, to get your bloated carcass to New Jersey! Now it's no skin off my nose but..." She looked at Bill. "I just know what's going to happen." She folded the letter, put it back in its envelope, and glared at Momma.

"Oh, all right, don't be such a huffy hissy, Missy," Momma said. "We all make mistakes. Just ask your Daddy or your Mommy, or whoever gave you that ass and poor attitude.

Billy!"

"Momma?"

"Front and center, honey. Go to the bureau and pull out the bottom drawer. Just pull it straight out."

Bill trudged over, bent, swept the drawer from its opening. He looked at its contents.

"I never saw you wear these," he said, puzzled.

"Not that," Momma said sharply. "Taped to the back."

Bill felt around, tore something loose from behind the drawer. It was an age-yellowed envelope. Nothing was written on it. He brought it over to Momma.

She took the envelope, opened it, licked her lips, reached inside and pulled out a torn piece of card stock. She held it up.

"The key to the castle," she said.

Bill and Nellie crowded around. Momma held the card as if it were a sacred relic. Bill took it. It appeared to be the top half of a card that had been ripped in two. The front showed a beaming Santa Claus, severed at the belly. One hand held up a hamburger from which protruded a pair of antlers. Off to the side, the face of Rudolph the red-nosed reindeer gaped in horror. The card opened. Inside, in cheerful holiday script, was a message that began: "Big Gus's Gourmet Meats wishes you a Tasty Holiday! Thanks for ..." The rest was missing.

"Hey," Bill said. "I remember this! You used to tape it to the wall at Christmas time whenever my Dads weren't around."

"Yeah," Momma said. "I thought you oughta have at least one card for Christmas. But that ain't why I kept it. Look on the back of the Santa part."

Bill did. In faded ink, it read: "Free meal. Present this card." It was signed "Joe" and then something else in Chinese characters.

"Never got back there," Momma said. "And I sure can't go to New Jersey now." She grunted with theatrical effort. "Could get a stroke or something. Billy, you know I'm close to dyin'."

Nellie said, "Oh, Jesus," and rolled her eyes.

Momma shot her a sharp look and continued, "You have to take that document to the court."

"I knew it!" Nellie growled. "Are we going to at least get gas money?"

"Nope," Momma said. "This ain't an imposition, sister. It's what kin are for. Right Billy, honey, you gonna do that for Momma?"

Then she coughed and patted her chest. Bill looked down at the card in his hand, then up at Momma, then at Nellie, then back and forth between the two. Nellie sighed.

"Of course we've got to go, Bill," she said. "I'm sure the boys will understand."

She pulled out her sequined cellphone.

"Let me call the lawyer," she said, looking at the paper. "I'll let him know we'll be there."

Bill and Nellie said their goodbyes to Momma. Bill slipped the card and the lawyer's letter into his leather jacket and zipped up the pocket.

"What do we do with the big guys?" Bill asked.

"Leave 'em here," Momma said. "They can fetch me stuff until you get back."

Bill stood up. "I'll have a talk with them."

He walked out of the room. A moment later, Nellie and Momma heard voices, protests, grunts and something heavy hitting something not quite so heavy, and a bit squishier.

Bill walked back into the room.

"I recommended they stay until we get back unless they want to lose actual body parts," he said sourly. "But I know they're gonna run the first chance they get." He shrugged his shoulders helplessly.

"Naw," Momma said. "They're paid muscle. Bribe 'em."

"We don't have any cash..." Bill began.

"Watch me," Nellie said, and sauntered into the living room, where the two thugs were seated on the battered couch, denting it so much that their knees framed their ears.

"Boys," Nellie said. "My man has offered the stick. Now let's talk carrots."

"Don't eat 'em," said Frankie, who was still rubbing his groin.

"What I mean is, you can keep doing what you were doing and maybe get a second paycheck out of it, too. Just watch Bill's Momma - and I'm not so particular about how you do that so long as there aren't any actual bruises."

"We're getting' paid to stay for three more days," Frankie said.

"So stay for three more days," Nellie said. "We should be back by then. Or maybe a day later, no more."

"What's the offer?" the other man said.

"Ever been to New Jersey?" Nellie asked.

"You wearing a wire?" Frankie asked.

"No" Nellie said.

"Then, yes," Frankie said.

"Well, there's a diner there, Joe's American Syrup & Fries Diner - heard of it?"

"You kiddin'" the other man said. "Biggest diner in the known universe. I ate myself unconscious there once."

"Well, gentlemen, that woman in there is about to own it, and she has authorized me to offer you payment in kind for your minor - and very short-lived - presence here."

"Like what?" Frankie asked suspiciously.

"Free fries - for life."

Frankie gasped. Tony sucked his teeth noisily. Their stomachs rumbled. They looked at each other. Nellie saw sneaky expressions try to work their way onto their faces but there just wasn't enough brain behind it to work. She guessed they were thinking of bargaining.

"Maple fries?" Frankie said at last.

"What are those?" Nellie asked.

"House special. Maple syrup on fries. See, it's the diner that serves "Syrup & Fries." Yum-yum." He made smacking noises and rubbed his belly.

Nellie smiled. "We'll see how you do. That's negotiable."

Tony got a shifty look in his eyes, which put them so close together Nellie was afraid they might touch.

"How about maple chili?" he asked.

"Which would be, I'm guessing,..." Nellie began.

"Maple syrup and chili on French fries." Tony's voice was thick with worship. "They serve it with a side of bacon!"

Nelly shook her head.

"Let me think about that one," she said. "Don't push it."

"But for life, yeah?" Tony pressed.

"Yeah."

"My life, or Frankie's?"

"I got cancer in my family," Frankie explained. "Testicular." He shot her an angry look.

"Look, guys, the deal is if you walk, hobble or get dragged into the diner at any time you aren't actually at room temperature, you get as many fries as you can stuff in those aircraft hangars you call mouths."

"Maple chili ..." Frank began.

"Oh, goddamnit, yes, okay, maple chili fries. Do we have a deal?"

"We will cherish that old bat like she was our own mom," the other guy said.

As they roared away from the house, Nellie thought she could hear Momma shouting for more pizza. And Coke. And buffalo wings...

"Worth it at twice the price," Nellie said. "Hey, why does your Momma call you Billy Lime?"

"It's my middle name," Bill said. "Momma says she loves key lime pie and she loves me, but too much of either gives her life-threatening heartburn."

"How sweet," Nellie said, shaking her head. "I just knew it had to be something like that. Good thing she didn't like coconut cream. William Coconut Cream Butcher. Or chili. You'd be Billy Chili, silly!" She guffawed.

In spite of himself, Bill laughed, and then wondered why.

Nellie slapped him playfully on his shoulder. "Okay, I'm done funnin'. For a mile or two. What now, William Boysenberry?"

Bill snorted, dislodging a tortilla chip. He decided he didn't care that Nellie was making fun of him. He had no desire to punch her in the face. He settled back, gripped the ape hangers firmly, and throttled up.

"We've got a junkyard date," he shouted as they took off.

"Yeah," Nellie said. "But I wouldn't tell anybody about this diner thing until it's all fixed."

"Why?"

"They might try to come with us. Slow us down. Let's just say we got business in New Jersey."

"Okay," Bill said amiably, glad to know a plan had been made.

"It's just a few days. I'm sure your boys won't have a problem with that," Nellie said, and squeezed him.

"Hell, no!" Reggie threw down his glove in macho rage, then bent, picked it up and dusted it off. He liked to keep a clean clubhouse.

Bill looked abashed. If he'd pissed off Reggie, it would mean a week of broom duty again.

"It's just for a few days," Bill said uncomfortably. He didn't like the feeling. He took a deep breath, inhaling the familiar junkyard miasma of grease, dust and hot metal. From outside came the comforting clang of cars being dismantled and the laughter of illegal workers.

The junkyard had always been the place he felt most at home ever since he'd walked by at fourteen and made friends with the dog, a Shepherd-Chihuahua mix named Señor Muerte that had as many fathers as Bill. They were both outcasts because of their size, although the dog was small and angry and had to be vicious to be taken seriously. He broke a tooth on Bill's arm, and they were friends. Bill spent hours picking fleas out of its mangy hide. One day, Old Man Felix had seen the dog licking Bill's face, swore in Spolish - Spanish and Polish - and yanked the dog away.

"That damn dog is supposed to be biting. You ruined my security system," the old man complained. Bill looked so crestfallen, though, that the old man let him inside.

Over the next few years, Felix let Bill stroll through the fairyland of chrome and rust, and even paid him a few dollars to haul stuff. Bill loved every acre of the derelict cars and motorcycles baking in the desert sun.

Bill's sneakers finally gave out, and Felix gave him a pair of motorcycle boots he'd traded with a biker who frequented the place. Bill loved them. They fit his sprouting feet. They were waterproof and had big steel buckles. He polished them every day and sometimes wore them to bed. Reggie had come through one day, stopped for a brake cable, and bought the junkyard. Felix retired to Florida, along with Senor Muerte, who probably was toothless by now and snarling at alligators. Reggie had taken one long look at Bill and made him a member of the club. Bill was grateful to fit in - above, actually, since he was tall - but sometimes he wished Reggie was more like Felix, who'd been comfortable with crud.

Bill looked around at the rest of the pack lounging on matching tartan-plaid couches and doily draped chairs.

"What is your problem?" Nellie asked Reggie. "It's not like you have a schedule."

"Rules are rules," Reggie squeaked ominously, as he unconsciously straightened an antimacassar. "And rule one is no PRIK goes east of Omaha."

"It ain't the whole gang," Bill reasoned. "Just me and her." He nodded at the ring of faces. They looked about as friendly as Senor Muerte's had been, if the dog had drooled more.

"You know the rule," Reggie said slowly. "And we can't make exceptions. You can't be going rogue, like an elephant. Then you'd be stomping around, killing villagers and destroying the good name of the club."

"And we damned sure don't go to New Jersey," Little Weenie added.

"Why the hell not?" Nellie broke in, irritated.

"Yeah," Bill followed. "Why?" He felt he should support his woman, since she was looking pissed and that meant he might not get laid.

The room fell silent at Bill's unaccustomed audacity. You could have heard a doily drop.

Reggie stroked his little mustache threateningly. His watery eyes glared, which actually made them seem like overcooked eggs.

The club held its breath, knowing Reggie was about to get profound.

"We don't go to Jersey," Reggie said carefully, his voice full of quiet menace. "Because it's Demon territory."

"Shit," Bill said.

The Demons In Konstant Kaos had split with the Princes and there was no love lost between them. Bill had mentioned once that the dividing line for the two clubs was Omaha but he'd specifically banned New Jersey. He'd called Jersey "the lint-filled Bellybutton of Damnation."

With dismay Bill realized he was asking the Pope for a pass to Hell. Or, actually, Satan for a pass to Heaven. Or something like that. His head was beginning to hurt. But he felt Nellie's hot glower on the back of his neck. If he didn't stick up for himself, those witchy eyes would put a brand on him - and that brand would say: "Pussy."

She was confusing him again. He raised a hand.

"I promise not to go anywhere near Demons," he swore. "It's just, I got to go to court. For my Momma."

"No. Way," Reggie said. "This isn't about family with a small f. It's about your real family - the big F. We're all big F's. If you go, you break our peace treaty with my broth—with the Demons. No way! And that is my final word."

"Please?" Bill said, sounding pathetic even to himself.

“I just said my last word,” Reggie pronounced reasonably. “Why are you still talking?”

Bill finally looked at Nellie, who looked disgusted in that way she had of making his testicles contract. It made him feel like a fourteen-carat turd.

Bill clenched his fists. Reggie took a step back and glowered. His hand dropped from his mustache.

“Reggie, I have got to go,” Bill said, and squared his shoulders, although he felt cold sweat dripping between them. “I’m going.”

"No," Reggie thundered. "If you go there - “ he paused as if unable to utter the words - “If you go there, you're not a PRIK. You're a DIKK!"

The insult hung in the air. From outside came the sound of cars being cut, crushed, torn apart. Bill felt as if he’d gone to teacher for a hall pass and been sentenced to death. Things had spun out of control so fast that Bill was reeling. He looked at the faces of his pack, his brothers. They were unreadable. They were only spectators. They weren’t about to take sides, although Little Weenie seemed to have an incipient wince brewing and was rubbing his head in anxiety.

Bill turned to Reggie and played his wild card. "You can't kick me out. I do all the beer runs!"

That brought grumbles from the crowd.

"He does get the beer," acknowledged Tiny, the newest, youngest, softest and fattest of the gang.

Reggie shook his head, and stroked his mustache so vigorously it threatened to detach. “We have to make sacrifices for the purity of the pack.”

He turned slowly around, making deliberate eye contact with each gang member just as that correspondence course in public speaking recommended. His eyes studiously avoided Bill’s.

“Gentlemen,” Reggie said. “I convoke the Ring of Judgment. Everybody outside!”

“What the hell is that?” Nellie asked but Bill just stood, feet apart and head down in shame.

He waited as the others left the clubhouse, one by one. Then he followed, his feet dragging as if his boots were gripped by invisible hands.

Nellie followed.

They stepped out into the blazing sun, its fierce rays reflecting around them like white stars from the chrome and windshields of the stacked cars.

Reggie and the other PRIKs wheeled their bikes into a circle. Bill trudged into the middle and stood, shoulders hunched. Nellie stood by but he didn't look at her.

"Gentlemen," Reggie said, shouting above the sounds of the yard. "One of our own has chosen to forsake his loyalty and intends to deliberately, with malice aforethought, break our code, codicils, policies, procedures and .... er... dogma. If he'd just killed a guy, that would be different. Then we might cut him some slack. But he's chosen to violate the most sacred taboo of the club. There is no precedent for showing mercy here. Bill there wants our permission to kick over our motors, shit on them and then make us ride them! So, as much as it pains me, I must call today for the ultimate sanction."

Reggie stopped, wheezing a bit. It was a long speech and the ground was dusty. "Gentlemen, start your engines!"

The ring of steel roared to life.

Reggie raised his hands. "All in favor of expelling William Butcher from the Princes in Konstant Kaos," - he turned to Bill and added, "Permanently." Reggie paused as if waiting for him to change his mind but Bill stood as silently as stone.

"All in favor," Reggie said, "Throttle up!"

Reggie twisted his throttle and gunned his engine. Slowly, one by one, the others followed. The chorus of chugging, racing and roaring drowned out the junkyard sounds.

The roar slowly died away to a thrumming.

"Now," Reggie said. "All opposed!"

Over the low rumbling, Bill could be heard sniffling.

Reggie raised a hand again, and said, "Judgment is passed. Sergeant at Arms, advance and do your duty!"

Little Weenie got off his bike and moved into the ring. His face was grim.

"Sorry, Bill. Really," he said, rubbing his head.

"I know," Bill said. "Do what you got to do."

"Bend down," Little Weenie said.

Bill, his face twisted in grief, bent over so that Little Weenie could reach his shoulders. Bill sobbed as his patches were torn away. His leathers were now as naked as they day they were stripped from the cow.

Little Weenie raised his hands, which were full of torn cloth, and said formally: “It is done.”

Then, biting his lip, he strode over to Reggie, handed over the patches, and returned to his bike.

Reggie stuffed them in a pocket, gave Bill one last look, and yelled: “This man is dead to us! Cortege assemble!”

Slowly, the ring of bikes broke apart and became two lines, with Bill in the middle. Then they began to move off, two by two.

"Wait!" Bill cried desperately "Ain't you gonna beat me up?"

Bill had enthusiastically taken part in many final beatings of departing club members.

Reggie turned and looked at him with remorseless eyes, one blue and the other pink.

"You have besmirched the club. We will not sully our fists on your treasonous hide," he said. “The next time we meet, you will be an enemy."

"And then you'll beat me up?" Bill asked hopefully.

"No. You will be invisible to us."

"Shit!" Bill said forlornly. Then he looked at Nellie. "Will you at least beat her up?"

The pack looked at Nellie, especially at her massive forearms and the handle of the Colt peeking from between her breasts.

Reggie cleared his throat.

"We don't beat chicks," he said. “New club rule.”

And they rode off in a cloud of dust.

Bill felt burning tears of shame course down his face. He felt like the time the club had ridden off and forgotten him in Boise. Only worse because this time, they wouldn't be coming back when they ran out of beer.

He was alone.

"Hey! Dumbass, we gotta move." Nellie said.

CHAPTER FOUR

Interstate 17, Black Canyon Freeway, Arizona

Bill cried for a half-hour straight as the bike sped along the blacktop. Nellie was spattered with his tears. Then, outside the Agua Fria National Monument, Bill went silent. She could feel the clenched muscles of his back.

Nellie squeezed him but it was like hugging a refrigerator; hard and unyielding and full of frost.

Nellie's brain told her that Bill was better off without his pack of losers. Her heart told her he was her Lancelot, who had sacrificed his previous life for a just cause, and for her. And her instinct told her he was hurting, and she had better do something to prop up his ego. Or she was sure he'd start blubbering again and she'd be sitting behind a lawn sprinkler for another thousand miles.

As they rose slowly into the Prescott National Forest, the flat, gray desert was broken up by cottonwood-lined washes and striated rock formations. Bill said nothing. The ground on either side grew a furze of green and scraggly stands of piñon pine and juniper, and finally became high ponderosa. But the desert remained in Bill's soul.

As they stopped for gas, Nellie tried to water it with praise.

"Honey," she said, "I just want you to know that what you did back there was the bravest thing I have ever seen. And I have seen cage fights between midgets and bears."

"I don't wanna talk about it," Bill said. "Who won?"

"Bear," she said. "It got ugly. But you gave up your old life, your Round Table, for your Momma, for the promise you made her. You are my hero, William Butcher. My smelly Galahad."

"I don't feel like a hero," he said. "I feel like somebody cut my dick off and fed it to pigs."

"No, no, Sweetie," she said. "It's still there. Let me show you..."

"Unh-unh," he said. "Sorry, Snowball."

Dear Jesus, Nellie thought with dismay. A blow job can't fix this!

Her heart went out to him. She'd never been with a man who cared about anything enough to cry over it for a half-hour – none had ever cried five minutes over her.

She didn't know how to help him right now, except to let him alone. She would just have to let him grieve. It felt uncomfortable not having an answer to his pain.

She wasn't sure how long Bill needed to come to grips with his ordeal so she tried the scientific method. Every fifty miles, she reached around and grabbed his crotch. Each time, there was nothing doing. It was like checking the pop-up thermometer on a turkey in the oven.

He wasn't done yet. So they rode on in a hard and uncomfortable silence through the forest and down again into the flinty desert.

They had just passed Winslow when they heard the whoop of a police siren. An Arizona Highway Patrol motorcycle backed by two patrol cars came up behind the bike, lights flashing.

"Oh shit," Bill said. "Snowball, I should have warned you. This happens a lot."

"You weren't doing anything!"

"Yes I was - driving while big. I saw the bike but he didn't hit the lights until he had backup." Nellie prudently pushed the handle of the Colt out of sight between her breasts.

A trooper got off the bike and walked slowly toward them, shiny boots crunching on the road shoulder. Behind him, the other troopers got out of their cars. They stood with their feet apart, cradling shotguns and watching warily.

Bill waited. The cop came up, took his time looking up and down at Bill and the bike, then turned his attention on Nellie, who smoldered.

"Nice bike," the cop said. "License and registration, please."

Bill reached into a breast pocket and pulled them out.

"Take them out of the holder, please."

"There's no holder. That's steak sauce." Bill wiped the papers with a leather-gloved hand. The cop took them between his finger and thumb, wrinkling his nose. His blue helmet and dark glasses glinted in the sun.

"William Butcher?" He asked.

"He's Bill," Nellie said. "Nobody calls him William."

"Mr. Butcher," the cop said.

"Trooper .... Reyes," Bill replied, reading his nametag.

"Do you know why I stopped you?"

The cop's head leaned forward confidentially, as if they were having a pleasant conversation.

"'Cause I am a scary-looking fuck and you're just doing your job?" Bill said it matter-of-factly.

The cop smiled with gritted teeth. They gleamed like his sunglasses. He glanced back at his buddies. They took a step forward and the tips of their guns edged up. Reyes shook his head and they stopped.

"Where are you heading?" Reyes asked.

"East. Got a job for my Momma."

"Your momma." The cop managed a tone of polite but contemptuous disbelief. "Are you carrying any weapons or narcotics on your person?"

"Boot knife and this..."

Bill reached into a side pocket. The cop jumped back and put a hand to his holster.

Bill pulled out a silver can.

"Beer," Bill said,

The cop's shoulders dropped but his hand hovered over the gun.

"You'll have to pour that out, sir," he said.

"Yeah, I know," Bill said regretfully. "It was warm, anyway."

He popped the tab and the golden stream splashed onto the asphalt. He crushed the empty and stuffed it back in his pocket.

The cop moved forward again. "The reason I stopped you, sir, is to ask about your helmet."

"My helmet?" Bill asked. "That's a new one."

"You're not wearing it correctly," the cop said.

Bill reached back and tapped the helmet. He wore it like a skullcap, the crown pointing nearly straight upwards. He pulled it forward and then tried to tug it down but the sides stopped at his ears and stubbornly refused to budge, despite his grunting efforts.

"It's the biggest size they had," Bill said apologetically. The cop looked skeptical.

"It's a religious thing," Nellie said quickly. "He's Jewish."

The cop actually smiled at that. Nellie lit up.

"Thought you might be a Buddhist," he said. He pointed at Bill's denuded jacket. "You're not flying colors. Who do you ride with?"

Bill was silent. Then in a hoarse voice, he said: "Nobody. Now." His big hand stole to the empty space on his shoulder and he sniffled.

Nellie patted his back. "It's all right, baby. You got me." She looked at the cop. "It just happened. He's still grieving. He gave up his friends for me. And his Momma. It's a long story."

The cop tried to scratch his head but his fingers met his helmet.

"Well, who did you ride with?"

"The PRIKs," Bilk said, between snuffles.

The cop snorted. He turned to his colleagues and waved them back to their cars.

"Sorry for your loss," he said. "You can go on, now. But get another helmet."

"Get another bike," Nellie said. "Those Kawasakis sound like their balls haven't dropped yet."

"Nellie ...," Bill warned.

But the cop actually was grinning.

"Have a good day, Mr. Butcher. Ma'am." he sketched a salute with two fingers as Bill gunned the big engine and pulled back onto the highway - not too fast, but fast enough.

"They had a lot of guns," Nellie said as they sped off. "Nice guys, though. For cops."

Bill said nothing. Loudly. After about a hundred miles, Nellie almost wished the cops had shot him. She was about reaching her tolerance for moping.

Nellie and Bill stopped for the night at the Silver Moccasin Motel in East Albuquerque, which was, in fact, painted silver with pastel blue and pink plastic blobs around the doors and windows to represent Indian beadwork. Bill rolled his bike up the tar-patched driveway, spotted the employee parking - it was the only carport - and pushed the bike in. Grabbing the saddlebags, he and Nellie walked into the lobby, which was decorated with imported knockoffs of Navajo blankets. He paid nineteen dollars in advance to the weedy-looking clerk.

"I parked in the carport," Bill told him. "I know the neighborhood. I'm a regular."

"You can't park there, sir," the clerk said tartly. "That's not for guests."

"Fine. I'll put it in the room, then," Bill said. The clerk began to say something, then took a second look at the black cloud that was Bill's expression and swallowed. He ran his tongue over his protruding teeth and decided that he wanted to keep them.

"No problem at all, sir," he replied, handing Bill a key and a roll of toilet paper.

The room smelled like stale cigarettes, vomit and cheap disinfectant. Everything in it was chipped except for the clock, which was broken. The window-unit air conditioner gasped. But the shower and the mini-fridge worked, the TV was mostly in color, and the bedsprings weren't quite peeking through the mattress.

Nellie gave Bill a wan smile. She was exhausted by the ride and by Bill's continued silence. Bill also seemed beat. He flopped onto the bed without taking off his boots. He sank five inches into the mattress.

Nellie pulled her spare pair of underwear out of a saddlebag. It was crushed and the lace was dingy. But right now, she needed to feel more like a woman than a road beast.

She held them up for Bill. He turned on his side and grunted.

Nellie said something under her breath that would have ignited the air if she'd said it out loud.

Never go to bed angry, she reminded herself. Or with the urge to disembowel your lover. Unless you really plan to do it.

She was seriously contemplating that thorny decision when her cellphone rang. The ringtone was a mooing cow.

"It's your momma calling," Nellie said. "I gave her my number."

"Momma?" Bill perked up, Nellie saw with a spark of jealousy.

She handed him the pink, rhinestone-covered phone.

“Momma,” Bill said, only semi-listlessly. One tooth peeked out in a quarter-smile.

“No,” said a gruff voice. “This is Tony. Do I sound like a chick? I mean, I know if you do too many steroids ...”

“Shut up, Tony,” Bill said. “What do you want? How’s Momma?”

“My momma? Fine. How do you know my momma?”

“No, you idiot, the woman you’re watching is MY momma.”

"Oh. Yeah. Well, uh, there's good news and bad news about that."

Bill felt his stomach lurch. In the movies, conversations that started like that never ended well.

"What's the good news?" he asked.

"You are about to become a property owner. You're gonna get the diner."

"Why am I gonna get the diner?"

"Well, that's the bad news. See, we like your Ma. Reminded me of my Dad. Anyway, we were watching “Cougar Town” and your Mom was saying she had way better jugs than that Courtney woman, and then she says she wants a snack.”

“That’s Momma,” Bill said. “So?”

“So we went to House of Pies and got ...."

"I know. Boysenberry, blueberry and Oreo cheesecake," Bill said, his eyes lighting with the memory.

“Those probably would have been better choices,” Tony admitted.

“But that ain’t what you got?” Bill asked.

“No. We got her what she asked for.”

Bill’s blood ran cold. “What flavor?” he said with rising horror. “Tell me it wasn’t...”

In a quavering voice, Tony said, “Bill, it was ... key lime.”

Bill felt like he’d been strapped to the front of a semi in a demolition derby.

"Key lime?" he said in a harsh whisper. "You did not give her ... key lime pie?”

There was an uncomfortable silence on the other end.

"She asked for it," the goon said in a tiny voice.

"She always asks for key lime," Bill said. "It's her favorite. She's allergic. We'd catch her smuggling it and wrestle it out of her fingers. I lost my first tooth that way."

"Well, we know that now."

"Everybody in town knows not to sell it to her."

"Well, we didn't say it was for her."

"What happened?" Bill struggled to remain calm. "Is she still in a coma?"

"Uh, not so much..." Tony said.

Bill felt a rush of relief.

"Man, you scared me. So what happened?"

Tony paused.

"Well, she ate three of 'em," he said at last. "Kind of fast. Then there was this ... smell and this sound, and she turned kind of purply. About that time, we kind of got worried but she was still breathing - and eating."

"So you called the doc?"

"No," Tony said. "'Cougar Town' was still on and your Momma said to shut the hell up so she could watch the end. So we did. Her eyes were kinda puffy by then but I think she saw the whole thing. Kept mumbling about Courtney Cox's boobs. Personally, I think they're pretty good for an old broad..."

"What the fuck happened?" Bill shouted, crushing the phone to his ear. Rhinestones flew like crystal dandruff.

"How do I put this?" Tony said. "She closed her eyes. She was *really* purple. Then she made this noise. I don't wanna describe it," Tony gulped. "And then she...she...Bill, she kind of exploded."

"You blew up Momma?"

"Well, jeez, guy, have some sympathy for us. We had to watch it. I still got some of her on my sandals."

"Momma's dead?"

"She is, Bill. I'm real sorry. We really did like her. She's the sweetest hostage we ever had. And she died doing what she loved. So you're gonna have to get back here and arrange the funeral - or the vacuuming, or something."

Bill responded, "She always said she never wanted to leave the house, and I guess she's a part of it now."

"Really, really sorry, Bill. We did treat her as well as we could. She died with a smile on her lips."

"Did she mention me?"

"I asked her, sitting there all exploded, if she had any last words. Something to say to you, maybe. She whispered: 'Fuck you, more pie!' Uh, you're not gonna hunt us down and kill us, are you?"

"No, you did the best you could. You couldn't a known. She's in a better place now."

There was a puzzled silence.

"On the ceiling?"

Bill hung up. He turned to Nellie, a look of pain on his face. He looked crowbar-stunned.

"Momma's dead," he said. "For real dead."

"Oh God. What happened?"

"She wanted key lime pie. They gave her key lime pie. She can't eat key lime pie." Bill tugged at his beard in sorrow. "They killed her with kindness. They gave her everything she asked for."

"Bastards!" Nellie said.

"No, it wasn't their fault. It was momma's insatiable appetite - and the key lime pie."

"We have to go back now so I can bury her," he added.

"No, we will not," Nellie said firmly. "I had to put up with your moping all the way from Phoenix, William Butcher. And we are damn sure not repeating that trip unless you can afford some seriously good hallucinogens to dull the pain."

Bill goggled at her.

"We got to go back. She was the only Momma I had."

"I'm your Momma now," Nellie said, crossing her arms. "And Momma says this: Let the dead bury their dead, as Jesus said. Look: If we go back, you lose the diner. Your Momma would never want that. She wanted you to have it."

"She wanted it for herself, for the pies."

"Well now she's dead, and you're her son and heir, and she'd want you to have it."

Bill thought hard about that. Eight long seconds passed.

"You're right," he said. "But I will never sell key lime pie at that diner. That pie must pay for killing my momma."

"Sounds like suicide by stupidity if you ask me," Nellie said under her breath.

But all she said out loud was; "Come to Momma. Baby needs a hug."

She swept most of him into her arms - as much as she could comfortably handle and Bill felt his pain dissolve in the enormous swell of her breasts. He reached around, put his hands under her bottom and hoisted her up until she was riding him in the air. The floor creaked. She smelled of sweat and taco sauce. The pain in his chest was still there but it was a different pain - actually it was the barrel of the gun poking into his sternum. He crushed her mouth against his, and most of her other parts, too. He wanted to say something to her, to let her know what he was feeling.

"Let's hump, sugar lump."

Much later and messier, the sun cast a blinding glow over cracked asphalt, dead rats and dumped bodies, bringing a new day to East Albuquerque. Bill and Nellie rolled off the splintered bed and prepared to hit the road. Nellie was sore in places she hadn't seen for several years and had almost forgotten existed. Bill seemed almost cheerful as he scraped some of the dirt off himself with the thin washcloth - even he wasn't about to risk the wildlife in the hotel shower. He was actually humming as he braided his beard. Nellie said a secret prayer of gratitude to the Sex Goddess, who had given females the Power to move men's minds. And to get them out of their goddamn moods, although She sure took her time on this occasion, Nellie told herself. But then, Bill was a deep feeler, if not a thinker.

Before they hit the road, Nellie handed Bill her phone.

"Call the cops, Sweetie," Nellie told Bill. "Tell 'em your momma's dead but you can't get to her. The coroner'll hold her until we get back. Then we'll do right by her."

Bill gave her a tooth-challenged grin so wide it was like looking down the throat of a railroad tunnel.

And for the rest of that day, as they hurtled down Highway 66, he told Nellie what kind of funeral they'd have. Nellie thought the cannons would be overkill.

CHAPTER FIVE

Joe's American Syrup & Fries Diner, New Jersey Turnpike, July 11, 2010

Norman Wuu sat at his shabby metal desk, rich with history and toilet paper inventories. Soon all of this would be his, he swore. The thought held an electric charge and made it hard to concentrate on balancing the diner accounts. He'd gotten a taste of ordering lackeys around but his heart was really with the paperwork. Masterminds were like that. They could hire people with people skills. Or slaves.

His cellphone gonged. He'd custom-downloaded the ringtone. It had the forlorn majestic tolling of a Tibetan temple - one where an insomniac monk was pissing off villagers.

Ah. That was the gong of fulfillment, the tone he'd selected for anyone handling his scheme to get the diner. His goon gong.

He smirked, in a mastermind sort of way. Chortling would come later; he'd been practicing.

"Hello," he said.

"Hi."

A moment passed.

"Umm," Wuu said. "You called me."

"Yeah. Sorry."

Another uncomfortable silence. Wuu toyed with the edge of a billing notice. Sixty cases of frozen hamburger patties. For a Monday? That didn't seem right. Mondays were fish days. His triumphant euphoria was sagging.

"You called me," Wuu said again, prompting. "So you probably wanted to tell me something important?"

"Yeah, but you're the boss so I thought, you know, you'd start the conversation."

Lackeys, Wuu thought. With people skills.

"All riiight," he said. "So, how's it goin'?"

The silence, somehow, spoke of bemused puzzlement.

"We're not goin' anywhere. Unless you tell us to. But we'd like to. It's pretty messy in here."

Wuu sighed. "I really don't need to know that. Is the bitch still there?"

Another uncomfortable silence. Wuu thought of the waste of his cellphone minutes.

"Oh yeah," came the reply at last. "She's not goin' anywhere."

"You're sure?"

"Ab-so-freakin'-lutely."

"Then why are you acting so weird?"

And yet another silence.

"Is there some kind of a problem?"

"Define problem ...."

"Goddamnit, just tell me why you called. I have work to do."

"Well, we just thought you should know - that nobody's goin' anywhere. But we'd kind of like to, like I said - because of the, um, mess. And the smell."

Wuu had an uncomfortable jolt.

"Like the smell of ... blood?" He whispered with thrilled horror.

"No. Key lime pie. Gone real bad."

"What?" he stared at the phone. Was it the connection? "So, you didn't kill her or something? She's alive?"

The phone was silent yet again.

"That's two questions," the caller said.

Norman's hard-fought icy composure was melting like a frozen meat patty in an unplugged fridge.

He said through gritted teeth: "Just answer the goddamn question. Both of them."

"Yeahhhh. So, no, we didn't kill her."

"Thank God for that."

"But she is dead."

"Oh shit."

"Not our fault. She died kind of happy."

Happy? Wuu quickly thought of all the possible options that could have made the woman happy. Every one of them was disgusting.

"Look, I don't want to know."

But at the same time, he felt a surge of joy. Problem solved! It was worth the extra message units. But they were waiting for instructions. He took a breath and adopted his mastermind voice.

"Okay. Your job is done now. I assume you'll make sure you don't leave any traces behind. You know, fingerprints, or ... yuck, whatever."

A nauseating image sprang into his mind. He shuddered and suppressed it.

"Um, that's kind of a big job," the caller said. "I think we'd need ..." There was a pause. "Oh, about five guys and five gallons of Pine-sol. And shovels. Maybe a fire hose. We can pick 'em up at the Home Depot but we don't have any cash."

Wuu drummed his fingers on the desk.

"No, no. no. This is a clandestine operation, get it?"

"Clan? We didn't sign up for a racist thing, man." The voice sounded offended. In a stupid sort of way.

Wuu sighed the sigh of exasperation he had perfected when talking to inferiors, which was pretty much everyone.

"Look, just clean up anything you touched or stepped in. Clear?"

"Well that makes more sense. Hold on a second..." the voice became muffled, as if the caller had turned away from the phone, and Wuu heard: "Hey Frankie, you see a mop around here?"

"You kidding? There wasn't even any toilet paper - 'course I didn't find no bathroom, either."

Wuu, unable to restrain himself, interjected, "It probably was outside."

"No, I looked, There's just this little shack. For chickens or something. Smells like a poultry graveyard. The old lady kept trying to make us go there."

"That's an outhouse, moron."

"Well, duh, of course it's an *out* house," Tony said. "It's outside. I just said that."

"Never mind," Wuu said irritably. "Just go get some cleaning supplies."

"Wait, I got an idea," Tony said. "Hey, Frankie, get on the horn and call Bill back. Maybe he knows where she kept her cleaning stuff."

"I hope it ain't under all this, er, all of her," Frankie said. "I ain't about to go sortin' through that mess."

Tony came back on the phone, sounding annoyingly chipper. "Okay, boss. We're on it."

Wuu's voice was frigid.

"Who is Bill?" he asked icily.

"Bill? Oh, that's her kid. He showed up. She sent him to the courthouse. That's before she died, of course. Nice guy. He didn't beat us up much."

"Except for my balls," Frankie said.

"I told you, just keep icin' 'em," Tony said. "Will you please make the damn call? You don't hear me complainin' about my tootsies. Butch up, for Christ's sake. You drop shit on yourself in the gym, you think the client's gonna wait while you bitch about it? Now I'm not so sure I want you to keep being my personal trainer."

"I never dropped nothin' on my balls, Tony. Maybe ice cream..."

Wuu cut in.

"The courthouse?" he said, his voice like the heart of Everest. The tone caught Tony's attention, apparently.

"Yeah," he replied slowly. "You know, the one you told us about."

"The one I paid you to keep her away from?"

The resulting silence seemed somehow to be laced with Tony's dawning comprehension of his utter fuckupped-ness.

"Oops," he squeaked. It was a tiny little sound.

Wuu heard a snap and felt a sharp pain in his hand. He looked down and saw that he'd broken his favorite, handcrafted Black Wing No. 2 pencil in half. And the point had disappeared into his clenched fist.

"Ow," he said.

"Did you say owl?" Tony asked, puzzled. "Is that, like, a code word or something?"

"Shut the fuck up," Wuu said. "I am in pain. That is not your concern. Your concern is to tell me about this Bill. Ow."

Wuu finally hung up the phone and only then did he reach into his drawer, extract a small pair of tweezers and remove the point of his favorite pencil from his palm. Now he faced a difficult choice. Glue the point back on, or sharpen the pencil? Undecided, he put it in an envelope in his top drawer for later consideration. He would have labeled the envelope "Pencil point" but his pencil was broken.

Then he turned to the most pressing problem. He cursed himself for using cut-rate labor. When he ruled the world, idiots like that would be relegated to circuses and children's TV.

To stop this Bill from usurping his birthright, Wuu would need real muscle, and for not too much money. For a moment he thought of calling in the Iron Pigeon Drop Fighting Ninjas but decided against it. Every member got one free assault but he didn't want to use it up, and he sure wasn't going to pay for the premium upgrade. Besides, he wasn't sure they were really all that lethal. Some of the people you met at Comic-Con weren't all that genuine. No, he'd have to hire minions.

But where to find them? And again, they had to be affordable. He'd almost tapped out his petty cash on the previous goods. Wuu sat for a moment, chin in hand, immersed in thought. Then he leapt to his feet. Of course! He was in New Jersey, for Pete's sake. Somebody at the loading dock would know somebody who knew somebody. Maybe that delivery guy who somehow managed to get fresh fish on a Monday ....

Ten minutes later, Wuu walked into the washroom and scrubbed the smell of halibut off his hand. He was smiling as he returned to the office. He opened his desk drawer, took out a brand new pack of index cards and pulled out a pink one. Pink was for threats to his plans. He grabbed a Sharpie and wrote on it: "Bill the Biker." He only used Sharpies for world domination details, not regular business.

As Sun Tzu (or somebody) said: if life doesn't go according to plan, change the plan.

Henchlings were *so* complicated, though. You had to tell them *everything*. Then they had to do it. Not like paperwork. With paperwork, if you had fifty extra rolls of toilet paper that didn't belong there, you just got rid of it, drew a line through it, marked it out. Why couldn't you cross out people like toilet paper?

Well, why not?

His eyes gleaming, Wuu turned and faced the hamburger invoice. He grabbed his approval stamp and poised it over the paper for a crushing blow, like the hammer of God.

The last words of his conversation with the dense goon echoed in his head.

"Why didn't you keep him there, too?" Wuu had asked.

"Cause you didn't tell us, and we didn't know he existed. Plus, he's big. Really, really big. I felt sorry for his bike."

Wuu hated motorcycles. The first thing he planned to do when the diner was officially his was to take a sledgehammer to the bike on the pedestal in the main room. Crazy Uncle Cho had had the thing custom-built in memory of the Slut. It was on a rotating platform that would have been better used as a condiment stand, Wuu thought.

Inside its Plexiglas cylinder, the bike was the center of a sound and light show every two hours. Wuu winced when he remembered the colored lights gleaming on the chrome, fake smoke roiling up around it as the roar of an engine rumbled through six speakers, rattling his fillings. Then, for five minutes, to the sound of a galloping Western bass line, a folksy voice actor told the story of the "Wild Woman," who blew into town one night and left behind a trail of love and mystery ... *and probably a venereal disease,* Wuu added sourly.

He looked at the phone number he'd inked on his palm and picked up the phone.

After two rings, a dry voice came on the line.

"Angel," it said. The voice carried the crackle of ice on a frozen lake. Wuu suddenly felt a chill.

"Um, I got this number from Alejandro." The man on the other end said nothing.

"Alejandro?" Wuu said again.

"What do you want?" Mr. Angel said at last.

"I have a problem. Special problem. I mean, not ..." Wuu lowered his voice to a stage whisper. "Exactly *legal.*"

"Uh huh."

"You're not a cop, right? You have to tell me if you are."

There was a low sigh on the other end of the line.

"No, I wouldn't. And why would anybody you know have the phone number of an undercover cop?"

"You have a point," Wuu acknowledged. "Unless, this is a double-cross."

"Tell me what you want or don't. But don't waste my time."

Wuu sighed in relief. A cop wouldn't say that. Salaried government employees always wanted to waste time. Those slackers loved to run the clock. When he was in charge...

"Hey, idiot!" Angel said. "Stop mumbling to yourself. This isn't a porn line. I'm not paid to hear you jerk off. So talk business or I hang up."

"It's Bill," Wuu blurted. "It's a guy I want you to grab."

"Ransom?"

"Not really," Wuu said. "I just need you to keep him over ice..."

"*On* ice," Mr. Angel corrected. "For how long?"

"Two days. Then you let him go and that's it," Wuu said.

"So short-term snatch. Right. That's ten thousand dollars, plus meals, gas and extras and a per diem."

"Per diem? That seems excessive. What if you cover food for the ... er, guest?"

"Are you trying to nickel-and-dime me? Have you ever done this before?"

"I'm just saying, is this like a vacation package, all included, or is it a la carte?"

"It's a freakin' buffet, OK? Where did you get this number again?"

"I'm from New Jersey. I negotiate this stuff all the time."

"Really? So you, what, ask the Mafia to offer a discount, like Dimple's? You think I take coupons?"

"Well, since you asked, do you?"

There was a long pause.

"Listen, dummy. Pay me what I want and I do the job. The terms are non-negotiable. I am not an Early Bird Special."

"Oh, all right. Soooooorry."

"Okay. Next order of business. If for some reason I can't grab him or hold him, do you authorize other measures?"

"What do you mean?"

"If everything goes to shit - which it won't - but if there are unexpected complications, can I proceed as I see fit?"

"Is that more expensive?"

"Yes. If he needs to have a permanent accident, say, that could run you ... $20,000 or more. Plus expenses, Chainsaw gas, cleanup, yadda yadda."

"Wow. Hold on ...." Wuu put down the phone.

Wuu's bank account was down to $25,000 and change. He started to sweat. Then he remembered: he had monthly invoices! Wuu turned to his desk calculator, mumbling.

"If I just add, let's see, two extra cases of hamburger patties, frying grease, truck gas - double that - doable!"

He picked up the phone.

"Ok," he said. "I'll authorize what it takes. If you can't hold him up then put him down. Uh, is this a money-back deal?"

"No. But we'll send you an itemized bill for your taxes."

"Really?"

"No."

"Oh. Well, OK anyway. So how do you want me to pay? Monthly installments?"

"You are joking, right?"

"Ha, ha. Yeah. So cash?"

"Visa or PayPal."

"Really?"

"Yeah. Or bitcoin. We're progressive."

"Ok. Thanks. Nice doing business with you. Bye."

But the line was already dead.

As dead as Bill would be if he put up a fight ....

Unbidden, Wuu released a perfect, evil chortle.

CHAPTER SIX

Interstate 40, Eastern Arizona

In the late afternoon, about the time rattlers were reconsidering their tanning options and damning the evolutionary path that left them without internal temperature regulation, Bill and Nellie came up on another police checkpoint.

An unmarked dark blue SUV with a flashing light bar blocked the highway.

"Oh shit," Bill said with a grunt. "Here we go again."

He eased off the throttle and let the heavy bike roll to a stop a few yards from the car. Two men got out of the SUV and walked slowly over. They wore dark military-style T-shirts and pants, long-brimmed baseball caps without insignia, polished combat boots, and their hands were on the thick butts of holstered guns. Both wore dark glasses and were ridiculously square-jawed. It was like watching a pair of life-sized G.I. Joe dolls, Nellie thought.

Joe No. 1 approached Bill.

"Stop the engine, sir, and step off the bike."

"Who are you guys?" Bill asked.

"Homeland Security," the man said gruffly. "Just a routine check."

"In the middle of nowhere?" Nellie asked. "Show me a badge."

The man ignored her and looked at Bill.

"Step off the bike, please," he repeated.

Nellie seemed about to say something but Bill gave her a glance that silently urged her to shut it.

She got down from the bike. The man ignored her but watched carefully as Bill dismounted. He was a head taller than either man.

"May I see your license and registration, please," Joe No. 1 asked. Bill dug them out. The man seemed to examine them carefully, looking from them to Bill and back. Then he looked over to the other man and nodded. Joe No. 2 came up.

"Mr. Butcher?" Joe No. 1 said. "Please turn around and put your hands behind your back."

"What? Why?" Nellie said shrilly. "He doesn't have to do that. He hasn't done anything!"

"Mr. Butcher, you are not being arrested. You are being detained for questioning on a matter relating to national security. I can't say any more but I strongly urge you to cooperate and we'll get this whole thing behind us as quickly as possible."

Nellie seemed about to change colors but Bill looked up and shrugged. "I told you this happens," he said apologetically. He turned around and crossed his hands. The man pulled a nylon band from his belt and cinched it around Bill's wrists. Then he patted him down thoroughly, removing Bill's beloved boot knife, which he slipped into his own belt.

"That's that," he said to the other man, who pulled off his cap and wiped his shining forehead. "For a second I thought this big bastard might give us trouble." Each man took an arm and they began to walk Bill back to the SUV.

"Hey!" Bill said. "What about my bike?"

"Your bitch can watch it," Joe No. 1 said. "We'll dump you back here in a couple of .... *urk!*"

Something large and furious hit him in the knees from behind and he went down. In the next moment, he felt the hard barrel of a gun pressed against his neck.

"Who's the bitch now?" Nellie said, and gave the Colt a cruel dig that made the man squeak. "And if Asshole No. 2 doesn't kiss the sand right now, you'll be breathing through the back of your head."

"Do it," Joe No. 1 cried. The other man cursed and went prone to the sand.

"Wait," Bill asked. "So these aren't cops?"

"No badges, no insignia, no manners," Nellie said. "The whole thing stank from the beginning. You're just too nice."

Bill looked shame-faced, then grunted, heaved and with a single jolt snapped the plastic cuffs.

"Who are you guys?" Nellie asked.

"Workin' stiffs," Joe No. 1 said. "Honest, we were just hired to hold your man for a couple days. We wouldn't have hurt him."

"I know, he's too cute," Nellie said.

She took Bill's knife from the man's belt, along with a couple more handcuff bands and tossed them to Bill, who trussed each man and took their guns.

Bill walked over to the SUV, pulled his knife and slashed all four tires.

Nellie stood up, still holding her Colt, and gave each man a firm kick. Their grunts echoed in the desert stillness.

"Don't come after us," she said, "Or I will lose my pleasant disposition."

"You don't know what you're doing," Joe No. 1 said.

"Neither do you, apparently," Nellie said. "Now you just share some quality time with the other snakes while we hit the road. Maybe you can start a support group: Belly-crawlers Anonymous."

She and Bill walked back to the bike. Bill gunned it to life.

Suddenly, from behind them, came shouts. Nellie looked and saw both men on the ground were writhing and yelling.

"That can't be good," she said. "Better get moving, lover."

As she said it, there was a bang and something that sounded like an angry bumblebee buzzed past her ear.

Nellie looked over and saw a third man, his pants around his ankles, standing up from a clump of roadside bushes and firing a gun with both hands.

Bullets made maddened insect noises as they swarmed past their heads. Bill gunned the throttle and the bike ate up the road. The gunfire diminished to a flurry of firecracker bangs and then to a scattered handful of sad little pops. In a mile, the sound of the Harley's deep thunder completely overshadowed them.

Fifteen miles down the road, Bill pulled the big bike into a rest area. Nellie unclenched her arms from around him. They both got off and beat at their clothing until they were standing in a cloud of dust.

Bill looked at Nellie.

"What the hell just happened?" he asked.

"Maybe those bozos at your Mom's house called their friends," Nellie replied but then shook her head. "Kinda find that hard to believe, though. People like that don't break a chili-fry commitment."

"They looked like cops," Bill said.

"Bill," she said. "They tried to *kill* us." She hugged herself and shivered.

Bill scratched his ear, dislodging more dust. "Who the hell has people killed over a damned diner? That's the trouble with people wantin' things."

He pulled Nellie to his massive chest. She stopped shaking and sank her face into the wiry strength of his beard.

"Listen," Bill said. "You didn't sign up for this. This ain't your fight."

Her head jerked back and she narrowed her eyes at him.

"If you think I'm leavin' you, you can just forget it."

"Hell, no," Bill said, surprised. "I meant let's forget the diner. It was your idea anyway."

Nellie pulled away angrily. For a moment she was speechless.

"Oh, now you're blamin' me?" she asked.

"Well, *you* made me promise Momma. I ain't blamin' you. It's just your fault." He shrugged as if that settled it. "So, how about Lubbock? They got a place where they got barbecued armadillos in the shell. You get a free meal if you eat five."

Nellie glared at him and blew air out of her cheeks. "Someone just *shot* at us. Food ain't gonna fix this."

Bill gaped at her. Then he said, reasonably: "Eatin' and runnin' away. I gave you two good options."

Nellie glowered at him, but it was spoiled by a snort. Nellie boiled over with laughter, a full-throttle guffaw that made her belly shake and left her gasping with her hands on her knees.

After a full minute, she looked up at the worried Bill and rubbed tears out of her eyes, streaking her dust-powdered face.

"Oh, lover, I can't stay mad at you. Come here. Give me some tongue."

The next few minutes were spent up against a sagging wooden outhouse. Small creatures that had nested there scurried for their lives or were crushed.

At last, Bill and Nellie returned to the bike.

Bill beamed at her. "Our first fight, and our first makeup sex."

"I feel all ... reality show," Nellie said with a grin.

"So," Bill said as he threw his leg over the hog. "We give up the diner, right?"

Nellie stared at him in disbelief.

"Hell no we don't."

"Awww come on," Bill said. "I don't wanta argue again, I'm makeup-sexed out."

Nellie mounted behind him and thumped his helmet.

"You are not givin' in," she said. "Paladins do not surrender to the forces of darkness and evil. Or dragons."

"What the hell is a paladin?" Bill asked. "This is a Harley."

"All that evil needs to conquer is for good men to do nothin'."

"It's a diner, Nellie, not the goddamn Statue of Liberty."

"Remember the bullets whizzin' past your head. That is an insult to your manhood and *I* will not stand for it."

"I'm really kind of OK with standin' for it, as long as they don't do it again."

"I wouldn't bet the house on that," Nellie muttered. "Now, giddyap!"

"Mr. Wuu?"

"Yes?"

"This is Mr. Angel."

"Ah hah!"

"Why are you chuckling?"

"It's not a chuckle. It's an evil chortle."

"Can you hear me?"

"You didn't say anything."

"No I didn't. So follow my lead and shut up."

Wuu's jaw clamped shut with an audible snap and he gulped.

"It hasn't been two days..." he began.

"No, there's been a complication," Mr. Angel said. "Your biker got through my people. Did you know he had a bodyguard?"

"What?" Wuu said. "No, I didn't."

"Built like a tank. She had a gun."

"Oh."

"Yeah. Oh." Angel's voice had cold iron in it.

"Well," Wuu said slowly. "Sorry. But you're going to try again, right?"

"I am. A deal's a deal. But since you seem to be concerned about payroll, I thought I'd let you know the price just doubled."

"What!" Wuu squawked like a sodomized parrot.

"Two people, twice the price."

"But I don't want *her*," Wuu said. "She's nothing to me."

"She's a witness," Angel said. "And she has a gun. So now she's part of the equation. I'm actually cutting you a break on the price. I'm going to have to hire a lot more people."

"Okay, okay," Wuu said, his mind counting hamburger patties. "What about per diem and all that?"

"I'll toss that in for free," Mr. Angel said. "They got the drop on my troops, and that hurts my pride."

"Oh. Okay, then," Wuu said. "Thanks. You're a real professional. I will definitely give you a good Yelp review."

"What are you talking about?"

"Just kidding. Ha. Ha."

The line went dead. Norman though that seemed to be happening a lot.

And somewhere 632 miles outside of Phoenix, Bill rode on in horny blissful ignorance. While ahead of him, bad people with guns and expensive suits began to mass, coalescing like a cyclone of killer scorpions.

CHAPTER SEVEN

Interstate 40, New Mexico

It was late afternoon as Bill topped a low ridge, his shadow sweeping ahead of him on the asphalt beneath an empty blue sky. The road ran down to a swath of desert that stretched for miles into clear distance.

Instantly, Bill killed the motor and backed the bike a few feet below the rise.

"What is it?" Nellie asked.

"Saw something, about a mile ahead."

"What?" Nellie asked with sudden fear.

"Cars and guys."

"What are they doin'?"

"Dunno. I'm gonna check." Bill got off the bike, and trudged up the little ridge. After a moment he came back.

"Well, what did you see?" Nellie asked anxiously.

"Four SUVs, two on each side of the road, and a bunch of guys standin' around."

Nellie caught her breath.

"Did they look like those other assholes?"

"They could be assholes," he admitted. "They got suits."

"If they're in suits, they are definitely assholes. I mean, who wears a suit in the middle of the damned desert? Unless it's a funeral and the hearse broke down."

"No hearse," Bill acknowledged.

"Did you see guns?"

Bill shook his head.

"Too far. But they could have weapons under their suits." He thought about it.

Nellie said something unfeminine but heartfelt. She reached out a hand and gripped Bill's.

"What do we do?" she asked.

"We can go back," he said hopefully.

"To find a way around, I presume you mean," Nellie said frostily.

Bill thought about it. "That's what I meant?" he asked.

"Yes, it is," Nellie said.

"Yep," Bill agreed.

He got on, kicked the engine to life, turned the Harley in a slow circle and roared off back the way they had come. After less than a mile they spotted a weathered sign on their side of the roadway. Bill pulled over. The four-by-eight sheet of plywood read: "Arizona's Original Petting Zoo" in faded paint. An arrow pointed down a dirt road. Beneath the words was a crude drawing of something with a long body, claws and lots of spindly legs.

"What's that?" Bill asked.

"I think it's a scorpion," Nellie said.

"I think it's a lobster," Bill said.

Nellie scoffed. "What would a lobster be doing in a petting zoo in Arizona? But, I'll admit, I could draw a better scorpion."

"I wouldn't want to be petting a lobster, anyway. Those suckers got mean claws."

Bill revved up the bike, turned and bounced down the dirt road, raising a rooster tail of dust.

The road ran over a downed barbed wire fence and petered off in front of a weedy, lumpy field stacked with junk, broken machinery and weathered lumber. Beyond that, a house that seemed to be held together mainly by rusty nails and faith stood in the weeds. Some places in the warped wooden siding had been patched with flattened-out tin cans.

Bill and Nellie got off the bike and walked up the sagging porch steps to a screen door. It was locked.

Nellie knocked and called: "Hello. Anybody home? "

Behind the screen door, an old wooden door cracked open. It was too dim to see inside but they heard a sound Bill knew; a shotgun being cocked.

"What you want?" a man's voice asked curtly.

"This road go anywhere besides here?" Bill asked. "We were looking for a...shortcut past the highway."

"Stops here. You best go back."

The voice had all the friendliness of a guy finding a Jehovah's Witness on his doorstep during the Super Bowl.

"We were looking for the zoo," Nellie said quickly. "Maybe we took a wrong turn." She looked doubtfully back up the road.

"It's customers, Radine," the man called over his shoulder. "I told you we needed to take down that danged sign."

The screen door unlatched and a shotgun poked out. Nellie and Bill took a step back.

"Philip, play nice!" a woman said. "You don't know if they need shootin'"

She laughed. It sounded like a squirrel being dragged by its tail across a tin roof.

A middle-aged man stepped out of the house, cradling the shotgun. He wore sharp-creased polyester slacks and a frayed hunting vest with no shirt. The vest pockets were stuffed with shells. His skinny chest was fish-belly white but his face and arms were a leathery brown. He smoothed the back of his mullet and attempted something that might, in dim light, have passed for a smile. But his eyes were cagy pinpoints of suspicion.

The door opened again and Radine stepped out. She was short, with close-cropped hair and wore men's clothing on a square-shaped body. She looked at them with beautiful brown eyes in a desert-weathered face.

"Hello," she said. "So you found us. We actually closed the zoo about a month ago. Tourist season was just too stressful for the critters. They don't like light."

"Well," Nellie said. "Maybe we should just go."

Radine stepped forward.

"No, I think it'll be fine. It's their nappy time. Just don't poke 'em. That'll be two dollar, apiece. The zoo's around back. Where'd you put the key, Philip?"

"It's on the hook where it always is."

"Excuse me."

Radine popped back inside, rummaged, and returned a moment later with a key on the end of a hefty chain. Bill and Nellie followed her down the porch steps and around the house and out back to a field strewn with big rocks. In the middle sat a large building of graying wood that might once have been a tractor shed. The door was secured with a sturdy padlock.

"Why do you lock up the zoo?" Nellie asked. "There's nothing 'round here for miles."

Radine shook her head and looked up at Nellie. "Varmints can sneak up on you. The human kind."

Just then a dusty, bearded man with a rifle popped up from behind a nearby rock.

"Lacho, arms down," Radine yelled at him. "These are customers come to see my babies."

"Damn," Lacho said. "I thought we was goin' to get to do some shootin'."

"That time will be coming soon enough. The signs are coming together."

She looked back at Bill and Nellie and rolled her eyes. "He just sort of sits out here all day. I keep tellin' him to watch the front but he likes his rock." She shrugged and unlocked the shed.

"Stand back," she commanded.

She grabbed the handle and threw open the door, hurtling herself sideways in the same motion. A rusty meat cleaver swung down and slashed at the place where she had been standing. It swung back and forth in evil little arcs.

Radine stepped forward and grabbed the handle, halting it.

She smiled apologetically.

"The angle is wrong to make a clean decapitation, but the scream and the thump will let us know we've got an intruder."

Radine stepped inside and snapped on a light switch next to the door. Above them, a half-dozen long fluorescent tubes flickered to life. They cast a pallid greenish light that made the shed seem to be underwater. Pools of light glinted off rows of tanks. Terrariums stood on wooden tables or on the floor in untidy rows. Smaller ones were stacked on metal shelves around the walls. They were filled with dark crawling things.

Nellie shivered and took a step back.

"Don't worry, they're harmless," Radine said, putting a hand on her arm.

"What are they?" Bill asked.

"My babies," Radine said. "Scorpions, snakes, spiders, centipedes, a few ant colonies. Started off collecting the local fauna for fun and just got hooked. Scorpions are my favorites. They are just so *elegant.* I don't like to boast, but I'd say I've got the most complete selection of venomous arthropods in the West."

She moved down the aisles and Nellie followed reluctantly past cages full of stingers, fangs and claws. It felt like being in a maternity ward for nightmares.

"There are 1,750 species of scorpions," Radine said in a tour guide's voice. "One of the largest, the Emperor Scorpion, is about eight inches long. You'll see one in the next cage. But that's nothing compared to the primeval scorpions. An ocean-going ancestor that lived 400 million years ago was bigger than a man." She eyed Bill. "Well, *some* men."

"I get 'em in my boots sometimes," Bill said.

Radine opened a cage and reached inside, withdrawing a dark orange scorpion with fat claws like a lobster's. It sat sluggishly in her hand.

"This is my Indian Red," Radine said. "My *Hottentotta tamulus.* They're considered the most lethal. They can be man-killers. Sometimes I let it loose in the kitchen to get rid of the roaches. Wanna hold it?"

"Pass," Nellie said.

Radine gently replaced the monstrosity in its cage. They moved past tanks containing rattlesnakes, diamondbacks, big centipedes and inch-long Australian bulldog ants with jaws like spiked scissors.

When they finally left, Nellie suppressed the urge to slap herself to make sure she wasn't covered in bugs.

Bill combed his beard thoughtfully.

Radine reset the cleaver and then carefully closed and locked the door. She led them back to the house.

"Well, that's it," she said. "I know I jabbered on a bit in there but I do love my babies. They're worth a lot, too. I can get twelve bucks wholesale for one of my Arizona desert hairies."

"How's business?" Nellie asked.

"Good," Radine said. "Sold out of all my giant Vinegaroons last month. I sell to dealers and stores all over. Got a shipment going east today, if that trucker ever gets here."

Philip stepped out onto the porch, holding the shotgun casually in the crook of his arm, muzzle down.

"Well," he said. "Whaddya think?"

"Amazing," Nellie said. "Just absolutely amazing."

Radine beamed.

"Should be, she spends enough time in there," Philip groused. "She loves them scorpions more than me."

"They bite harder," Radine said.

"Do not."

"Do so, besides, they got a stinger you can't match."

Philip gave a lop-sided grin. Nellie decided she liked these people. They reminded her of herself and Bill, if a lot older and more desiccated. And *crazy*.

"Sorry we're out of souvenir T-shirts," Radine said. "Say, it's hot, you wanna try some scorpion tea?"

"Radine," Philip warned. "They's customers, not houseguests. There's the *equipment* inside." He jerked his head knowingly at the door.

"Oh, poop, pardon my French," Radine said. "If they were feds they would have busted us by now. Brought in a black helicopter."

Philip looked up at the empty sky.

Radine looked at Bill and Nellie. "He's a little suspicious of folks," Radine said. "But I know you're good people. The radar didn't ping so you don't have those tracker things in your heads." She shook her head. "Still, like the Boy Scouts say, be prepared. Which reminds me. I got to go feed Lacho. Why a grown man can't just walk to the fridge, I do not know. All kinds, right?"

"Riiiiight," Nellie said slowly.

Radine took Nellie's hand in both of hers and held it warmly. "If you don't mind my prying, what really brought you out here today? And don't tell me you were just looking for a roadside attraction."

"We saw one of those," Bill said. "We're trying to get away from it."

"Huh?" Philip asked.

"He means," Nellie said. "There are some men and some cars up the road. And we'd prefer not to make their acquaintance."

Radine and Philip gave each other meaningful looks that meant nothing to Nellie but still worried her.

"Honey, were they police?" Radine asked. "Are you outlaws?"

Bill looked uncomfortable.

"Not the way you mean," Nellie said hastily. "And I don't think cops would be wearing suits."

Phil's eyes went wide and jiggled.

"Did you say ... *suits?*" he breathed in a tight whisper.

"We think so," Nellie said. "They're about a mile or so off so it was hard to tell but they didn't look like they had uniforms."

"Oh, dear God," Radine said and put her hand to her mouth. "I was right about the signs coming together. You two are harbingers."

Nellie looked at her face.

"Um, actually, we were just hoping you could show us a way around so we can, you know..." she stared at Radine's hard, eager expression. "Listen, thanks for everything. We really have to go." She took Bill's arm.

Radine stepped forward.

"You weren't brought here to run away," she said with breathy determination. "You were brought here to *show us* the way!"

"No, I really don't think so ..."

"Really? Then why are you afraid of those men on the road?"

Nellie sighed. "It's kind of complicated."

Radine put a hand on her arm. "It's a hot day, and there's a porch, and I got two ears," she said jauntily. "Feel better if you get it off your chest. " She stumped up the porch and turned with a wicked smile. "Besides, sweetheart, you ain't goin' nowhere unless we help you."

"She has a point," Phil said, and then caught their expressions. "She didn't mean it menacin'-like. She only *looks* like a rattler." He winked at Radine, who gave a screechy laugh.

"Phil," Radine called. "I think we need to put eyes on those folks up the road. Don't you?"

"I'll get Lacho," Phil said. "He's the best spook we got. Whenever he decides to leave that damned rock."

Phil trudged off around the corner of the house. A short time later, a rusty, half-primered pickup truck bounced around the side of the house and disappeared down the dirt road.

Philip came back onto the porch.

"Well, he's off," Philip said.

"He sure is," Radine said, rolling her eyes. "Man can't even make himself a sandwich."

Philip shrugged. He'd heard this argument before. He went over and stood by his wife.

"Won't be long," Philip said. "Meanwhile, you probably need to tell us what's goin' on. Like I said, if you're part of what we think you're part of, we're all in this together. We need to know what you know, because we all need to know...uh, stuff ... that needs knowin'." Phil caught himself and shook his head. He stuck a hand in his vest pocket and rattled the shells. "Sorry, where was I?"

"You were about to get us all some tea," Radine said soothingly. "And take your meds."

"Yeah," Phil said, embarrassed. "Forgot again." He opened the screen door and disappeared inside.

Radine plumped herself down in a broken rocker and motioned Nellie and Bill to a wooden bench. Nellie sat gingerly. The bench bent under her weight.

Phil returned holding some plastic cups and a sun-tea jar of some slightly oily liquid with ice in it. It looked like the aftermath of an Alaskan oil spill.

"Help yourselves," Radine said. "It's got a kick but it goes down real well. It's slightly alcoholic. You're not Mormons, are you?"

Nellie eyed the dubious liquid.

"Yes ma'am, we are," Nellie said and tried to look disappointed.

Radine looked deflated. "Oh. Well, Phil will get you some well water. Meantime, do you mind if we...?"

"Oh, no, please, help yourselves," Nellie said.

Radine cheered up. Eventually, everyone was sitting with a cup in hand.

"Well, this is pleasant," Radine said. "Are you ready to tell your story?"

Bill looked down at his hands.

"The PRIKs kicked me out and my mom exploded yesterday," he said sadly.

There was dead silence on the porch.

"Um, what he means," Nellie interjected hastily, and in brief words described their journey.

At the end of it, Radine drained her cup of scorpion tea.

"Well," she said, and reached for the jar again.

"That is a hell of a story," Philip said. "So this is all about a diner?"

"Yeah," Bill said. "I was just tellin' Nellie – who the hell tries to kill someone for a diner?"

Phil glanced at him with disbelief. "You don't know?"

"Do you?" Nellie asked.

"I have my suspicions about *who,*" Philip announced. "And I dang sure know *why.*"

Philip jumped to his feet with springy energy. Apparently, the meds were taking effect.

"See," he emoted. "It's an old-fashioned American diner that was owned by an immigrant who built the American dream."

"Yes?" Nellie said.

"Well, that's it, ain't it?" Philip said. "Obviously, he died and wanted his business to go to real hard-workin' Americans. Otherwise, it might get tore down and replaced with one of those fast-food chains."

"Like McDonald's?" Bill asked. "I like Mickey D's. My mom took me there when we had money. I still got a paper hat and the cookie from a 1987 Happy Meal."

"Not McDonald's," Philip scoffed. "Everybody likes McDonald's."

Nellie asked. "Uh, Chick-fil-A?"

"Who the heck doesn't like Chick-fil-A?" Radine said, genuinely puzzled. "They're owned by true Americans."

"Oh, for..." Nellie began.

Philip looked grim as he peered around at each of them.

He said in a quiet voice: "What do you think about ...Starbucks?"

The porch went silent again. Radine spat on the floor, leaving a tar-like lump of tea.

"The horror," she said.

Just then, the rusty pickup bounced back up the road and swerved to a stop in front of the porch. Lacho jumped down and ran over.

"I been down the road," he said. "Those guys didn't bother me, so it ain't a sobriety checkpoint, 'cause I never passed one of those in my life. I just cruised past, back and forth, a couple three times. They didn't even look at the heap. Didn't seem interested in anybody drivin' past in a car, although I saw 'em check a semi-trailer."

"That's because they know what they're looking for," Nellie said. "A motorcycle."

"What they'd look like?" Phil asked.

"Like lawyers with guns," Lacho said. "Suits, suits and more suits. I counted about sixteen guys standing around. Four big black Chevy Suburbans with dark windows. One had the back hatch open. I could see a rack of guns inside. Maybe a couple MP5s and I swear one was a combat shotgun." He licked his lips. "She was sweeet."

"Shit," Nellie said. "What do we do?"

"We got to be sure before we act," Radine cautioned.

"The jackets," Lacho said.

"What?" Nellie asked, puzzled.

"Lacho, stop buildin' up the melodrama," Radine warned.

Lacho sighed.

"All right," he said. "Like I said, a lot had suits but some had camo and boots and all, and there was some in those cop windbreakers with the letters on the back." He waggled his eyebrows significantly.

"CSI?" Bill asked. "Good show."

"The Miami one is good," Phillip said. "The Las Vegas one kind of sucks. I don't like that red-headed woman."

"No, it weren't CSI," Lacho said irritably. His voice dropped to a hoarse whisper. "It was FBI."

Radine nodded. Philip cursed.

"Uh," Bill said haltingly. "I don't think they're really ...."

Lacho turned on him.

"Well, hell, of course it ain't the *real* FBI. We ain't stupid." He looked around solemnly at the others. "They're aliens!"

"Say what?" Nellie said.

"Space aliens," Lacho said, looking scornful.

"Oh, yeah, they took over the government a long time ago. Now they's cleanin' up the opposition. We may be the last rebel fortress."

Nellie looked at the junked washing machines in the front yard, stacks of bald tires and the sad strings of barbed wire that had once been a fence.

"Now," Philip said, holding up a reasonable hand. "Let's not be hasty. Maybe it *is* just chance. Maybe they don't know we're here. We do maintain radio silence."

"We just use a CB," Lacho explained. "It's too primitive for their sophisticated technology to track. Same as we use the old truck. No electronic ignition, so an EMP can't kill it."

"Plus it was only fifty dollars from my nephew at the salvage yard," Philip put in.

"What do we do?" Nellie asked.

"We could lie low," suggested Philip.

"*Et tu*, Philip?" Lacho said. "This is our chance to strike a blow, maybe a decisive one."

"Really, guys, I don't think..." Nellie tried to intercept.

"They're here for us," Bill boomed.

"Well, of course they are, man!" Lacho said, wheeling on him. "They gotta stop your diner. It's free market. And them aliens are Communists."

"Didn't think there was no more communists - except for Obama, of course," Phil said.

"Oh yeah," Lacho said firmly. "Hive minds. Ain't a free-thinking consumer among 'em. They all dress alike. I seen it." His eyes gleamed like new bullets. "First they'll take you out, and then they might be coming for us."

"How long have we got?" Bill asked.

"I say if they're waitin' for you, they may be there all night."

"We have to start planning," Radine said.

"For what?" Nellie asked.

Radine leaned over and thumped Bill in the chest with a calloused finger.

"To get you out of there," she said. "You got to go and get that diner, and then spread the word. And if we fail, then it's up to you to be the last beacon of sanity and freedom in this world."

Philip wiped a tear from one twitching eye.

"And even if we have to give up our bullet-riddled, anally-probed corpses for zombification and CIA slavery, we will have struck a blow," Radine said.

Bill's beard shook with emotion.

"I will name a milkshake for you all," he swore.

"What flavor?" Phil asked.

"Licorice?" Bill said.

"A licorice milkshake?"

"I like licorice," Lacho said. "But them Twizzlers are better."

"Can we please stay on topic?" Nellie asked. "So Radine, what is the plan?"

"Well, we got about a dozen contingency plans but first thing is to call in the troops. Lacho, get on the horn. We'll need everybody."

"Timmy, too?"

"Why, you don't think a ten-year-old can shoot straight? I said everybody! This is the big one."

"Wait, wait," Nellie said hurriedly. "You're thinkin' of shooting sixteen guys?":

"At least," Lacho said confidently.

"But if they're government..."

"Aliens," Philip said. "Government aliens."

"Anyway, right now they just want Bill and me. I don't think they know you're here. But if you kill *anybody,* then they'll bring in, I don't know, tanks or something."

"Like Waco?" Lacho asked.

"Worse," Nellie said. "Maybe they'll bring nukes. Flatten the whole desert."

Radine put her hand to her mouth. "My babies!"

"Soooo," Nellie pushed on hurriedly. "I think you can still strike a blow if you just distract them so we can get on our way."

"I dunno," Lacho said. "I still think this is the last stand. Radine, what do you think?"

"The signs don't lie," she said. "But sometimes they do tease you a little." She looked at Nellie and shrugged. "Little girl there may have a point. No reason to draw attention to ourselves until we're ready. Lacho, you're still looking for a Stinger missile, right?"

"Well, that's true. I reckon we'll need something to take out the black helos." Lacho scratched his head. "I'll ask Timmy to check eBay again."

"Well, there it is," Radine said. "So no killin.'"

"How about wingin"?" Philip asked.

"Well, the ideal thing would be to leave no bullets at all so forensics can't track 'em," Radine suggested.

"Well, what the hell are we gonna use?" Lacho asked.

Radine suddenly looked up at the deepening red sky. "There's something," she said. She took a deep breath and looked solemn. "It'll be night soon." And she walked up the porch into the house without another word.

CHAPTER EIGHT

Interstate 40, New Mexico

The desert sky had gone from blood to black in a heartbeat. The air was dry and warm and full of mesquite and the tiny rustlings of animals. But the men at the roadblock hadn't heard the sound they were all waiting for: the deep rumble of a motorcycle. Some had unbuttoned their suit jackets and lounged against the Suburbans. Others were eating MREs or smoking cigarettes. But half of the men were detailed to remain on guard. Mr. Angel walked from car to car, making sure they were on their toes. One guard with night glasses sat cross-legged on the roof of an SUV, cradling a rifle and scanning the dark desert.

The surveillance work was tedious and the bike was way overdue. It had blown past the first checkpoint hours ago. Mr. Angel swore softly. He would send out yet another sweep to see if this Bill character had tried to go off-road. He didn't think so. He couldn't see the man driving a fully-loaded Harley through the desert, even on baked hardpan. A half-ton machine with only a five-inch clearance would be sure to lodge in a sandhill or hit a buried rock.

So where was it?

Out of habit more than anything else, Mr. Angel strolled over to the perimeter. The only noticeable feature was a narrow wash that flanked the left side of the road, then bent and ran underneath it. It was about five feet deep but not worth guarding because a Harley would bog down in the loose, sandy bottom. Mr. Angel frowned. The bottom now gleamed in the half-moon. Something liquid trickled there.

"That wasn't there before," Mr. Angel said. "What the ...?"

The wash erupted in a river of fire and the sky turned white. Mr. Angel, blinded, threw himself backward. He heard yells and smelled burning kerosene.

The next instant, he heard a *whoosh*, like some great animal expelling air from its lungs. Six more followed, there was the crash of glass, and great bonfires of flame bloomed all around the perimeter.

"Molotovs!" somebody screamed.

"Sir, we're under attack!" somebody yelled.

"No shit," Mr. Angel said under his breath.

He rolled to his feet and stumbled back into the center of the road. People were scrambling around with guns - always a bad idea. He grabbed one man by the shirt collar.

"Hendricks, get Squad A to cover the left side. Tell them to use the vehicles for cover and lay down suppressive fire. Go!" He shoved the man, and without waiting, ran to the right shoulder of the road. "Squad B, I want two men on either side of the SUVs. Suppressive fire. Hernandez!"

He looked up at the top of a Suburban but the man with the night glasses was gone. Angel looked around and found him lying face down in the dirt. He'd been blinded by the sudden flash and toppled off, beaning himself. Mr. Angel swore, stepped over his unconscious body and took his rifle.

There was more whooshing. Mr. Angel thought it might be the sound of air cannons. Then the men on either side opened up with short chattering bursts into the darkness. At almost the same instant, metallic canisters arced from the darkness, bounced on the road and blew up in vast explosions of noise and light and gas. Mr. Angel's ears popped. He held his breath and closed his eyes against the brilliance.

His troops dissolved into chaos. Men ran, threw themselves down, fired shots but they had no targets and no idea whether to run into the desert or keep to the road.

Mr. Angel, his ears ringing, dropped down behind one of the Suburbans and swore.

First Molotovs, now flashbang grenades, he thought. Who the hell did we piss off? This is a freakin' war.

And then the snakes arrived.

More gushes of air, and suddenly a dozen twisting forms were landing on cars, men, and tarmac. There was hissing, rattling, curses and screams. It was like a bad horror movie. A cobra with a hood like a spread black glove landed a foot in front of Mr. Angel's face. He scrambled back, picked up the rifle and let off a ratcheting stream of bullets that caught the snake and made it dance, cutting it in two.

Around him, the whole camp was a tableau of glare and shadow, moving forms, moans, shouts and screams.

Waiting back at the ranch, Apollo Martinez popped the CD of Eddie Rabbitt's "I Love a Rainy Night" out of the player and listened. From up the road, he was almost sure he could hear screams and gunfire.

"Son of a bitch," he said. He popped the CD back in the player and decided to take a nap until things calmed down. After all, those crazy bug guys had told him to stay put. And they'd torn down their stupid sign with the lobster on it.

He turned up the music.

He loved rain songs when he was driving the desert. It cut the dust somehow.

Mr. Angel needed to regroup his men.

He shouted at the top of his lungs: "Squads, to me! Retreat! Follow my voice!" and he turned and began to walk back up the road, which was now blazing in half a dozen places.

Out of the darting shadows came knots of men, concentrating on his voice. Some were limping or scorched and their eyes were wide with the confused fear of soldiers who couldn't see the enemy. Eight men clustered around. He got them to face outward and they began backing up towards the wash.

And then they heard the helicopters. To anyone who had seen combat, the rhythmic chopping of blades was unmistakable - although these sounded small and tinny. Mr. Angel looked up. Silhouettes were darting across the half-moon. They *were* helicopters - three squadrons of three each. Each triad had a black box slung beneath it. He couldn't tell if they were close and small or big and just far away.

One of the men, an old Vietnam vet, gave a scream of pure terror.

"It's the Vietcong!" he shouted. "They're twenty feet above us!"

"No, they're a thousand feet!" someone else said.

"It's the black helicopters! The fucking black helicopters!" somebody shouted with an edge of panic.

"There are no black helicopters!" Mr. Angel yelled. "There's no Vietcong in Arizona, either!" Not for the first time, he wished he hadn't used nutjob mercs. But then, sane people usually didn't do this job.

The vet, drool coursing down his ragged gray beard, fired straight up with his aging AR-15. Then all hell truly broke loose. Everybody opened fire in all directions.

White and orange tracers screamed skyward, glass terrariums shattered and a deluge of spiders, scorpions and bulldog ants showered the men. Helicopters exploded into shattered plastic parts, their tiny buzzing motors spiraling to the ground.

From a ridge six hundred feet off in the darkness, Timmy put his remote-controlled helicopters through their paces. Radine, standing next to him with Philip, let out a sob.

"My babies are dyin'" for us," she said.

"No, darlin'," Philip said. "For freedom."

The situation had gone cluster. Mr. Angel had no choice now but to save his own hide. He sprinted for the end of the road, planning to throw himself into the wash until the shooting and panic died down.

Just as he turned, he heard the sound he'd been listening for all day.

A Harley roared straight through the flames, screams and snakes. Mr. Angel opened fire, shooting the rifle from waist-level in a guttering arc. But the bike swept by, ridden by a huge apelike shape. Behind the rider sat a woman, her hand on the trigger of an air cannon that rested on the biker's massive shoulder. The last thing Mr. Angel saw as the bike charged by was her hair streaming behind her like a flaming banner.

Wuu was awakened in the middle of the night by a telephone call.

"Hello?" He asked groggily.

"You're dead, A-hole."

"Whuh? Why?"

He pushed away the love doll and sat up.

"You said it was one guy and a woman."

Wuu snapped into semi-alertness.

"You mean Bill?"

Mr. Angel's voice held a bitter edge.

"Yeah. One biker. But he's not. He's got a freakin' army."

"Bill?" Wuu was having trouble with the concept.

"He hit us outside of Albuquerque. They had guns, bombs. They had bugs. Lots of bugs."

"Bugs?"

"Air support. Death from above." The voice was cold with contained rage.

"Are you on something?" Wuu asked.

"I've got a dozen guys down with scorpion bites, snake bites, ant bites, self-inflicted gunshot wounds. Your lone wolf has cost me three SUVS and about fifty gallons of calamine lotion."

"I swear, as far as I know, it was just him and his witch."

"Well, he hooked up with somebody." There was a pause. "So this is no longer our war. Unless you want to pay ...."

Wuu felt his stomach churn.

"Um, How much?"

"Open checkbook."

"Last time you said this was a matter of honor."

"Let me tell you about honor," Mr. Angel said coldly. "When your 'one guy' takes out a dozen of mine, it makes me think someone wasn't being entirely honest about the job."

"You think I lied?"

"Why, yes I do."

"That's hurtful."

"You set me up for a war. So now honor dictates that I come after *you*."

Wuu knew he should have had paperwork. These ad hoc deals never worked.

"I swear I didn't know. Look, what can I can I do to make this right?"

Again, there was a pause. Wuu was getting to dislike those.

"Two options," Mr. Angel said. "If it was an honest mistake, you pay with money. If it was a dishonest mistake, you pay with your blood. *Capisce?"*

Wuu wondered if *capisce* was a kind of fish. He'd known a guy who was into fish porn. He'd gotten fin rot.

"I'll go with honest mistake," Wuu said after a moment.

"Nope, sorry. You're a lying bastard. You thought you could hire me on the cheap. Well, that's a really bad business decision. Because they attacked us with bugs!" Mr. Angel's voice was rich with loathing. "If it weren't for the bugs, I might let you off."

Wuu glanced in alarm at his Sinead doll. Would this be the last time that he saw her sweet latex face? No. He was a mastermind. He felt his brain ratchet into gear.

"Do your guys have medical insurance?"

Another pause.

"What?"

"Your guys. Are they covered?"

"No. They're subcontractors. What the ...?"

"I'm thinking what the true cost is here. Speaking as a businessman, revenge is sort of a non-starter. You lose a potential client, you don't get your money. See where I'm going with this?"

Mr. Angel thought.

"The East river?" he suggested.

Wuu let the comment pass.

"Here's what I'll do. Fifty thousand - that's more than double - all medical expenses (but I want receipts) and ..." he sucked in his breath. "...a ten-percent stake in the diner chain if you complete the mission."

The pause that followed wasn't just pregnant. It had triplets.

"You have got some balls," Mr. Angel said at last. "Fifty percent."

"Fifty!"

"And you keep your balls."

"Thirty."

"Thirty. And you keep one ball."

Wuu didn't answer.

"You're actually considering it?" Mr. Angel asked in disbelief. "What is wrong with you?"

Wuu sighed.

"Fifty then. But you don't get the diner unless you get Bill."

"Whatever it takes."

Mr. Angel snapped the phone closed and stared in disgust at the road where the bike had vanished. Behind him, the screams and curses weren't dying down.

"Shut up, you pussies!" he barked. "Act like professionals!"

The screams descended to whimpers. Shaking his head, Mr. Angel turned around and walked back to the carnage.

He saw a man lying on the ground.

"You hurt, Jimmy?" he asked.

"Nope." It was a whisper.

"Then what are you doing on the ground?"

"Not moving."

"Why not?"

"There's a scorpion on my chest."

Mr. Angel thought about that.

"So?"

"If I move it might sting me."

"So?"

"I could be allergic."

"Are you allergic?"

"Won't know unless it stings me."

Mr. Angel nodded, raised a boot and brought it crashing down on Jimmy's chest. There was a crunching sound - from bug or bone. Jimmy made a noise like a deflating balloon.

"Sting you?" Mr. Angel asked with polite concern.

"No" Jimmy wheezed.

"Glad to help."

Mr. Angel walked through the confused wreckage. Sound ceased as he approached. Mr. Angel shook his head.

God. What a shitstorm.

Mr. Angel was a soldier. He'd been in disasters before. Missions failed. But he'd never learned to like it. And he'd never seen anything like this screwup. Fifteen of his men on a simple grab and they wound up burned, bitten and battered. Then to make things worse, they'd started spraying rounds in all direction, wounding each other. Classic death blossom.

He didn't look forward to starting all over again. And the possible damage to his reputation gave him heartburn.

He thought about chasing the targets but they were on a bike. They could outrun his vehicles and go where he couldn't.

No, they were long gone.

Shit.

He decided he couldn't be around these losers or he'd lose his cool and do something unprofessional. He turned back from the roadblock and walked out onto the empty road ahead. He looked up at the stars, scintillating like diamonds on velvet. He took a lungful of clean desert air - and coughed.

It smelled like gasoline.

Mr. Angel turned around, wet his finger and stuck it into the air. The breeze was blowing back towards the roadblock, so it wasn't from there. He walked ten feet up the road, stopped, sniffed.

Gasoline.

Ten yards more.

Gas. Definitely.

Mr. Angel pulled out a cigarette lighter from his pocket. It had a winged skull on it. He squatted down, flicked the lighter.

A pencil line of flame erupted and streaked out into the night.

The flame vanished as quickly as it had appeared but not before it illuminated the fierce smile on Mr. Angel's face.

"Got you," he said.

He stood up, marched back to the roadblock.

"Casey, Bashir, any of you others that can still walk, get your guns and get into the SUV."

"What about our wounded?" somebody asked.

"Leave 'em," Mr. Angel said. "We're going hunting. This mission is not over."

Ten miles down the road, they saw metal glinting in the desert.

"Stop," Mr. Angel said. The SUV lurched to a halt. Mr. Angel grabbed a flashlight and opened the door. "Get the green eyes. Cover me," he said.

He jumped down and walked towards the shoulder. Behind him, there was the soft squeak of boot leather and the hard clatter of Russian weapons as the others followed. One man waited by the SUV and two followed Mr. Angel, their guns drawn.

Off the road, the desert became soft sand. Mr. Angel's boots sank with each step. Ten meters and he found it. The motorcycle was lying on its side, half-buried.

"Son of a *chupacabra,*" Mr. Angel said softly. He called to the others and they hauled the bike upright.

Mr. Angel looked at the gas tank and found what he was expecting. He put his pinkie finger in the hole.

He turned quietly to Casey.

"They took a bullet," Mr. Angel said. "So now they're on foot. Probably hiding in those hills." He swept his hand to indicate low shapes. He peered out into the night as if he could see his prey, then cleared his throat.

"Well lookie here," Mr. Angel shouted into the darkness. "I found me a bike."

He waited as the echo rebounded.

Then he shouted back to the SUV: "Jimmy! Give me some light here."

A spotlight flared over Mr. Angel and his shadow shrouded the bike. He stepped around to give whoever was watching a good view.

"When a man leaves his motor, I guess he doesn't want it anymore," Mr. Angel yelled. He stroked the saddle. "Let's see, Harley softail, maybe late seventies, nope, early eighties, I'd say. Heavily customized. Limited edition?"

He walked slowly around the bike.

"Ooooh, modified legpipes, suicide shift. Damned ugly seat though. I'll switch that out—unless you want to come and get it?" He waited but heard nothing. He nodded, not expecting anything.

"Oh, wait a minute," he said. "What the hell? This bike's defective. Why it's got a hole in the gas tank. Gosh darn."

He turned to the other two men. "Split up," he said quietly. "You see any footprints, follow them. Otherwise, circle that hill at two and ten." They moved off silently. Mr. Angel reached into his coat and drew a knife. He looked thoughtfully at the bike and then plunged it downward twice. There was a hiss of escaping air.

"Oh look, somebody's slashed the tires," he said. "That's a pity."

"Did I call this thing a classic?," he continued. "Now that I look at it, I'm finding more problems." He waited again, ears straining. There might have been the faintest sound of someone's breath hissing out between teeth. Or not. Maybe it was the wind. Or a javelina. He shook his head, returned his attention to the bike, thought for a moment, then walked back to the SUV. Jimmy was standing outside, holding an assault rifle.

"Hand me that," Mr. Angel said.

Jimmy handed over the gun. Mr. Angel loudly and unnecessarily pulled the banana clip and jacked it back in place. He returned to the bike.

"Like I said, this machine has issues," he called. "The paint job, for instance, is really bad."

He stepped back to avoid ricochets and unloaded a full clip on the bike, methodically spraying it from end to end. The gun roared and coughed shells onto the sand. The bike sparked as bullets gouged divots and cratered the frame.

"Better," Mr. Angel shouted. "But now the engine block's no good."

With poetic slowness, the wounded bike toppled. Mr. Angel let the echoes of gunfire die away.

"This thing looks like a carcass," he yelled. "You know, I don't think I want this buzzard bait between my legs after all. Of course, you might have different tastes. So I'm told."

One more time he paused, listened. *Nothing.*

Oh well. He took a final look at the bike's ravaged frame.

"Wait a minute'" he said loudly. "Huh, how could I have missed that?"

He made a show of crouching down and examining something, then straightened up.

"Wow, a custom tail light. A chrome skull. Classy. Bet its little red eyes even light up. Now *that* I like. I'm a fan of the angel of death theme."

He fished out his lighter, held it in the spotlight beam. "See? Got it on my lighter."

Without turning, he shouted "Jimmy!"

"Sir?" Came the reply from the SUV.

"Come up here and bring me a spare gas can."

Bill watched from the crest of a low hill across the road and a hundred yards from Mr. Angel. He heard the *whumpf* as the gas caught and a pillar of flame erupted from the bike. Bill threw an arm over his dark-adapted eyes to hide the glare. When he looked again, his hog was blazing in the middle of its own funeral pyre.

Bill's neck bulged. He began a bellow of rage and challenge and loss - and found himself struggling to breathe as Nellie fiercely crushed his face against her leather- and sweat-encrusted love sacks. Her arms encircled and clamped his head like steel eels.

All Bill could manage was a muffled gurgle like a nursing baby moose.

"Don't say a word, lover," Nellie whispered, her nacho-scented breath hot in his ear. "Or we're dead."

She clutched him tighter to emphasize the point. Bill's skull creaked.

He whimpered, trying to nod.

The crushing pressure eased slightly.

Bill took two burning lungfuls of air and then prepared to shout again - and found his face instantly clamped against Nellie's breasts. He struggled, half-smothered, but Nellie rolled him over and pressed her full weight on his face. Bill's skull sank into the hilltop. He felt sand filling his ears. He struck out and he punched blindly, hitting soft flesh. Nellie grunted but held on. Seconds passed as he feebly struggled. His red rage began to pale. There were white sparkles at the edge of his sight. His head began to jerk involuntarily. Blackness flowed into his mind.

And suddenly he could breathe again.

"Shhhh," Nellie said, and patted his chest. "Remember the bad guys are still there."

Bill lay panting quietly, looking up at the half-moon. He heard voices from the road. Bill rolled onto his stomach and peered down. The men, turned to shadows in front of the burning bike, were moving towards the SUV. One stopped momentarily, hands on hips, and looked up, scanning the sky.

"Sleep tight, you two," Mr. Angel shouted. "Hope you have a blanket. It's gonna be really cold out here. Tell you what, we'll be back on the morning to thaw you out. Nighty-night." The other men laughed.

They got into the SUV, which roared to life and skidded around, its high beams cutting a bright arc on the hill just below Bill and Nellie. Then it was down the road and gone.

The fire had caught nearby bushes. Now they burned in a ring around the bike. Smoke rose from its blackened, twisted shape.

"Okay," Nellie said quietly. "They're gone. Go ahead."

Bill trembled but didn't yell.

"Nellie," he said quietly.

"Yeah, baby," she said.

"They executed her."

"I know, lover. I know."

"I want to tear them apart." He looked into her face. "Is that okay?"

Nellie shivered. “It’s okay, but we need to get moving.”

"I got to bury ‘er. She deserves that."

"They're gonna bury us if we don’t get out of here. They could have just circled around and be coming back."

But she followed silently as Bill rose and trudged to the wreckage. Bill stood over it, his head down as if in prayer. Then he fell to his knees. His huge shoulders shook. He scooped up handfuls of sand and flung them in the air. The bellow Nellie choked off earlier now erupted from his throat.

Nellie clapped her hands over her ears. She hadn’t thought a human being, especially Bill, could release so much pain. Someone was tearing open the heart of the world. She wanted to bury herself and hide, like a child from a thunderstorm.

The roar stopped. Nellie realized she could breathe again.

Bill was still on his knees, with his hands raised. But he held something in his fist. He extended his fist to Nellie and uncurled his fingers. Nellie saw it was the tail light. The chrome skull was blackened and the sockets where its red eyes had been were empty. Nellie shook her head. Bill rubbed the still warm metal against his jacket to scrape off the soot.

"My heart is now as black as your face, little skull," he said. "But I will make them pay. And I swear one day, you will be grinning behind my ass once more."

He planted a hairy kiss on it and slipped it into his pocket.

The saddlebags were charred. Bill reached into one and came up with a blackened boot. It fell to pieces in his hand.

Bill looked at the remains in despair.

"It's all I had to remind me of Grandpa," he said. His tears fell, turning the fragments into lumpy black oatmeal. He reached into the other saddlebag, fished around and grabbed something.

He pulled out a half-melted toothbrush. He pawed away his tears, stuffed the toothbrush into a pocket of his motorcycle vest pocket and got to his feet.

"I'm ready," he told Nellie. "Let's go."

CHAPTER NINE

Somewhere off Interstate 40, New Mexico

The moon was down and the desert had turned silent and dark gray in the predawn. Bill and Nellie trudged along the road. They staggered with fatigue. Bill was sweating despite the chill, his big body fighting its own gravity. Nellie was coated head to foot with dust and was nearly asleep on her feet. They moved drunkenly, their boots dragging through the gravel at the highway's edge.

They'd been moving for hours. They'd talked about cutting cross-country but Bill knew this country and there was nothing for miles on either side except dust devils and tarantulas.

"We got to go forward," he said. "They're waiting for us back there and there's nothing out in the desert."

"What's ahead?" Nellie asked.

"About fifteen miles on there's a rest stop."

"Won't they go there if they don't find us here?"

"Maybe," Bill acknowledged.

"Well if I have to die," Nellie said. "It's gonna be in a place with flush toilets. Besides, we could call the cops there."

"That, too," Bill said.

So they had walked for hours with no water. Every time lights flashed down the highway, they scrambled down into gullies thick with scrub. Bill's face bore bloody scratches and his beard was torn. He looked like he'd lost a fight with an insane parrot. Nellie's red hair was caked with grit.

They were staggering down a small slope when twin spikes of light flared behind them, casting their own shadows in front of them.

"Down," Nellie gasped despondently. They lurched into a gully and dropped like dying draft horses.

The lights were accompanied by a throaty grumble. Something mechanical was grunting up the grade.

"That ain't a car," Bill said, sitting up suddenly. He listened intently. "It's either a low-rider or ...." He listened again. "Yep. Truck."

"They could have a truck," Nellie said.

"No," Bill said. "She's a long-haul diesel. Pulling an empty trailer."

Nellie rose to her knees. "Then that's our ride," she said.

Bill stared at her dark silhouette blearily. "That trucker's not gonna stop for hitchhikers in the middle of the desert in the middle of the night," he said.

"He'll stop," Nellie said confidently.

Apollo Martinez was exhausted, achy and pissed. He was supposed to pick up a load of tarantulas and scorpions from those desert rats but they wouldn't give him the shipment.

"Emergency," they said. Something about the government or aliens or some bullshit. Then they wouldn't even let him leave.

"Too dangerous. Bound to be shooting." Holy shit, they were all batshit crazy but they had guns so he'd parked his rig, grabbed his portable CD and beloved Eddie Rabbitt disc and sat on a rocking chair on the porch of their weird little compound while they scurried around and moved big tanks of bugs.

He'd drunk a couple of *cervezas,* put Eddie on repeat and taken a nap. After dark, he'd gotten up to pee but from up the road, he was almost sure he'd heard gunfire. And more gunfire. And then, lots and lots of screaming and cursing.

"Son of a bitch," he'd said, turned up the volume on the CD and decided to resume his nap until things calmed down.

Later, in the dim glare of something burning, he'd called his boss and told him he'd be behind schedule.

"Apollo, this is coming out of your pay," Snyder had said.

"Better than out of my hide," Martinez said. "There's some kind of war going on here."

When some of the singed survivalists finally limped back and said it was safe to go, all he'd seen on the road were some scorch marks and a few suspicious stains.

So here he was after midnight, hours behind schedule, with an empty trailer, and all he'd eaten for six hours was some turkey jerky, a Mars bar and tap water. He hadn't slept in those hours, either, and so he'd have to fudge the swindle sheets, too. Worse, Snyder had punished him for losing a load by having him drive empty clear across the country for a pickup.

The whole trip was turning to *caca.*

He downshifted and came down the rise with his high beams sweeping across the empty road.

And suddenly he saw something.

Standing by the shoulder was a statue of a woman that looked like it had erupted from the brown desert. It was dirt-colored from head to toe. The statue moved. Its hands reached up and pulled at its clothing. Suddenly, two massive breasts erupted. They gleamed white in his headlights, like colossal scoops of ice cream.

"*Madre de Dios,"* Martinez said. It was either a miracle or a mirage.

Without conscious effort, his foot jammed the brakes and his tattooed hand grappled with the shift lever. The airbrakes screamed and the truck groaned as it ground to a halt.

The vision walked toward him, stuffing her boobs back into a very dusty leather top.

He looked down. She was - well, to a tired trucker, the stuff of dreams.

The smart Martinez, the lonely little guy who lived in the back of his head under tequila bottles, half-eaten cheeseburgers and used condoms, shouted in a muffled voice: *This isn't normal, cabron! Women do not magically appear in the desert! Floor it!"*

Martinez rolled down his window.

"Well, *hello*," he said. "Need some help?"

She looked up and beamed. And then something lumbered around from behind the truck, and he was looking at a huge, bearded, bloody face like a pirate's.

"Aaaaah!" Martinez screamed. "Hijacker!"

He mashed the window button but a hairy arm like King Kong's reached right through the window opening and grabbed the wheel.

"Shit!" Martinez swore and hammered at it. "Look, I got nothing. The truck's empty!"

"You got a valve problem," the pirate said.

"What?"

"One of your valves. Needs a lash adjustment. Tappet's noisy, too." It was said in a thoughtful voice. "I'd give you another five hundred miles before you got yourself a really big problem."

"You a mechanic?" Martinez asked.

"Bikes, mostly," Bill said. "But I've done some diesels. Where you headed?"

"Maine," Apollo said.

"We're joining you," Bill said.

Nellie broke in quickly.

"What my boyfriend means is that our bike broke down in the desert back there, and you're the first vehicle we've seen on this road in hours. We'd appreciate a lift to wherever you want to take us."

"You could have just used a thumb," Martinez said.

"You're a trucker," Nellie said. "You would never have stopped for a thumb."

Martinez nodded in agreement.

"You're not gonna get me in trouble with the cops, are you?"

"Cross my heart," Nellie said, and did so. Apollo's eyes followed her fingers across her breasts.

The smart Martinez moaned softly as the dumbass Martinez said: "Hop in."

At Martinez's direction, Bill took the bunk behind the seats and Nellie wedged herself into the co-pilot's seat.

"How long you been broke down?" he asked.

Nellie shook her head. "Seems like half the night. I can't thank you enough for helping."

"Yeah, about that," Martinez said. "Got some ground rules. One, I'm going through the night. We don't stop; I gotta make up lost time. So your job is to make sure I stay awake. Got any whites?"

"Sorry," Nellie said.

"All right, then, keep an eye on me. Talk to me if my eyes start looking at my belt buckle. Now, you look like you got problems."

"That's for sure," Nellie said.

"I don't want to know about 'em," Martinez said. "And don't ask me about mine. And no talkin' trash about the D-backs."

"No problem," Nellie said. "Anything else?"

"Yeah," Martinez grabbed a fistful of CDs. "I got Eddie Rabbitt, Mariachi Hits of the '70s, and the Grateful Dead. Which you want first?"

It was late afternoon of the next day when the truck, blaring mariachi hits for the seventh straight hour, pulled into Ozarkland Village in Sarcoxie, Missouri.

"I got to stop here," Martinez said. "They got the best saltwater taffy in the world. I got a taffy addiction."

"You might want to get some new CDs, too," Nellie said.

"Why?" Martinez asked.

"You know, switch it up, try something new, a little variety."

"Well that doesn't make any sense. I know all the words to these."

"We all do now," Nellie said.

Martinez climb out of the cabin and headed to the store.

Nellie rubbed her gritty eyes and woke Bill.

"We have to get out of here," Nellie whispered urgently.

"Why, are we in New Jersey?"

"No, we're in hell," Nellie said. "I got to listen to that trucker sing off-key to the same three CDs since Arizona."

"I didn't hear anything," Bill said.

"You slept through the whole damn ride!" Nellie said, an edge to her voice. "But if I have to listen to that shit anymore, I may have to kill someone."

"Not the trucker guy," Bill reasoned. "He's been good to us."

"Let's stretch our legs," Nellie said bitterly. "And hope they sell Jack Daniels or something. I don't want to get back in this rig unless I am well and truly stoned."

Nellie and Bill climbed down and walked across the road towards a red-painted general store fronted by a split-rail fence with signs advertising mugs, fudge and fireworks.

Nellie, though, stopped short in the parking lot.

"Bill, wait," she said. "Look at that."

She pointed to an old VW bus. Painted in broad crimson letters across its sides were the words: SNARFEST OR BUST.

"Lover," Nellie said. "I think I've just found our next ride."

They stood by the bus. After about five minutes, the door of the general store opened and out stepped two couples and a little girl. The adults had armfuls of souvenir T-shirts, cups and bags of candy. The little girl's right arm was in a sling and she looked sour.

They saw Nellie and especially Bill and stopped short. The little girl's mouth went wide as she squinted up at Bill.

"Hi," Nellie said.

"Howdy," said one of the men, who had scraggly long hair under a fake coonskin cap.

"I'd forgotten SNARFEST was coming up," Nellie said.

"You're a SNAR fan?"

"Nope," Nellie said. "I'm a – SNARLIE!!!" She snarled, squatted in a Sumo wrestler stance, put her thumbs to her nose, flattened it into a pig snout, wiggled her pinkies in the air and began grunting and squealing.

The four adults looked stunned. Then they dropped their bags and candy and souvenirs, raised their hands to their noses, and the land was filled with snorts and squeals. The little girl looked disgusted and shook her head at Bill.

"Yeah!" one of the women said when everybody had come up for air. "It is so great to meet another SNARLIE!"

She went forward and hugged as much of Nellie as she could reach around. "I'm Amber."

"Nellie," Nellie said.

Amber pointed to the others.

"That's Justin. We just got married and we're honeymooning at SNARFEST."

"Yeah," Coonskin Cap said. "We met there two years ago. Amber says it was love at first lust." He made a sound that might have been a laugh or a cat coughing up a hairball. "And these are our best buds, Ashley and Josh."

Everybody exchanged nods.

"And Tina," the little girl said, extending her hand to Nellie. "I was the flower girl. Mom made me go on this stupid trip with Auntie Amber. Blechhh."

"Well, if you hadn't tried to ride your brother's dirt bike off the school roof and busted your arm, you'd be on that rafting trip with your folks right now, missy," Amber said.

Bill, whose arms were crossed, turned slightly and gave Tina a secret thumbs up behind his elbow. She smiled.

"Well," Amber said. "This is a real pleasure. Maybe we'll see you tonight."

"Wish we could," Nellie said with a sigh.

"What?" Justin asked. "You're not going?"

"We hitchhiked," Nellie said. "But we're with a trucker who just likes country music."

Ashley put her hands to her mouth and went pale.

"Dear God," she said with a gasp. "How long?"

"All night and day," Nellie said, and shivered melodramatically.

"Oh, Jesus, I'm so sorry," Amber said. She turned to Justin with an imploring look. "We have to help these poor people. We have to take them with us. It's our SNARLIE duty."

"I don't see how we can," Justin said, casting a tape-measure eye over Bill. "There's not much room left."

"She's a SNARLIE, Justin. That makes her family. We have to make room somehow."

He shook his head. "We only have one extra seat. And everybody has to be belted or I'll wind up with another $800 ticket in one of these speed-trap dumps."

"Then think of something else," Amber ordered. There was a pause while everyone did. Then, their eyes swiveled at the same instant.

"Tina," Amber said. "Get your suitcase."

Justin rushed to the van and hauled out a child-sized flowered suitcase with a big stuffed bear tied to the handle. He put it down in front of the surly child and pulled a twenty-dollar bill from his pocket.

"Take this," he said. "Go back to the store and wait for us. Buy anything you want."

"I want taffy."

"You can't. You have a retainer," Amber called.

Justin overrode her. "Make you a deal, we won't tell your mom you had taffy and you don't tell her that we left you here."

Tina nodded her head.

"Great." Justin stood up and patted her on the head. "We'll be back in two days. If anybody asks you, tell 'em your daddy's in the bathroom."

He walked to the bus and flung open the side doors with a melodramatic gesture.

"Fellow SNARLIES," he said in a sepulchral voice. "Enter the realm!"

The Chattering Otter Water Park was fifteen acres but much of it had fallen to ruin. It had been built intentionally on a political no-man's land; due to some surveyor error or ancient graft, the property lay outside of both city and county jurisdictions, so the thrifty owners hadn't had to worry about health and safety rules or pesky fire marshals. The parking lot was poorly laid and the low spots were sometimes submerged. The hot dogs had the occasional bone chip and greenish hue. Several years back, the poorly-paid and unsupervised staff neglected to chlorinate the giant children's wading pool. By mid-season, it was filled with leeches. The resulting furor led to the owners closing the park for good in the middle of the night and fleeing to an undisclosed South American country.

These days, the wading pool was choked with weeds and was a famous flyover for migrating waterfowl, who'd left it covered with feathers and guano. When it rained, the concrete rafting river filled with water and then became a stagnant creek that bred mosquitoes as large as helicopters. Here and there, the ruins of derelict waterslides - decapitated by seasonal tornadoes -poked up like the stumps of blackened teeth.

But once a year, loyal SNAR fans - the SNARLIES - brought it all back to life, like fairy godmothers on crack. They dredged the river - sometimes waging pitched battles with birders who tried to stop them - patched the concrete, got the park's recirculating pump system back on line, opened the capped fire hydrants, hooked up fire hoses, set up generators and stage lighting and in general devoted months and thousands of dollars that would have been better spent on college educations, dental care and nursing homes for their aged parents.

And now, as the summer mosquitoes swarmed like squadrons of blood-seeking missiles, SNARFEST was reborn.

Bill and Nellie walked through the main gate, which was streaming with fans. Nobody was checking bags for drugs, booze or weapons but there was a sign that read: "Troublemakers will be eaten." Volunteers with lighted batons shepherded people into semi-orderly rows and thus thwarted the thrusting crowd's efforts at mass extinction.

DEET misted over the throng like a toxic magic spell. Roaring diesel generators juiced strings of carnival lights that crisscrossed the grounds like giants' jump ropes. Every so often, a costumed SNAR fan on stilts or wearing a towering dragon's head would hit a strand and there would be a scream and a puff of smoke. Bill kept ducking.

They walked through a gathering throng past portable toilets, a medical tent decorated with axes and iron maidens and booths selling beer, handmade band souvenirs, food and, of course, inescapably, incense. The sweltering, humid air reeked of the cloying smell mixed with the skunky odor of cheap pot and sweat.

"Smells like the clubhouse," Bill said nostalgically.

"That, or a Chinatown whorehouse," Nellie said.

"Nope, those are usually more of a 'spunk-and-perfume thing,'" Bill said.

"Ewww," Nellie said, eyeing his enormous bulk. "Did you break anyone?"

"A couple," Bill said.

"You had a ménage a trois?"

"No. I was a bouncer. Summer job. No freebies for the staff," Bill added.

Nellie felt indescribably better.

The last rays of the sun died, leaving hot darkness filled with the crowd's anthem of shouts, screams and laughter.

Nellie and Bill crossed a bridge over the rafting river, which was lit by lanterns on poles. People were swirling down it, some on inner tubes, some gripping pool noodles and one or two riding small replicas of the famous SNARPIG. There was the occasional thud and curse as someone on the bridge tossed a badly-timed beer into the water.

The crowd surged on, leaving the river behind. After what seemed several blocks Nellie finally caught sight of the stage.

Volunteer crew- the SNARRIORS- had built a canted platform out from the original smaller stage that, rumor said, was haunted by the ghost of

Milli Vanilli. It was whispered that on dark nights, hobos camping in the ruins would suddenly find themselves uncontrollably lip-synching "Girl You Know It's True." Nellie shivered and clamped her lips together.

The stage was crowded with amplifier stacks, instruments and cabling. Near the back was an enormous pile that looked like a deflated balloon. SNARRIORS, some already wearing their stage orc heads, clustered around as if it were a huge sow about to give birth and they were the midwives. Others shouted orders, checked lights and mikes. The speakers screeched with feedback. It was the usual pre-concert chaos.

On either side of the stage were functioning water slides. The original framework had been bought from mob contractors. The fiberglass had gone brittle and was crudely patched with ribbed plastic sheeting and old street signs. Here and there the rusting trestles had been spot-welded, apparently by three-fingered monkeys on Ritalin, and bore long silvery scars. Yet the slides had held together for five years of SNARFESTS. They were floodlit and towered fifty feet high. Fire hoses kept the water rushing. SNAR fans grouped on either side, waiting for the chance to climb makeshift ramps and plunge down, screaming. From speakers came the SNARFEST ballad "Dragons Don't Do Dogs." It was from the band's Philip Glass period and consisted of two repeating bass chords followed by someone shouting "Monkeys!"

Security guards had strung out along the front of the stage to hold back the swelling crowd. Bill bulldozed his way up to them. Nellie smiled.

"We're here to see Stan," she said.

"Who?"

"Stan. Stan Poindexter. The lead singer?"

"You mean Satan," the man replied sternly. "He who has stolen the Infernal Music and brought it to Earth."

"Yep. Anyway, could you get a message to him?"

"Look, lady, we're a little busy here," the man said. "Just go find a place to stand and enjoy the show, okay?"

Bill stepped forward. "Say that again, asshole." he said.

The man looked up at Bill and swallowed but held his ground.

"It's okay," Nellie said, and turned back to the man. "I know he's busy but if you'd just tell him it's Nellie from Duluth. I think he'll see us." She smiled her most becoming smile. Behind her, Bill smiled too.

The man looked at Bill and shuddered. "Wait here," he said and disappeared.

A few moments later, he came wending his way back.

"Follow me," he said. Nellie and Bill were led to a small building to the left of the stage that housed the Green Room. The man pushed opened the door, let them in, and hurriedly closed it behind them.

The first thing they saw was a woman's ass. She was clad only in her underwear and bent over, retching noisily into a bucket. Two band members in full mutant makeup and costume hovered over her, holding back her long blonde hair and looking as if whatever she had might be contagious.

Satan was pacing and looking annoyed. He was holding a gigantic fanged headpiece in one hand. He slapped it against his scaly thigh irritably.

"Is she done yet?" he asked.

"I think..." one of the band members said but was interrupted by a groan and the sound of splashing. "Er, nope," he added, "She missed again." He shook one of his boots. "Ewwchh!"

"Goddammit!" Satan said, and addressed the woman. "Gwyneth, why would you eat something called The Devil's Feces? You should have just waited for the pizzas!"

He shook his head in disgust, then caught sight of Nellie and Bill. His teeth gleamed.

"Hey, hey, hey!" he said, clumping over on foot-high boots, and gave Nellie a crushing hug. The giant erect plastic nipples on his chest piece poked her so they ended up a foot apart.

Satan stepped back. "God, it's good to see you! Been what, two years?"

"Just about," she said. "I've been travelling. This is Bill." Bill nodded.

"Jesus, so it is," Satan said. "Hi. Just passing through?"

"Sort of," Nellie said. "It's a little complicated. Basically, we lost our bike and our cash and we need to be someplace. I was hoping you could loan us a ride for a couple of days."

"Oh, sure, anything for you," Satan said. Just then, Gwyneth gave another groan.

"Oh God," she gasped.

"Is she all right?" Nellie asked worriedly.

Satan made a noise of disgust. "She ate from one of the food trucks. I warned everybody not to do that. That's for the fans. 'Stick to the Domino's' I said." He glanced at Gwyneth again and shook his head. "She's anorexic. You'd think she'd be used to vomiting."

"She should lie down," Nellie said. She looked at the hovering band mates. "Soon as she's done, put her on the couch. Get her lots of water and get a bouncer or somebody to watch her." She turned back to Satan. "I've been there," she said. "At least she has a bucket."

"And she's not in a moving vehicle," Satan added. They both guffawed. Bill looked perplexed. It was the universal expression of a man whose lover is sharing a private joke with an old friend.

"Hey," Satan said, snapping his clawed fingers. "Nellie, you're a godsend. You can help us out. Then we help you out. How about it?"

"No sex, Stan, I'm with Bill," Nellie said.

"No, no," Satan said, sizing up Bill, whose head nearly touched the top of the Green Room. "Gwyneth was supposed to be our ritual sacrifice to the SNARPIG. It's the show finale."

"Oh, yeah," Nellie said. She explained to Bill: "They wheel the woman out in a cage and she gets eaten by the big balloon."

Satan looked at the vomitress, who was rising shakily to her feet.

"Gwyneth was our ritual sacrifice but I don't think she can handle it. And if she explodes at both ends it would really spoil the moment." He turned to Nellie, arms extended. "How about it, Nell? You want to be our stage goddess?" He glanced up and down her pillowy vastness. "You're a lot more, er, visible than her anyway." Bill growled and put a beefy hand halfway around Nellie's waist.

"And Bill can be head of security!" Satan added hastily. "If we can find a SNARK T-shirt that fits."

"If we do this, you'll give us a ride?" Nellie asked.

"I was going to, anyway," Satan said, looking offended. "You're a friend, Nellie." He looked at Bill. "We ran out of gas and cash in Duluth. Nellie was working a bar there. She gave us everything on the house." He took on a mockingly spooky voice:

"Gooey, shrouded carcasses of slaughtered bovines..."

"Cheeseburgers," Nellie interpreted.

"Flagons of rotted hops..."

"Beer," Nellie said with a grin.

"...And tip money to get us on the road."

"Got to run away again, right?" Satan asked her.

"Rode with them all the way back here," Nellie told Bill.

"And she helped design the first SNARPIG...aaaand she wrote the lyrics to our first hit, 'Pygmy Babies from Hell.'

"By the way, Stan, I've still got five dollars in royalties coming," Nellie said.

"She's good people," Satan said. "Even if she is expensive." He winked.

"You good with this?" Bill asked Nellie.

"I think it'll be fun, lover," she said, and added, "Plus, we don't have that much choice."

Bill nodded.

"Great!" Satan said. The door opened and a security guard popped his head in.

"You're on in ten, guys," he said.

"We're ready," Satan said, then added: "Hey, Gary, I've got another security guy for you. Bill, follow Gary. Gary, see if you can find him a shirt."

"Jesus Christ," Gary said, but added, "Follow me."

Bill gave Nellie a quick kiss - which actually covered most of her face, took thirty seconds and included large amounts of tongue. Then he left.

Satan looked on in shock. "Wow," he said. "So that's your new Humpmeister Five-thousand. I can see why. And may I add, 'Yuck!'"

"Fuck off, Stan," Nellie said sweetly. "Let's do this."

Ten minutes later, the stage went black. There was a moment of silence, during which the band members took their marks. Suddenly, a drumbeat began. It was deep, slow, foreboding. It pounded over the exalting crowd like iron spikes being hammered into their spleens by a mentally-challenged Thor.

A guitar gave a single, cosmic harpy screech, the note long and drawn-out and begging for release. In the dark, The voice of Satan arose.

"We are the mutants!" he growled. "We are the damned spawn of a corrupt universe that ejaculated into the womb of God! We have come to bring horror and decimation upon a cowering mankind! Only those who worship us will remain! And now, as our clawed feet stamp on the slime-covered necks of our foes, and their small, furry pets..." He paused and his voice became conversational. "...Especially poodles, or those stupid pocket pets those rich bitches in Hollywood carry around like, I don't know, fuckin' accessories, or something. What's with that?"

A drumstick hit the back of his head. "You're losing them, Stan," a disembodied voice said. "Stick to the monologue."

"That hurt, douchebag," Satan said, but his voice lowered an octave and he resumed.

"We call the Chosen to join us in our Infernal Orgy. Mutants, mutants all - mutant orcs and mutant dolls, mutant nuns and mutant souls - It is time to kneel before your masters and lick the knob of Destiny." Some in the crowd actually knelt and began licking the ground and nearby fans.

Stan's voice boomed: "I say unto you now: Arise!" The crowd surged to its feet.

"Raise your hands to the night!" The SNARLIES raised them over their heads.

"And embrace the DARKNESSSS!"

At that moment, the entire stage was lit in an unholy glare by the erupting flare of a dozen firework mortars. They showered the front of the stage and sent up pillars of sparks. Several fans caught fire but guards grabbed them and threw them into nearby water features.

The concert had begun.

SNAR rocked through a half-dozen songs. Meanwhile, behind the band, the balloon was slowly filling with hot air from two burners, tended by crew in orc heads.

During a break between "Zombie Whore Thrill Kill" and "Botulism Babies," an orc-headed SNARRIOR rushed onstage and thrust a can of Red Bull at Satan, who grabbed it, took a gulp and then spat it out.

"What the fuck!" he said. "This tastes like piss." He glared at the SNARRIOR, who turned to run but tripped on a cable and went sprawling.

"Security!" Satan bawled.

Instantly, the stage was full of SNARKs in yellow shirts. They hauled the SNARRIOR to his feet and gripped him firmly by both arms.

Satan strode forward and reached for the mask. The SNARRIOR bellowed and clung desperately to the headpiece. It took three guards to yank his hands away.

The latex head ripped in half and fell away. Beneath it was a pasty, adenoidal man. His bulging, watery eyes were full of hatred.

"Rog?" Satan said. "What are you doing here? Dude, was that .... did you..." Satan looked at the can and tossed it into the crowd. There was a scramble for the souvenir.

"Yep, asshole!" Rog said gasping. "I did it for Cynthia! And it's just a start!"

"Who's Cynthia?" a guard asked.

"An angel from heaven corrupted by this fiend!" Rog gasped.

"His girlfriend. He says I slept with her. I don't remember."

"You violated her!" Rog said.

"Rog, if I did her, it's because she came onto me, okay? And I don't remember and she probably doesn't remember, and why she even told you I don't know, but you can't keep stalking me."

"She won't stop talking about it!" Rog said. "Mourning her defilement ... making comparisons ...," he stopped, and suddenly blushed and looked down.

"Oh, Jesus," Satan said. "Look, we're in the goddamn middle of a show here, Rog. So can we please just settle this? I'm sorry for whatever I did to your girlfriend. *Mea culpa, mea maxima culpa.* If you want to take a punch at me, go ahead."

But Rog shook his head.

"Oh no, my friend. This was just the start. The finale is yet to come. Revenge is a dish best served cold."

Satan sighed. "You brought this on yourself," he told Rog. "Throw him out. He's banned from SNARFEST. For life."

Rog stared at Satan.

"Not for life?"

"You pissed me off, Rog, and in fact, you sort of pissed *in* me. Yuck. I could have you arrested for assault."

"Nooooo!" Rog said as he was dragged offstage.

"And tell Cynthia my dick says hello!" Satan shouted after him. He turned back to the band. "Sorry guys." He spat and rubbed his mouth. "Ucccch. Can someone please get me some Lysol?"

The rest of the show went without incident. The band, with Satan on string-busting rhythm guitar, tore through the instrumental "Death Bunny Boogie" followed by "Hamsters of Hate" and the crowd screamed so enthusiastically after "Mummy Don't Mind" (the ballad for necrophiliacs) that they did an extra three-minute reprise. The press of bodies created so much heat that SNARRIORS briefly turned a hose on the crowd.

And in the background, the SNARPIG continued to slowly rise as the band played their non-symphonic version of "God Between the Ducks."

Nellie, watching from the wings, tugged at her sacrifice outfit, a sort of clingy bed sheet, and wondered if she would fit in the cage. She was sweating furiously in the heat and wondered if the costume would become transparent. Then she grinned. That would be memorable for the fanboys, she thought.

She peaked past an amplifier stack and squinted at the stage. She could just make out Bill's silhouette, looming in front. It made her feel warm and squishy. She wondered if Stan would let her keep the outfit. Bill might like it - and she would love him peeling her out of it. A little drool gathered at the corner of her mouth.

During a drum solo, Satan stepped into the wings and joined Nellie.

"Jesus, Nellie, how'd you meet this guy?"

"At a bike rally. I saw him riding into town, and he stopped. Then he put his fist through a car window."

"Phew. What, was he on meth or something?"

"No," Nellie said. "There was a dog in the back. The windows were all rolled up and it was 110 in the shade."

Satan scratched his head in bewilderment.

"So, you both like dogs?"

Nellie felt her own IQ dropping. That happened when you tried to explain things to Stan.

"I like dogs," Satan said. "They can lick their own balls."

Satan returned to the stage and resumed shouting. Approaching the three-hour mark, SNAR launched into "Pygmy Babies from Hell." The frenzied crowd went wild.

The bile-colored SNARPIG, fully inflated now, loomed over the park. It was a salvaged Pink Floyd pig, 40 feet in diameter, modified by additional claws, tails, and three anuses that jetted colored smoke. An enormous horned dragon's head crowned a six-foot-wide, scaly pillar of a neck that bobbed menacingly between the water slide towers as if it were alive as SNARRIORS on either side of the stage tugged on guy ropes. The head had a gaping mouth full of Day-Glo teeth and its eyes were ruby-colored mirrors that caught the spotlight beam and flashed red rage over the audience.

A SNARRIOR came up to Nellie. "You're on," he shouted over the music. "You signed the waiver, right?"

"I'm ready for my close-up," Nellie shouted, adjusting a shoulder strap.

As the last power chord died away, Satan raised both hands and strode to the very lip of the stage. He paused and waited until the roar died to an excited murmur.

"SNARLIES, SNARETTES, SNARSLAVES," he said. "The SNARPIG has risen! Our Mutant Lord is well-pleased by your worship! He lay dreaming for millennia but your fervent voices have awakened him!"

On cue, the drummer began a slow series of triplets, building in intensity. The bassist, Ooze, and lead guitarist, Burn Ward, began a melody line. Satan's voice became low and intense.

"He was awakened from the sleep of eons. *And he is hungry!!!*"

Roars and shouts erupted from the crowd.

Satan stalked the front of the stage.

"Our twisted god *must have blood!*" he shouted.

He stopped again, dead center, clenched both fists and lowered his head. The stage went dark except for a spotlight on him.

"Our Unholy Father demands - a sacrifice! A virgin sacrifice!"

Suddenly, he threw out both arms, tossed back his head, and spun around to face upstage. A second spotlight flared on.

Nellie stood in her virgin outfit, her head lowered. Her fiery hair fell over her face fetchingly. Her hands were clasped together as if in prayer.

Satan strode upstage, walked behind her. He put a hand on her shoulder, stroked it, looked up and leered at the crowd, sticking out his tongue like a snake licking the air.

"Tasty," he shouted. "She will well please our Dark Lord!"

He stepped to her side, raised his arms and shouted: "Bring the cage!"

From above them, a dented and tooth-marked shark cage descended from the lighting catwalk by ropes. It hit the stage with an audible thump.

Like a stage magician, Satan made mysterious gestures. Two orc-headed stage crew members appeared from the wings, carrying what appeared to be an iron chain with shackles at one end and an industrial hook with a latch at the other.

With a flourish, Satan stepped over and pulled open a door that was crudely welded into the side of the cage.

The orc-heads clamped the shackles on Nellie's wrists, then led her to the cage. They squeezed her inside and clipped the big hook to a top bar. The position raised Nellie's arms above her head. Her breasts thrust out and pushed tautly against the fabric. She looked appropriately scared and vulnerable as Satan slammed the door and slid the latch home.

All this time, the music kept up its insistent, sinister rhythm.

"Raise her!" Satan commanded.

The SNARRIORS grabbed the lead rope and hauled away. The cage went up six inches - then thumped heavily to the floor again. The SNARRIORS braced their feet, grabbed the rope again, and heaved. They grunted and hauled. The cage rose again, swaying slightly with the struggling SNARRIORS groaning and planting their feet. A moment later, the cage again thudded to the floor.

"Jesus Christ," one handler said. "How much does this chick weigh?"

He nodded to the other SNARRIOR, who nodded back. They turned and waved into the wings, beckoning. A moment later and two more orc-heads rushed out. All four grabbed the rope and strained. The cage, illuminated in the spotlight, slowly rose fifty feet into the air and dangled beneath the catwalk, under the inflated jaws of the SNARPIG.

Ropes attached to either side were held by SNARRIORS on the catwalk. The center rope for the cage was attached to a pulley that rolled on rails the length of the catwalk. One orc-head pulled and the cage slowly rolled left along the stage. On stage, other SNARRIORS tugged on ropes attached to the SNARPIG's head, shifting it in time with the cage. To the crowd, it appeared that the beast was following its prey.

When the cage reached the end of the stage, another SNARRIOR hauled it back. The cage rolled back towards the right. The SNARPIG's head followed it greedily.

The music rose a notch in tempo as the band broke into "Dragon with A Maiden's Heart."

Inside the cage, Nellie was getting nauseated. As the cage shifted back and forth, it slanted and her big body was thrown against the bars, contributing more momentum.

Nellie grunted. Show business wasn't as glamorous as she thought.

"For God's sake," she shouted to nobody in particular. "Can somebody please just eat me already?"

The music roared, and the pace increased, back and forth. The cage began to swoop erratically and take on a life of its own. The SNARRIORS strained to control the ropes. Three more ran out from the wings, bumping into each other and scrabbling for the cables.

Satan, roaming the stage, stopped by the cluster of panting orc-heads.

"That's awesome, guys!" he shouted. "Looks real scary. Just fucking great!"

"It is scary," one said. "We haven't got this. We never practiced with this much weight."

"Wh...Wha...what?" Satan said, faltering and puzzled.

"Stan, grab a rope or get the hell out of the way," he said. "Now! Guys, slow it down! Grab it!"

One of the ropes tore free of a SNARRIOR's hands and he tumbled backwards. The others held on, a knot of struggling bodies wrestling with ropes that seemed suddenly as malicious as the tentacles of an enraged octopus. The handlers waltzed around the stage trying to regain control of the cage.

Suddenly, there was the sound of rending metal and the catwalk tilted.

"Oh shit!" somebody yelled.

Above, an orc-head was catapulted over the railing. His safety harness saved him but he let go of a control rope and the cage yawed far out to the left, swinging in a dizzying arc. It swung clear back across the stage and slammed into the side of the right-hand waterslide. The fiberglass slide split and support framework buckled. Rusty girders and pieces of slide rained down, bouncing off the cage and littering the ground and the side of the stage. Water cascaded from the gap, nearly drowning Nellie as it poured through the cage bars and dumped onto the speaker stack. Sparks exploded.

Nellie screamed and spluttered, gasping for breath as the flood engulfed her.

Bill, looking up, saw the cage imbedded halfway in the waterslide six stories up. Half of the cage jutted into thin air. Bill could dimly see Nellie's silhouette through a torrent of water. Her arms were still chained above her. Her head was bent as if she were measuring the distance between life and death. Bill felt, rather than saw, the terror on her face.

"Nellie!" he roared and vaulted to the stage in a single leap.

Satan was looking up, mouth agape, when Bill bowled him over. He tumbled across the stage like a satanic rag doll.

The crowd cheered.

Ooze, Burn Ward and the drummer, Disciple, faltered as the speaker stack erupted into sparks and flame and water roared down in a curtain to their left. They couldn't see Nellie nor the top of the slide but they could see Bill bowl down Satan and SNARRIORS rushing about onstage like crazed chickens.

Shockdog, who was playing tambourine, shouted: "Looks like the fire hose broke loose!"

"Let's get the hell out of here before we're all electrocuted!" Burn Ward shouted.

"No!" Shockdog shouted. "If it was gonna happen we'd be French fries already! Just keep playing! Let crew sort it out!" He jingled his tambourine menacingly. "The show must go on!"

"Why the fuck must it go on?" Ooze shouted. "We're not even getting paid."

"Because if we stop, that crowd out there panics," Shockdog yelled. "And even if they signed waivers, anybody who dies is going to have family who will come after us with lawyers, guns and money."

Burn Ward unplugged. "Fuck this," he said.

Shockdog desperately played his last card.

"Wait!" he yelled. "Stan's down. You know what that means? Solos for everybody!"

The band members gave each other thunderstruck looks. Then a fierce, animal joy dashed across their features.

"Dibs!" the bassist said.

"Second!" the drummer shouted.

Burn Ward looked sour.

"All right! From the bridge!" Ooze shouted.

Bill reached the left side of the stage, which looked as if it had been chewed by the SNARPIG. Debris had smashed a large chunk of it into splintered wood. A speaker stack had fallen over and lay in a foot-deep stream fed by the waterfall pouring from the skies. Bill slipped and stumbled over the edge of the stage, leaped through the waterfall and splashed through the swirling debris.

Above him, the waterslide leaned crazily toward the stage, its twisted meshwork outlined against the sky like some broken-backed insect. Nellie's cage jutted from it, blazing in the spotlight. A sheet of water was pouring over it. Bill couldn't see what was keeping the slide from tipping all the way over and collapsing. Maybe the fire hose, full of incompressible water, was acting as a prop. *Until it tears free*, Bill thought.

The slide tilted another degree as one of the water slide's support legs bent.

Nellie, half-drowned, thrashed frantically at her shackles but the hook held.

Bill heard her shrieks over the sound of the groaning metal and the nightmare of a badly-tuned guitar.

There was no time.

He reached out a paw-like hand, grabbed a strut on the water slide and began to climb.

Satan staggered to his feet. He was half-stunned and one foot-high boot heel had snapped off, so he was lurching like a drunk. His head was foggy. Something had hit him, he was pretty sure, possibly a runaway buffalo. Some of the rear stage lights were off and the sound had cut out from the left speaker bank. Around him, orc-heads were scrambling, some leaping offstage like lemmings.

Satan turned around to face the crowd. Through the spotlight glare, he could see only the faces closest to the stage. Their eyes bulged, their mouths were open. He followed their gaze.

He saw Nellie's cage, hovering over nothingness. He saw the damaged slide list farther, its girders protesting. When it collapsed, somebody was going to die.

"Oh," Satan said.

He wondered why the band was still playing. He also wondered whether he could make it out of state by morning, before the lawsuits began. He began to lurch offstage.

And then he heard gasps and cheers from the crowd. He looked at the slide again and just made out something crawling on the framework. It looked like a huge, misshapen beetle. But it moved powerfully, with a bestial grace.

"What the fuck is that?" Satan asked, forgetting his mike was live. "Spot! Somebody get a spot on that thing!" and he pointed to the bottom of the water slide.

A circle of blazing light erupted, panned over the legs of the slide and finally stopped, pinning the mysterious thing in its beam.

It was Bill, yellow shirt hanging in shreds, his beard and hair streaming. He clawed his way up the girders like an ape, his massive arm and shoulder muscles bunching as he grappled.

Satan's jaw dropped. *This is a disaster*," he thought to himself. *Somebody's gonna die. But fuck me, it's great theater. How can I get in on this?*

Bill swarmed up the skeleton of the water slide. The spotlight dazzled him and made it hard to see the next hold. His boots skidded on the wet, corroded steel. Rivulets of rusty water streamed down his arms, mingling with the blood from his torn hands.

Below him, Satan's amplified voice bellowed: "He goes! The Servant of Darkness rises to, er, salvage the sacrifice. She shall NOT escape her SNARLY destiny!"

Nellie's shrieks turned into coughs and choking as she fought for air but inhaled water. She was disoriented, blinded by the torrent. She threw herself back and forth against the bars, struggling to break the chains. *Who the hell,* she thought dimly, *puts real chains in a stage show? Nobody could tell if they were plastic.* She tried to move her head around to get out of the water but she couldn't find much space. She began to weaken. She put her head down, managed to get a half-liquid breath or two but no more.

Her vision began to narrow, a diminishing ring of reality enfolded by darkness, irising closed like the last scene in a silent movie.

My final scene, Nellie thought. She tried to speak, to say her final words. They were supposed to be "Goodbye, Bill" but they came out *glug glug.*

Bill climbed relentlessly, moving like a pile driver. In less than a minute, he was below the cage. Water drenched him and the force of it plowed against his chest.

Huge red eyes glared at him. To his left, a dozen feet away, the head of the SNARPIG had been caught by one of the cage cables and towed off-center. Its eyes were level with the cage and its gaping mouth seemed to be straining upwards to reach the morsels within.

Through slitted eyes, Bill looked up at Nellie. Her arms hung suspended from her chain but the rest of her body was pressed limply against the side of the cag, which had become a sloping floor. Her eyes were closed. Bill couldn't tell through the gushing water if she was breathing.

The slide rocked as another support joint bent. The cage slipped half a foot.

Bill reached up and grabbed the latch on the cage door and tore it away. The door didn't open. The lower half was wedged into the shuddering side of the slide.

Bill groped at the bars but he couldn't get enough purchase to pry them back.

Half-blinded by water, he looked into Nellie's face, only a couple of feet from his own. The waterslide was beginning to seriously wobble now. Shrieks came dimly from below. Satan was shouting something that echoed from the speakers.

Bill wondered how to say goodbye. To Nellie. To everything.

Something that felt like a boot hit him in the back of the head. Which was weird, because there was nothing but air behind him.

Bill looked back and down just to make sure.

He saw the frenzied crowd, the torn-up stage, and Satan in front, still shouting something that echoed in the night.

Suddenly, Satan's voice became clear and close and oddly familiar.

"Hey, stupid!" it said. *"It's a converted shark cage. It's got a top door!"*

Then the voice blurred back into nonsense.

Bill looked at the cage again. It was half-buried in the water slide and tipped out and up at a sharp angle. The half-buried door where Nellie had entered the cage was facing out and down. Her hanging weight had pulled the chain taut where it hung from the top bars, which now were on the left side of the cage - the part that jutted out into emptiness.

"Fuck me," Bill said. There *was* a top door. He could see where the opening had been welded shut. The top corners had hooks attached to hold wrist-thick ropes, three of which were tangled in the bars and blocked the door. The last rope had broken free of the cage and was tangled in the SNARPIG.

Bill hauled himself up the ripped metal, heedless of his gashed hands and face, then hoisted himself with a grunt onto the bars that now formed its slanting roof. Water from the fire hose gushed down on him. He scrambled for purchase, lost it and was carried over the edge.

There was instant of drowning and falling, both at once, then Bill flailed and one hand caught a bar. He dangled out into the air, kicking his legs, and choked out a curse along with a lungful of water. Heaving, Bill got one leg up and hooked one boot into the cage bars. Then he reached up and began to climb out sideways, his drenched and slippery hands and feet fighting him at every precious inch.

He managed to reach the left side of the cage – what used to be the top.

Bill hacked at the ropes, each movement making the unsteady cage bounce and judder. After an eternity, he cut the ropes free. Their ends dangled near him, jerking in the waterfall like thrashing snakes. The cage, now held only by the wreckage of the water slide, gave a sudden jerk and tipped down another half-foot. Bill felt his heart leap into his throat and was suddenly aware of his massive weight.

He found the spot-weld on the top latch. It was a crappy job. Bill made a fist and punched, and the weld snapped.

Bill yanked on the door. It didn't budge. Cursing and spitting water, he tugged and hammered futilely. The cage trembled but the door held.

It took a desperate minute before Bill understood what was wrong. The industrial hook was latched to the center bar of the door. Nellie dangled from the attached chain. Her sagging weight inside the cage was pulling the door tightly closed. To open it, Bill would have to force it open against her entire weight - and he'd have to do it without losing his balance.

He took a wild glance down, wished he hadn't and jammed his booted feet more firmly against the bars.

He grabbed the hook with both hands and heaved. Nothing happened. He snatched at the chain but it was taut and unyielding.

Then he saw the shackles on Nellie's wrists.

Bill slithered back along the side of the cage until he was even with her hands. Balancing, he reached both hands through the bars. He grabbed the shackles and with a single motion tore them from the chain.

Nellie collapsed in a heap at the bottom of the cage and Bill fell outwards before he managed to grip the bars again. Then he scrambled back to the top of the cage. He flung open the shark cage door, reached down, grabbed some soft part of his lover and a hank of limp hair.

Grunting and tugging, Bill pulled Nellie's massive body from the cage and hefted her across one shoulder.

She was pale and deathly cold.

The cage, now topped by more than a half-ton of Bill and Nellie, finally tore free of the water slide. Bill turned and lunged at a girder, as the cage tumbled away in a glittering cloud of shrapnel and water. He held on, his shoulders aching, as above him the brass snout of the fire hose - which had been tangled in the cage bars but was suddenly free – thrashed wildly, eviscerating the remaining framework of the slide.

Bill looked around, hoping to find somewhere to climb. The slide lurched, kept lurching. It was coming down.

There was nowhere to go. Bill closed his eyes and prepared to go there. He hoped the pain would be over quickly.

Satan's voice blurted in his ear again. Why was it so familiar?

"Jump!" it said, peevishly. *"Now, moron!"*

"Where?" Bill asked but then he knew. He saw the glaring red eyes of the SNARPIG.

Bill tensed, crouched, and exploded in a leap toward that malignant gaze.

The crowd saw Bill and Nellie, bathed in the white glare of the spotlight, arc outward and plunge earthward like falling stars.

They tumbled into the gaping jaws of the SNARPIG.

Satan saw the dragon teeth of the big balloon snap closed, as if it really were devouring them. Bill and Nellie's momentum had imploded the head. A patched seam gave way with a sound like a shrieking macaw. The head drooped, the huge neck bowed. The jaws were a dozen feet above the stage when the seam tore completely. Air gouted out in a roar and the SNARPIG's head plunged groundward.

It slammed to the stage with a jolt. The balloon collapsed in billows of fabric, covering Bill and Nellie like a shroud.

The air seemed to echo from the concussion. The entire back of the stage was full of garish fabric. The SNARPIG's great red eyes were shattered into glittering pieces. The muzzle was torn and flattened, the half-inflated teeth poked up at wild angles.

Satan gulped, then turned to the crowd.

"It is done!" he shouted. "The Beast has been sated. That's our show! See you next year!" and finally pulled his mike free and threw it down.

Ignoring cheers and claps and shouts for encores, Satan ran towards the remains of the SNARPIG. The other band members and a couple of SNARRIORS joined him. They hauled frantically at the fabric, prying apart the jaws.

Nellie and Bill lay motionless.

"Stan?" Burn Ward said. "What do we do? Are they...?"

Stan knelt by Nellie. He tore off the SNARMASK and put his ear to her face but felt no breath. He put a hand to her throat, feeling for a pulse. Her flesh was ice.

"Shit," Stan said. "Anybody know CPR?" His voice cracked with panic. Nobody stepped forward.

"Shit, fuck, shit," Stan said. Hazily, he recalled a high school video on first aid. He put his hands between Nellie's breasts, felt for a heartbeat, couldn't find it, and pushed. Nothing moved. Stan swore again, shifted his weight, tried again with the same results.

He straddled her, threw his back and shoulders into it, and pumped with all his might. Her breasts bobbled.

Stan, sweating, his makeup running, let up, leaned over and put his lips to hers.

Nellie erupted in a gout of water that caught him squarely in the face.

She coughed.

"Stan? What the hell are you doing? Get off me!"

She kneed him. Stan gave a choked scream, crumpled and tumbled off Nellie. He lay on his side, groaning.

"It's okay," Shockdog said. "He was helping you. He gave you CPR!"

"He gave me some tongue!" Nellie said. "He's the one who needs CPR!" She paused, looking around for the first time, aware suddenly that the water had made her outfit almost transparent. She wrapped herself in a corner of the SNARPIG. "What happened?"

"The cage hit the waterslide," Shockdog said. "The waterslide collapsed. Bill rescued you. You both hit the SNARPIG."

"Bill?" Nellie said. "Where is he?"

Shockdog looked away for a moment, swallowed, then said: "Behind you."

Nellie twisted. Bill lay flat on his back. His chest wasn't moving, although it was hard to tell because his water-logged beard covered most of it. His face was hidden by a seaweed-like mass of wet hair.

"Is he ..." Nellie began. Her face screwed up in anguish.

"We don't know," Shockdog said. "We don't want to touch him."

Nellie crawled over to Bill's prone form. She felt his chest, stroked his face, and finally put a hand down his pants.

Bill groaned. His eyes snapped open. He raised both arms and crushed Nellie to his chest. She squeaked.

"Your hand is really, really cold, Princess," he said. "My balls feel like igloos."

"Sorry," Nellie said. "I just wanted to say good-bye to my favorite parts." And she kissed him until they both ran out of breath.

Stan, looking somewhat chartreuse, was helped to his feet by Shockdog.

"Wow," Stan said. "You do someone a good turn ...ouch." He put a clawed hand to his crotch and gasped.

"Well, to be fair, man, you did put her in the cage and almost kill her," Shockdog said.

"She signed a fucking waiver," Stan said. "Besides, she cost us a waterslide." He looked around. "Hey, where did it go? I thought I heard it fall but everything moved so fast, and ..." he looked around at the stage. "It should have flattened us like bugs. Where the hell is it?"

Only then did he notice an odd sound coming from behind the stage. It was a chorus of honks and bleats, like the road rally of the damned.

Or a hundred car alarms going off at once.

"Uh," Shockdog said. "We were amazingly lucky. The tower collapsed all right, but it mostly fell backwards. I mean, you know, there's a big chunk missing from the stage, and a speaker stack but you know, tons and tons of shit just missed us. It's like a miracle."

"What's that sound?" Stan said.

"Sound?" Shockdog said. "I don't hear anything." But he looked evasive.

"Yeah, you do, *Arnold*." Shockdog winced at the use of his real name. It meant Stan was beginning to be really upset. "You hear...what do you hear?"

"Cars," Shockdog admitted.

"And why?" Stan said. "Where did that tower land, *Arnold*?"

"Er, behind the stage, like I said."

"And what's behind the stage?" It almost wasn't a question.

Shockdog sighed. "Just open field...with some cars parked on it."

"Ooooh, crap!!" Stan said.

"But hey," Shockdog added hastily. "It's where we had the volunteers park. You know, close to the stage, easy access, yadda yadda."

Stan looked visibly relieved. "Oh, that's all right, then."

"Yeah, and we pulled the SNARmobile around to the other side exit. Not a scratch."

Stan clapped his band mate on the shoulder. "Good thinking, *Shockdog*. I knew there was a reason you handle logistics."

"And tambourine," Shockdog said.

CHAPTER TEN

Chattering Otter Water Park, outskirts of St. Louis, Missouri

The SNARmobile loaded up before dawn. Nobody had slept. Shockdog had overseen salvage operations and let the volunteers handle the rest. He and Stan agreed it would be prudent to leave before daylight. They rolled east towards the brightening sky, leaving the wreckage behind them.

The SNARmobile was a vintage bus that Shockdog had bought from a parochial school in Juarez, Mexico. The front was decorated with SNARPIG ears and the grill was painted to look like the gaping mouth of the beast.

The sides read: "Santos de ..." in faded black paint but the rest was blotted out in dripping slime-green letters that said: 'SCHOOL'S OUT!"

Bill and Nellie had the back of the bus to themselves because they wouldn't fit anywhere else. A row of seats had been replaced with a plywood sleeping shelf with a mattress on top and storage space underneath. It could be curtained off for privacy. Every member of the band claimed to have brought a groupie or two back there but it was like Bigfoot - there were no witnesses and just a few grainy photographs as evidence.

Most of the other seats had been pulled to make room for gear storage, a small fridge, and other necessities.

Shockdog had given Bill and Nellie the tour, even pointing out the secret dope panels.

"Those nuns must have been freaks," he said.

"No, asshat," Stan said. "It's Juarez. Drug-runners used this. Then they gave it to the school."

"Oh, that explains the price," Shockdog said with a flash of insight. "And the bullet holes."

"Mmmm, nuns," Disciple said.

Nellie yawned and leaned her head against Bill's chest. He'd fallen instantly asleep but was still upright, his head lowered so that his beard swept over her face like a bristly comforter. His snoring made a deep rumbling that vibrated pleasantly against her body and harmonized with the throaty diesel engine. She felt like a kitten nestling against her mother's purring warmth.

The bus was filled with the calm and magical quiet that accompanies predawn trips, before the coffee and strain and excitement - or sheer boredom - kicks in.

A few seats ahead, Ooze played a bass line over and over, just noodling. Burn Ward was driving, his calloused guitarist's fingertips tapping lightly on the wheel, making patterns as if he were pressing strings. He drove exactly at the speed limit.

Shockdog yawned.

"Man, this is the life," he said.

"You got that right," Stan said. "I know I'm never gonna get rich at this..."

"You think?" Shockdog said with a grin.

"...And I don't give a shit," Stan continued. "Seriously. It could be just for beer and smokes, on a vomit-stained stage, but it's rock 'n' roll. I never wanted to do anything else and I never will."

"That's an anthem," Shockdog said. "You gotta keep the faith. Do what you were born to do."

"Do what you gotta do to be comfortable in your own skin," Stan agreed.

"Like a shark - it stops swimmin', it dies."

"Yeah," Stan said. "I'm a rock shark."

"And I'm a road shark," Shockdog said.

"Yeah, bro. And we sharks gotta ... flock together."

"A flock of sharks," Shockdog said.

"That's deep," Stan said. "If we weren't SNAR, I'd call us Flock of Sharks."

"Dude," Shockdog said. "That's probably gonna be the name of one of our tribute bands."

Bill slept through the first hours as the SNARmobile rolled through featureless farmland. The bus slowly filled with candy bar wrappers, empty plastic water bottles and the smell of weed.

Nellie slumped on Bill's chest, snoring.

"Hey, Disciple," Stan told the drummer. "They're in rhythm. Why the hell can't you keep your beat that steady?"

"'Cause I'm trying to cover you," Disciple said.

"Well, I'm trying to cover Burn Ward," Stan said.

"Maybe I can't always remember what order them three chords go in, but I know women," Burn Ward replied smugly.

The other band members nodded in the affirmative.

"He does know women better than music," Ooze said.

"Why the hell do you think we let him join the band?" Stan said. "He brought two chicks to the audition."

A shaft of sunlight woke Nellie as the SNARmobile approached Terre Haute. She blinked heavily. She was still lying against Bill's chest. She moved aside the curtain of his beard and glanced up. Bill gazed down at her.

"You awake?" she asked.

"Yeah."

"How long was I out?"

He shrugged. "Few hours, I guess. I woke about an hour ago."

"Where are we?"

"Someplace with lots of nothing," he said.

She yawned and rolled off him. "Bet you have really gotta pee," she said.

"Yeah," he said.

She called a restroom stop at the next gas station.

Everybody got stiffly off the bus, leaving behind Shockdog, who paused to gather up armfuls of debris from the bus floor and dump it in a trash bin.

With the band emptied and the bus filled up, they got back on the road.

Bill and Nellie got the back seat again. Nellie playfully reached over and tugged the front curtain closed.

She gave Bill a flirty smile. "Hey, lover, whatchya doin'?"

"Nothin'," Bill said, glancing out a side window.

"Exactly," Nellie said, and squished her big body closer. "And that seems a damned shame, since we *are* sitting on a bed. All alone. Hint hint." She gave an exaggerated wink.

"Mmmm hmmmm," Bill said, eyes on the landscape.

She gave him a concerned look.

"You okay?" she asked, with an edge of worry.

"Not sure," he admitted.

"You know," Nellie said, and put a hand on his arm. "I dreamed about drowning and falling. Never thought I could do both at the same time." She laughed weakly. "But you didn't let that happen. You just go ahead, lover, and deal with what you've got to deal with."

"I don't know how to deal with it," Bill said.

"I know," Nellie said, nodding. "That's natural. We almost died. That's got to mess with our heads."

"Naw, that's nothin'," Bill said.

Nellie jerked her chins up. "*Nothing?*" she repeated.

"Not really," Bill said with a distracted glance. "Shit happens." He shrugged and turned back to the window.

"Bill," Nellie said softly. "Listen. Everybody deals with this stuff in their own way. But it ain't healthy to bottle it up. You can talk to me. If you want."

She waited. The silence stretched.

"...And if you don't, that's okay, too," she added.

She scooched a little ways on the seat to give him space. After a moment, Bill sighed and turned to her with sad, basset hound eyes.

"I never been without a motor this long before," he said.

Nellie started. "What?"

Bill nodded thoughtfully and tapped the glass of the window. "It's between me and life," he said.

"The window?" Nellie said. "What's that got to do with...anything?"

"When I'm riding," Bill said. "My wheels keep me above the earth. It keeps me from thinkin'. And now I'm thinkin' too much."

"You're thinkin' about the road?" Nellie asked, puzzled. "Oh, you mean the road of life. The shock of nearly dying has made you think about living. Wow. I'm still learning about you, lover. You are a deep well."

"Best bike I ever had," Bill said.

The well of sympathy in Nellie's eyes suddenly froze over. Ice crystals began to glint in her gaze.

"William," she said quietly. It was the first time she'd used his full name. It sounded like a threat. "Are you thinking about that motorcycle?"

Bill nodded, missing the daggers in her tone.

"That bike was a part of me. Like a kidney."

Nellie's mouth formed a scary line. "You saved my life, and almost lost yours - and you are dreaming about your Harley. Do I understand that correctly?" His vast unconcern hit her like a rock.

"You can't lose a kidney and feel whole," Bill said. A tear welled up in his eyes and he knuckled it away. "Once a kidney's gone, it's gone."

"They can replace kidneys," Nellie said sharply.

"Yeah, with somebody else's kidney! But that's not your kidney. You're still short a kidney. You can't hop on that kidney and ride it the way you can your own kidney. It doesn't feel right. It don't have the history. It's not a part of you."

Nellie tamped down her rising wrath. Either this man was complicated or stupid. The odds were diminishing for complicated. Either way, she should be supportive.

"Give it time," she said. "We'll replace your bike."

"No," Bill said. "You can't replace history."

Nellie gritted her teeth. There was an Arctic grinding sound for a full minute before she spoke again.

"Well," she said at last. "*I* ain't been a part of you for all that long. What are you saying about *us*?"

Bill got a look on his face like a man who takes a sip of beer and finds a rabid ferret clamped to his lips. Nellie looked like a 350-pound puma with death in her eyes. Bill thought that stare was peeling the skin off his face. He went red and began to sweat.

Nellie stood up and flung aside the curtain.

"Stop the goddamn bus! Now!" she roared.

The SNARmobile jolted to a halt in a squeal of tires. Dust flew up from the highway. Nellie marched to the front.

"Let me out," she told Shockdog, who was at the wheel. The doors gasped open and she stomped out.

Every eye on the bus turned to Bill. He hesitated, then slowly got up and followed her. The band trooped behind him.

Nellie was standing in the middle of a field, arms crossed. A shaft of sunlight glowed in her red hair, which was raging. Bugs swarmed around her but dared not alight. She was kicking half-grown honeydew melons. They burst into sticky shrapnel.

The band clustered near the bus in terror. Bill walked forward like a man crossing a minefield.

He didn't bother to understand what had happened or complain that he didn't deserve it. His gut told him there was no time.

The band followed him but stopped short when Nellie suddenly turned and eyed Bill. Bill hunched his shoulders, and kept coming. He dodged a hurled melon and stopped a dozen feet from Nellie, who had picked up another and held it menacingly.

"Hi," Bill said.

The band, which had closed up behind Bill, backed away slowly as if Nellie had started ticking.

Bill wanted to back away, too, but knew instinctively that you don't break eye contact with a maddened feline. He didn't know what was going on but he knew this was one of those rare situations where size didn't matter. In fact, he felt very small.

"Princess," he said cautiously.

He raised his hands placatingly as she cocked the melon. "We was just talking about bikes and kidneys, right?"

He said it softly and slowly, the way he might talk to a man with a broken bottle and a four-hour drunk.

"Were we?" It was a cold question.

Bill looked behind him frantically but nobody was offering more support than he'd get from a bad jock strap.

"Yes." He said tentatively.

Silence.

"No?" he tried.

Heavier silence. Nellie's eyes got harder, if that were even possible.

She balanced the melon in her hand.

Finally, Bill said: "Honey, I don't know the answer you're lookin' for."

Her face was a mask.

"That was the wrong one," she said. She let the melon drop, turned and walked away.

Bill stood there like a man who'd been suddenly decapitated and was holding his own head in his hands. He turned to the others.

"What the hell just happened?"

Shockdog finally took pity on him. He stepped forward.

"There was no right answer," he told Bill. "The right answer was to grab her and kiss her and squeeze her until she couldn't breathe."

It took the better part of an hour to convince everyone to get back on the bus. Nellie commandeered the front seat. Bill lumbered to the back and slouched stickily on the mattress.

The rest of the day passed in tense, brooding silence. Eyes glanced nervously, lighting on Bill and Nellie and then darting away like terror-stricken sparrows.

The smell of honeydew filled the bus, became cloying and then rancid.

Nobody spoke, as if words were sparks and the floor was covered in gunpowder.

After a while, Stan tried to ease the mood by turning on the radio. A synthesized beat thumped from the speakers.

Bill, silent for hours, suddenly roared from the back of the bus.

"Turn off that disco shit!"

"That's Miley Cyrus," Disciple said. "It's not disco. It's hip-hop."

"You can put lipstick on a pig but it don't make her a whore," Bill said. "Shut it off."

Stan slapped the radio console. The beat died and the nervous silence that replaced it stank worse than the melons.

Two pee breaks, a lunch stop and several iced cases of beer did nothing to ease the mood in the bus. Nellie sat like an angry mountain, pointedly ignoring Bill the way a smoldering volcano ignores a village .

Anyone with the courage to look at Bill saw a man working hard to understand what he'd done as he was slowly roasted over a fire.

As if Nellie's thoughts had congealed, by three p.m. the sky had begun to darken with thunderclouds.

Around five p.m., Stan called a halt. Everybody was exhausted from eight hours of emotional tip-toeing. The bus was ankle-deep in junk food and the opened windows had barely eased the melon miasma.

The SNARmobile pulled off the highway onto a grass shoulder that expanded into a small field. It was edged by a copse of trees. A stack of chopped wood sat near a split-rail fence.

Everybody stepped out into the gloom, stretching and lighting up joints.

"Hey," Stan said, looking at the woodpile. "We can build a campfire." He looked up at the sky, which was now purple. The sun had nearly vanished and the air was rapidly chilling.

"Shockdog, give me a hand with the wood," he said. "Ooze, go get the marshmallows."

The bus springs groaned as Bill stepped out. Nellie had her back to the vehicle, looking at the trees. The gloom turned her red hair to the color of dirty blood.

Bill advanced cautiously, stopped a couple of feet from her back.

"Princess," he said quietly. "I'm sorry."

Nellie said nothing. Her shoulders tensed, though, and after a long moment she asked: "For what?"

"For whatever I did. I know it was wrong."

"How do you know that?"

"Because you're not talkin' to me," Bill said.

"Oh, really. So the only thing you know is that I'm unhappy."

"That's all I need to know," Bill said. "That's what matters."

Nellie sighed, and turned. Bill couldn't read her face; her eyes were in shadow.

"Try to figure this out: What did you do to make me unhappy?"

"That was a while ago..." Bill said uncomfortably. "Something about a kidney?"

Nellie took a short step forward, halving the distance between them.

"The *bike*, Bill," she said. "I was right there, and you were mooning over that goddamned bike."

"And I called it a kidney?" he asked.

"You said you can't replace a kidney," Nellie prompted, arms crossed.

"Yeah, I did," Bill said. But he looked confused. "I meant the bike."

Nellie frowned. "But I was right *there*, Bill. Right there next to you, and just before that you saved my life, and it's like you didn't care about all that. Just your damned bike. Like it was your ex-lover."

“No way,” Bill said. “Princess, you’re a kidney, too. Swear to God!” he reached out his arms to embrace her but she stepped back.

A stray gust of wind sent her hair flying.

"I'm not a kidney Bill. I should be a heart."

Bill thought about it and then said: “But you can’t replace a heart."

"Yes, goddamnit, you can’t replace a heart," Nellie said. “I should be a heart."

And she turned and stalked off across the field.

Bill stood, arms out, and watched her retreat. His eyes followed her back. Then, slowly, he lowered his arms.

“You can’t pee without a kidney,” he whispered. “It’s important, too.”

Why don't I ever learn? Nellie thought. She reached the tree line and rested her forehead against a trunk.

She'd have thought by now that she wouldn't throw her heart away. Every time she did that, someone threw it back in her face, and she’d sworn to toughen up, to hold something back.

And she never could.

And now Bill, her knight of the road, was pining over a damned motor. True, he'd ridden that bike for a lot longer than he'd ridden her. And that just made her jealous. It was a rival she couldn't handle, because it was gone.

And you can't fight a ghost, she thought bitterly.

She felt the cold muzzle of the gun against her chest and briefly toyed with shooting him.

In the end, though, she just decided to leave. A man had disrespected her, and that was one time too many.

Again.

But she’d thought he was a keeper this time. From the moment when he’d put his fist through that car window, she’d known. Who else would do that to help a dog? Right then and there, she’d left the guy she was riding with. It was the first time she’d ever dumped a guy. She’d felt good, grown up, finally making good choices even if it was painful.

And then her prince had turned out to be another slimy, putrid, fucking amphibian.

"Fuck frogs," she said out loud.

Wait, she thought to herself. *This isn't me. I'm in charge. I'm not somebody to be dragged around by a man. I was, but that girl grew up. So bitch up and consider the choices.*

Nellie turned and slid down the trunk until she was sitting with her back against it. She raised a hand and counted, folding down a finger for each option:

1. Leave.

2. Give Bill another chance. He'd hurt her but he hadn't meant to. He had a pretty good heart. Like most men, he was just stupid and needed guidance.

3. Slap the shit out of him.

4. Get even. Show Bill what he's missing.

She stopped. Her middle finger stood stiffly extended.

Bill needed to be shown what he would miss.

She hefted herself up, loosened the drawstring of her peasant blouse and pulled down the shoulders. Her breasts, sensing imminent freedom, strained like caged hippos against the fabric.

She straightened her shoulders and stalked back to the bus.

A small campfire was crackling in a cleared space in the middle of the grass. A tub filled with melting ice and Budweisers stood nearby. Bill and the others were standing around in a rough circle, nursing beers and looking shell-shocked.

"All right," she bellowed. "Listen up, boys."

They turned like antelope startled at a waterhole. One or two flinched. Bill caught the determination in her eyes and looked - *hopeful?*

"Nellie!" he said.

With a huge stride, arms wide, he reached to embrace her.

A quick hip thrust and a well-timed knee and he was rolling on the ground, grunting.

"Shut up," she said. "You are not my man any longer. You have defiled me with your contempt."

"I did what?" he gasped.

Nellie put her hands on her hips and strutted slowly around the circle.

"Gentlemen, I am now auditioning suitors, since my previous consort has besmirched my honor. So here's how it's gonna work. You will fight for my favors. And the one who wins can have me."

The band members looked tentatively around, apparently wondering who would be brave enough to bolt first.

Stan cleared his throat.

"You mean like punching and kicking and like that? Cause we're kind of pacifists."

Bill staggered up and slammed one meaty fist into a palm.

"I'm ready," he said, wobbling.

"I didn't say you were invited," Nellie said.

"I'm in, whether you like it or not." He winced but stopped himself from rubbing his aching crotch.

Nellie felt a flush but suppressed it.

"Suit yourself. Just to make it interesting, I will permit Mr. Butcher to compete."

The rest of the ring drew a little further back.

"Pacifists!" Stan squeaked again. Then added: "Although you *are* hot."

Nellie grunted in disgust. Then she looked over at Bill. He could *fall* on them and kill them. Her heart did a little flip-flop. But he wasn't going to get off that easily. How to make it a fair fight, though?

"Hold up your hands," she said.

They did. Stan's arms were corded with muscle from hacking at his guitar. Burn

Ward, the lead guitarist, had arms like doggy chew sticks. Disciple had forearms that would put Popeye's to shame. And Ooze - well, she didn't want the bassist. He was scrawny.

"Arm wrestle," she declared. "Two falls out of three and you have got yourself a woman."

She cocked a meaty hip. "Who goes first?"

Stan, licking his lips, flexed his fingers and got a look of renewed interest.

"Uh, you are serious?" he asked.

"Trial by combat," she said. "It's traditional."

"Then, my lady, bring it on."

Shockdog, Disciple and Ooze went back to the bus and came out with speaker stacks and amplifiers to serve as chairs and a table.

Disciple was first. He squatted down on an amp, rolled the sleeves of his red T-shirt over his shoulders and raised his right arm, flexing the fingers. A tattooed rat on his forearm twitched its whiskers.

“Bring it, Bill,” he said.

Three and a half minutes later, there was a huge slap as the back of Bill's hand hit the top of the amp. Disciple laughed. His nose ring glittered in the campfire light.

Bill looked stunned and rubbed his wrist.

"I ain't never done this before," he said.

"Two out of three," Nellie said.

Bill shook out his hand and placed his elbow on the speaker box. He and Disciple locked hands.

“One, two, three. Go!” Stan said.

The drummer moved his shoulders back and forth, trying for better purchase. Bill was planted like a stone gargoyle. Not even his eyes moved. His enormous neck veins bulged.

Disciple started turning colors. His eyes, already a bit pop-eyed, started forward like two loose eggs. After three minutes, he began gasping for breath. He looked like a beached koi.

At four minutes and eight seconds, Bill turned his wrist as if he were gunning the throttle of a bike.

Disciple yelled and his arm slammed down on the speaker box. Bill let go, and Disciple slumped to the ground, whimpering and clutching his arm to his chest.

"Fuck!" he yelled.

"One even," Nellie said, and the look she gave Bill was not entirely venomous.

"Nope," Disciple said, staggering up. "I forfeit. I gotta use this arm to play." He staggered off and plunged his arm into the beer bucket.

Bill rubbed his wrist.

"I'm getting the hang of this," he said.

Burn Ward and Ooze looked at their fingers and begged off for artistic reasons.

Stan looked impressed with Bill's performance but quickly covered it. It wasn't just strength, he knew. It was leverage and psychology. He glanced at Nellie, then brazenly let his eyes crawl up and down her body.

Nellie caught the look and almost rolled her eyes, but checked herself, glanced at Bill to make sure he was watching and blew Stan a kiss.

Stan seemed to grow a couple of inches. He strode over and looked down at Bill with a confident sneer.

"You took the drummer," he said. "But I'm the front man. I am the face of SNAR."

He drew it out in a snarl. He sat, slapped the makeshift table and raised his arm. "Bring it!"

They locked hands.

"I don't want to hurt you, buddy," Bill said. "You been a good friend to us. But this is for my woman."

"Bill, she ain't yours unless you win," Stan said. Then he caught the look in Bill's eye, and released his hand.

"Wait!" he said. "Point of order."

He looked at Bill again.

"Hey, man, no hard feelings, okay? When I get your woman, I mean. You won't come back and kill me?"

"As long as you fight fair," Bill said.

The men shook hands gravely and then clasped them again.

"One, two, three. Go!" Nellie said.

Stan won the first round with a quick, surprising snap of his wrist. Bill didn't fall for it again. In the second round, he spent four minutes grinding Stan's arm, forcing it relentlessly down inch by inch. At the end of that round, both men took a brief halt. They panted, rubbed their arms and gave each other glances of admiration.

"Come on," Nellie said. "Let's get this over with."

They renewed the battle. Their locked arms were rigid except for tiny, almost invisible tremors, as if they were steel beams under unimaginable stress.

Full dark came on and the campfire light picked out their hard faces and hunched shoulders. Something creaked - possibly tendons.

"Bill," Stan said, between gritted teeth. "You're a good man. Nellie doesn't know what she's missing. And I won't hold it against her if she screams your name when I'm plowing the fields of the Lord."

Bill frowned and his fingers cracked. His eyes shot to Nellie for an instant. Stan made a snakelike move with his wrist, thrust hard at an angle, and suddenly Bill's arm was halfway to the tabletop.

Stan gave a fierce shout of glee and threw all his weight against Bill's arm, struggling to close the gap. Bill's wrist began to bend and his cheeks were bright red. Air whistled through his distended nostrils.

The rest of the band hooted and cheered.

Stan heard a gasp, and despite himself glanced up.

It was Nellie. Her face had gone pasty in the firelight. Her eyes were deep wells of worry. And at that instant, Stan suddenly realized how much she cared for Bill.

That was rare in a person, he thought wistfully, that joy and love. What bastard would want to stand in the way of that? But then he looked at Nellie's amazing hooters. And remembered why he'd gotten into rock 'n roll in the first place - and it wasn't for the music.

"Fuck it," he said, and surged forward.

Bill turned his eyes on Nellie. His shaking arm stopped its slow descent. His knuckles hovered an inch from the tabletop.

"I don't deserve anyone as good as you," Bill said clearly. "Never did."

Stan crushed him. Bill's hand slammed down on the speaker box with the finality of a gunshot.

Bill leaned his head down on his arms and buried his face in defeat and sorrow.

Stan leapt up and stood, weaving slightly.

"Holy shit!" he crowed. He raised his clenched fist over his head in triumph.

It was the left fist. His right arm hung uselessly at his side.

Stan shook it. It flapped pitifully. He shrugged and looked at Nellie. "I'm gonna be your one-armed lover tonight," he said, and flopped unconscious onto the grass.

The rest of the band moved up and hauled Stan away to the bus to recover.

Bill didn't raise his head.

Nellie came over. Hesitantly, she reached out a hand and stroked his hair lightly.

"I'm sorry," she said. "Jesus, I really am."

"Naw," Bill said. "He's the better man."

"No, he ain't," Nellie said with a bitter smile. "He's just the better arm wrestler."

She bent and put her chin on top of his head. Her eyes were moist.

"I wouldn't have done it if I thought you could lose," she said quietly.

"I can lose," Bill said, his voice muffled by his arms. "I lost twice tonight."

The door to the SNARmobile wheezed open and the band members stepped out. Stan came last, holding onto the door railing with his left hand.

"Hey, hey!" he said. "Did somebody order a sex god?"

Nellie looked up, wiped her eyes and wrenched a smile onto her face. She left Bill and walked regally to Stan.

She reached out and took his right hand.

Stan winced.

"Maybe it'd be best if you took my other hand," he said.

Nellie led him back into the SNARmobile. The door shut behind them with a soft gasp. Through the windows she could see the band members looking up with pale faces. Bill hadn't moved.

She pulled Stan to the rear of the bus and tipped him backward onto the mattress. She raised her arms, crossed them over her head and began to slowly swivel her hips. Her breasts heaved like tugboats jostling in a stormy harbor.

Stan stared, resisting the temptation to lick his lips. He forced himself to look at her face.

"I've seen the way you look at him," he said.

Nellie leaned over and pressed her hands into the mattress on either side of Stan's head. Her arms caged him and her breasts brushed his chin.

Parts of Stan wanted to sing.

"Let's just say you won fair, and it's not like you're not man enough for me," Nellie said throatily. "Truth be told, I've always thought about what it would be like with you."

Stan's eyes lit for a moment and then he frowned and scooted back on the mattress.

"Damn, you're wrecking this," he said. "If we didn't have history, this would be different. You can't lie to me. I know where your heart is."

Nellie's smile faltered but she pasted it back on and pressed herself to him. The mattress sank several inches.

"We ain't talkin' about hearts," Nellie said. "There's better parts. So shut your mouth and let's do it."

Stan's dick seconded the motion but the rest of him felt strangely cold and squirmy. Behind Nellie's eyes, he caught misery. It glinted like moonstruck tears.

"Oh fuck," Stan said.

"Yeah, baby," Nellie said, and reached down. Stan jerked at her touch.

"Oh, crap. Shit, fuck, piss," Stan said. "Why do I have a fucking conscience?"

He reached up with his left hand. It wanted to grope one amazing boob but by sheer strength of will he made it push against Nellie's shoulder, stopping her.

"Sorry, little guy," he whispered to his dick, then said to Nellie: "Wait, wait....seriously wait."

She paused. Her breath came in hot, panting bellows. Stan cursed himself again and wondered what asshole - probably in Catholic school - had drilled into his head that virtue was its own reward.

"Tell you what," he told Nellie. "My arm's hurting bad. Let me up for a second."

Puzzled, Nellie took her weight off him. Stan struggled upright, and realized with mixed emotions that his Little Fireman had gone into the firehouse.

"Look," he told Nellie. "I need some pot. My arm is killing me."

Nellie look frustrated. "We have to do this. I made a vow."

"Yeah, but I really took a hit out there. You wouldn't be getting the full Satan experience. And I've got a reputation to uphold."

Nellie looked at Stan for a long moment. Stan patted himself on the back, inwardly.

"How about a BJ instead?" Nellie said, and licked her lips.

Stan groaned as his Fireman heard the alarm. *Oh man,* he thought. *Now you're just fucking with me, God.*

"Nope," Stan said in a husky voice. "I'm not big on delayed gratification but really, I think we'd better give it a pass this time."

"Well," Nellie said, flipping her hair back. "I am yours, now, to do with as you please."

"Yeah, well, about that," Stan said slowly. "I'm not really into long-term relationships, either. Twenty-four hours is really stretching it. So, why don't we just call it a day?"

Nellie stood up. "You sayin' you don't want me?" Her eyes gleamed with hope but her nostrils flared with indignation.

"No, God no, I really want you," Stan said quickly. "But I couldn't give you all of me. Truth to say, my heart belongs to the music. So I must decline your enormous...generous offers. And my God, am I sorry for that. Go back to Bill."

Nellie crossed her arms. Tears glinted in her eyes.

"Stan, I don't know what to say. I was going to fuck an asshole within an inch of his life and now I can't even give a blowjob to a good guy."

"Oooh, yuck," Stan said. "Let's just not talk about body parts, please?"

"Tell you what," Nellie said. "You deserve something." She thought for a moment. "How about I let you cop a feel?"

"I could live with that," Stan agreed.

"Right," Nellie said. "One OATG coming up."

"OATG?"

"One-armed titty grab." She pulled down her blouse.

Stan's eyes bulged. He raised his good hand, then dropped it.

"Naw, the other hand's always gonna be jealous. But you know what I've always wanted?"

"I just know you're gonna tell me."

"If Bill gives me his stash, and I bury my face between your torpedoes, we'll call it even."

Ten minutes later, they emerged from the trailer. Stan ran to the beer bucket and thrust his arm into the ice water. Nellie went over to Bill.

"What the hell?" Bill asked. "I didn't hear anything break."

"He's a gentleman. He respects us and what we've got. I gave him a little titty action. And, by the way, you owe Stan your stash."

"You said *us*."

"I meant us."

"Be right back," Bill said.

He went over to Stan and handed his stash to him, then stuck out his hand.

"We can shake when I'm not hurting so bad," Stan said with a groan.

Bill nodded and returned to Nellie. She took his hand and pulled him to the bus.

"Boys," Nellie called over her shoulder. "We're gonna need a little privacy."

"We'll be right here," Disciple said cheerfully. He sat down on a speaker. "Any beer left?"

"Yeah," Shockdog said. "But now it tastes like Stan's armpit."

Not long after that, it began to rain. Cursing, the band dragged the speakers under the trees and tore off their shirts and jackets to cover them.

Then they trudged back to salvage the beer. The campfire sizzled and died.

They all sat under the dripping trees in the dark. Moans issued from the SNARmobile as if it had indigestion.

"Damn," Burn Ward grumbled. "Even the pot's soggy. And it's in a baggie. In my *pants*."

"Stan, you're a fuckin' idiot," Ooze said.

"Can't argue that one, but I'm thinking we get a great song out of this."

"Right, if we survive the night," Disciple said, shivering. "It's getting colder."

"It's gonna be big," Stan said. "I think it'll be our breakthrough, bigger than 'Prairie Dog Apocalypse.'"

"That could have been you rockin' the bus," Ooze said.

"I couldn't rock it like that," Stan said. "I hope they don't break the shocks."

The next day, the rain stopped and the SNARmobile pulled out onto a gleaming road. The rain had filled the potholes with silver. Bill was quiet - not worried quiet or scary quiet. He had a beer in one hand but he wasn't drinking.

"What you doin', sweetie?" Nellie asked in her brightest post-fuck voice.

"Just thinkin'" That brought her up short.

"Thinkin'? Why?"

"Dunno."

Nellie began to be worried. This was a side of her man she had never seen - although being he was so big, it was easy to miss a side or two.

"What are you thinkin?"

"The road looks different out a window."

For just a second, Nellie felt the dragon of resentment lift its scaly snout. But she bit her tongue. Bill had proven his love for her, and a biker's woman couldn't but grieve for the loss of a motor. Now that she'd made him prove his true desires - repeatedly - and hopefully taught him a lesson or two, she was willing to be charitable. As long as he didn't fucking *mope* about it.

"You mopin'?" she asked.

"Nope."

She looked at him. He wasn't. All the mope of the last few days was gone. But she had no idea what had replaced it. She didn't like not being able to read a man. Never happened before, she thought.

She listened a second to Ooze three seats up, who was struggling with the bass line to "When Warthogs Cry."

"Are you sad?" Nellie asked.

"Naw." Bill looked contemplative- another first, Nellie thought.

"It's more like ...." he struggled. "It's like you're on a road, and you don't know where you're going."

"You want to know where we're goin'?"

"No," he looked puzzled. "I want to know why I care where the road goes."

"Wait. Are you saying you're thinking about the future?"

"I ...." Bill couldn't finish. But he did take a sip of the beer, which emptied the bottle.

He looked thoughtful.

"I lost my bike, I lost my gang, I lost my Momma. That's a lot of things to lose."

"Yeah?" Nellie asked.

"But I got you."

Nellie smiled. "Right answer."

She kissed him, heaved herself up from the crushed mattress, walked forward and slapped Ooze hard across the back of the head.

"Play something else!"

The SNARmobile had made only two hours when Shockdog begged for a halt.

“Sorry guys, I think we’re lost,” he said.

Everybody looked out the window. They were on a smallish road flanked by frame houses. Women in gingham dresses and men in big hats, holding pitchforks and unnamable farm implements, peered at them with suspicion.

“I don’t think we’re on Highway 78 anymore,” Ooze said.

“Sorry, man,” Shockdog said again. “I’m just toasted. The rain and some people’s FUCKING MAKEUP SEX kept me awake all night.”

“Yeah,” Stan agreed. “Why don‘t we pull over and crash for a couple hours? I’ve got only one functioning body part.” He raised his left hand and wiggled his fingers. “And that’s thanks to six Red Bulls and a bottle of Motrin.”

“And you two,” he looked pleadingly at Nellie and Bill. “No more makeup sex?”

“We’re good,” Nellie said.

“What?” Bill said.

“Seriously, sweetie, everybody wants to recharge.”

Bill grumbled, tilted back his head, his mouth gaped and he was instantly snoring.

“Oh dear God,” Burn Ward said, and stuffed fingers in his ears. “I hate him.”

But the bus pulled over and somehow, everybody fell asleep.

CHAPTER ELEVEN

Joe's American Syrup & Fries Diner, New Jersey Turnpike

Norman Wuu was in a funk. He stalked around his lair - a closed-off section of the diner office hidden behind a supply shelf - scowling at his knick-knacks. He was having an attack of *minionitis.*

When it came right down to it, whoever you hired was bound to screw up. They were only human.

That's why Wuu didn't like humans.

He looked at his evil plan corkboard, straightened an index card. He walked over to the cabinet holding his finger collection and toyed with a rhesus digit. He'd ordered them on eBay. They were much smaller than they'd looked in the picture. He wished he could return them but the seller couldn't be found. He had no interest in midget fingers.

Wuu snapped his own fingers. That reminded him. It was time to feed Killer Boo Boo.

Wuu knew that, as an aspiring super villain, he'd needed a pet. But he'd felt that the Blofeld character in the James Bond movies was stupid because he had a Persian cat. What super-intelligent person would want an animal that shed, clawed the furniture and made you sneeze? His Killer Boo Boo was a dwarf komodo dragon.

They were supposed to grow to six feet but Killer Boo Boo was only twelve-point-two inches and never grew, although it ate a substantial number of bugs. He thought maybe he'd been sold a *dwarf* dwarf komodo dragon by mistake. It actually resembled a common iguana but if you couldn't trust a web ad, what could you trust in life?

He went to a terrarium full of sawdust, reached in and grabbed a handful of mealworms, then went to another shelf where his pet was snoozing under a sunlamp.

The fat lizard eyed him, opened its jaws, lazily clamped down on the mealworms one at a time, then went back to sleep.

Wuu patted the horny head then flopped down in his World Domination Chair, a Staples discount item with five roller legs and easily-cleaned artificial leather. When he was feeling like this - when the whole world had let him down - there was only one thing to do. He tapped a key on his computer and signed into his LoveDoll© "Head of the Month Club."

It was $39.99 a month well spent. He kept the doll body in a garment bag under his bed.

Wuu perused the online biographies. Schnitzie came in a box with a plastic Swiss cow and tiny milk bucket. She was raised in the Alps and liked to gambol among the edelweiss, wear low-cut peasant blouses and yodel.

"Hmm," Wuu said. He clicked on Missy. She was a former Dallas Cowboys cheerleader who was kicked out for violating hygiene rules. She was a sassy Southerner who wanted a gent who was "finger-lickin' good."

Wuu wanted somebody more exotic. He clicked on the Third World section. A globe appeared and he used the cursor to stop at each country. He passed the Asian section - he already had Ming, an escaped child sweatshop worker whose little fingers had nimbly assembled smartphones and were good with delicate manipulation. He turned to Africa.

"Keeza" grew up in a lovely little Rwandan farming village, where she herded goats and learned about the tribe's rich traditions, until her family was massacred and the village burned during a regime change. She made her way to New York where she studied library science at Columbia (the box included a sexy pair of horn-rimmed glasses) and pole-danced by night to pay for schooling.

Wuu was smitten. He checked the order box with a triumphant jab of his finger - and only then realized that he still hadn't opened last month's box. He'd been too busy with the Bill thing.

He stood up, shoved aside the supply shelf on its rolling casters, and walked out into the back office of the diner to his desk, where he collected his mail. The unmarked brown cardboard box was shoved in the well of the desk. He picked it up and took it back to the Lair.

He sat on the bed and eagerly tore open the package.

"Sinead!"

She had freckles and a stub nose. Her strawberry blonde hair gleamed under the cheap fluorescent lights. He would place her on the shelf next to Lawanda and Buttercup. There was a neat gap there where Stacy had been. He'd thrown her away. She'd had a disturbing resemblance to the last real girl he'd dated. He shivered. He still nightmares of being forced to take tango lessons. Interruptions. Demands. Questions. A lot of talking. And hair everywhere - sinks, bathtubs .... He began to get queasy and had to sit down.

Girlfriends were worse than minions. In fact, he made a new rule: No *female* minions. That would cover that. He scrawled it on an index card and pinned it to the board. He'd need to add that to his Conquest of the Planet manual. He'd have to find a role for girls, though, because they were necessary to continue his dynasty. Plus, they were essential for producing minions. Unless ... He made another note to have his scientists work on an improved version of females. The pop-off heads were really a good idea ....

Absorbed, Wuu forgot Sinead's head and grabbed his laptop. He began working out the details, pausing only to scratch absently at his latex rash.

Bill was dreaming. He was standing at the edge of a field of ripening wheat. It was morning and the sky was a crystal blue streaked with ragged white clouds. He heard a sound.

Something ominous rustled the wheat stalks. It was moving toward him with a dragging step - and a god-awful smell.

Bill's nose twitched, but in a familiar way.

"William ...." said a reedy, ghostly voice that just might have been the wind - if the wind was particularly cranky that day and smelled like rotting bologna.

Bill shivered. Now he knew what was coming.

A skinny old man emerged limping from the wheat field. He was wearing only one boot.

He came up to Bill, his eyes sparkling.

Bill's eyes welled with tears.

"Gramps!" He shouted and opened his arms to embrace him.

And took a horny little fist to the ear.

"William, you dumbass, where's my other boot?"

Bill staggered back, rubbing his head.

"What?" he said.

"My goddamn boot!" Grandpa said in his usual voice, which always seemed to contain a note of irritation. He raised one bandy leg and wiggled the foot, which was encased in an athletic sock gone gray with grime. His big toe peeped through a hole like a timid chipmunk.

"I can't walk around for eternity like this. It's embarrassing. As if the way I died wasn't embarrassing enough," he added. "They never let you forget that here."

"I don't have it," Bill said, perplexed. "It got burned up when they killed my stee... er, bike." Nellie had gotten him into the unnatural habit of calling his hog a steed. It was confusing.

"Focus, idiot!" Gramps said, and clocked him in the knee with the unbooted foot, then gave a yelp of pain and began dancing, holding his toe and defiling the air with curses.

"Son of a cow cunt!" He said. "Ow. Ow. Ow. This is why I need the boot."

"But Gramps," Bill said, trying to mollify him. "Look, you have at least one boot, right? "Where did you get that one?"

"The first intelligent question to come out of your piehole this whole dream," Grandpa said. "This actually is the boot you lost. You lost it, I got it. There's some connection between us."

"Wow," Bill tried to get his head around that.

"And before you ask, no, I can't give you stuff," Grandpa said. But he looked shifty.

"Hey," Bill said after a moment of deep thought. "Have you got my bike, too?"

Grandpa's eyes darted from side to side. He paused.

"Noooo," he said slowly.

"But the boot was in the saddlebag. Didn't they, uh, reach the other side together?"

"I told you I don't have it!" Grandpa snapped. Under his breath he added, "Now."

His right hand crept slowly over his left wrist, covering a gold Rolex.

"Oh," Bill said regretfully. "I sort of hoped she was in a better place."

"Oh, forc ... Get off my back already! I said I didn't have it," He said it a little bit louder for at that moment, there was the ghostly sound of an engine ripping by and a thin voice saying "You still owe me a taillight for this beast, Adolf!" Then it was gone.

"That sounded just like ...." Bill began.

Grandpa struck out quick as a snake, and Bill's other ear burst into pain. He suddenly recalled that Grandpa'd always been a fast little bastard.

"Focus, stupid! I wish to God I *had* that boot."

Bill let the nausea pass. He thought Grandpa might have made a great cage fighter. Trying not to piss him off further, Bill said helpfully, "You could kick me with the boot you're wearing."

"Naw, That boot's for kickin' enemies, dumbass. That's the HATE boot. The one I need's for kickin' family."

Bill suddenly felt a warm glow and rubbed the back of his pants, his fingers tracing the hidden letters EVIL, imprinted from contact with a boot sole in childhood. Bill suddenly remembered the hundred or so times when he found himself doing a face-plant without warning as Grandpa addressed some shortcoming with percussive correction.

"Look, sonny, stop going off like that," Grandpa said crankily. "I don't have all the frickin' time in the frickin' universe for you to zone out, William."

"But you're dead."

"Oh, so my time is less valuable? You say things like that and you wonder why I need my boot. And you were the *smart* one in the family. Maybe I should have kicked your mom more." He shook his head in disgust.

"Oh," Bill was suddenly hesitant. "Gramps, I've got to tell you something." He paused and then said: "Mom is dead."

"Yeah," Grandpa said in disgust. "Everybody knows. I guess she's gonna visit. Everybody but me is wondering about that key lime smell in the air. But enough old homes bullshit. I have a mission for you, William."

"You want me to deliver stolen TVs?"

"You were the only kid in the neighborhood who could actually carry one, but no. Stop reminiscing, goddammit. Anyway, focus! I can't tell you what the mission is, exactly - some dumbshit rule they have. Prophetic dreams and portents all have to be big fuckin' puzzles. Don't ask me why. It's like import laws. Just bullshit. But I can say, 'William, when you wake up, keep on the road about ten miles, get off on Saddleboro Road, then turn left and look for a sign that says "Yoder's Farm." There you will find your destiny.'"

He said the last word in an echoey voice that resonated with fate and foreshadowing - although it was a squeaky foreshadowing. Bill felt that some majestic clouds should have swept up and covered the sky, like in bad Bible movies.

"Which is what?" he asked.

Grandpa's mouth snapped shut. The majestic tone screeched to a halt like a derailed boxcar full of parrots.

"Which is what *what?*," Grandpa asked.

"What's my destiny?" Bill asked, tugging at his beard.

"Did I just not get through telling you I can't tell you that? *Jeeezus.* I wish I'd lived long enough to kick some sense into you. Just trust me on this. May I continue, please?"

"Sorry." Bill felt his face glow with familiar humiliation.

"So," Grandpa's voice attempted to regain its majesty. The sky trembled with portentousness.

"Oh, fuck it," Grandpa said, and threw up his hands. "Look, take the exit. Go to the farm."

"Then what?"

Grandpa turned and shuffled off into the wheat, limping and muttering. Just before vanishing, he shouted over his shoulder.

"Tell that farmer he's an asshole."

Bill woke with a jerk. The jerk was Stan, who'd been leaning over him, apparently watching him sleep.

"You were screaming," Stan said. "If that was a sex dream, you are one weird freak."

Nellie came up behind Stan and peered over his shoulder.

"Leave him be, Stan," she said. "You're not the only one who dreams about me."

Stan blushed, then hurriedly squeezed past Nellie and went to the front.

Nellie sat down next to Bill and took his hand.

"What is it?" she asked. "Nightmare?"

"Prophecy," Bill said. "Grandpa spoke to me."

Nellie sucked in her breath.

"Your dead grandfather? What did he want?"

"He wants us to go to a farm near here and talk to the farmer."

"Did he say why?"

"He said he couldn't say. They have some dumbass legal code in the afterlife."

Nellie nodded. "Oh, I know. That's why the food won't ever give me a straight answer. You'd think God had better things to do than make up shitty puzzles." She patted Bill on the knee and stood. "Well, if that's what we gotta do, let's go do it."

Yoder's farm was a neat white, two-story clapboard with a big barn and a silo, surrounded by fields in strips of green and gold. It was prim and pretty as a calendar painting. The SNARmobile blew through it like a farting guest at a fancy dinner. Brass-colored stalks of wheat dipped their heavy heads as the bus swept by, as if they were embarrassed.

The bus pulled up a short distance from the house, just where the paved roadway became gravel. Bill and the others stepped out. It was peaceful. The breeze carried the rustle of wheat, the sweet scent of hay, and the explosive sound of Stan sneezing. It took nearly a minute before he stopped.

"Goddamn nature," he swore, and wiped his streaming nose. "Back in a second. I'm gonna get a Benadryl."

"Well," Nellie asked Bill. "What do we do now?"

"Find the farmer," Bill said.

"Why don't we knock on the door?" Shockdog said.

"Yeah, it's not like they'll think we're wandering Bible salesman," Burn Ward said, fingering his nose ring. "I think we might scare the crap out of these folks."

"It's harvest season, and it's daylight," Nellie said. "The farmer will be in the field. Everybody look around."

"We didn't see anybody coming in," Stan said, returning.

"Wish we knew his cell number," Burn Ward said.

"He's Amish, dork," Shockdog said. "He doesn't have a phone. Probably doesn't have socks."

"He might be way off at the end of a field," Nellie said. "But maybe we can hear him. Everybody shut up for a minute."

They clammed up, except for Stan, who snuffled quietly. The wheat made soothing sounds like a mother's lullaby. It very nearly drowned out the sound of somebody swearing in German.

They followed the sound, walking around the edge of a field and down a small hill. They saw a farmer sitting on a horse-drawn combine in the middle of a stubbled row. The four horses had their heads down and their tails swished lazily. The big paddle-wheel blades of the combine were quiet but the farmer wasn't. His wizened face was bright red and he stamped his feet angrily on the splashboard. He didn't even seem to notice them until Bill stepped forward and his shadow fell on the contraption.

The farmer stopped mid-swear, eyed the biker, moved a plug of tobacco thoughtfully from one cheek to the other, then bent over the seat and spat a brown jet that looked like something that would come from a mule with diarrhea.

"Jehoshaphat, son," he said to Bill. "Your *Mamm* must have been a Clydesdale. If I hadn't just broken my harness, I'd hitch you up and turn Annalie out to pasture."

"Are you Yoder?" Bill asked,

"Good question," the farmer said. "Let's see, this is the Yoder's Farm, according to the sign on that road up yonder, and I'm thinking by my outfit and the fact that I'm harvesting wheat that I'm a farmer, and you put two and two together, and what do you get? Just stamp your hoof on the ground the right number of times." He chawed and spat again. "I thought Clydesdales were smart animals."

"Well," Bill said. "Now that I met you, I guess I know why Grandpa had that message for you."

"What message?"

"That you're an asshole."

The farmer gaped. His chin beard waggled ferociously.

"I'll be a gelded goat," the old man said. "Tell me, was your *groossdaadi* named Butcher?"

"Adolf Butcher," Bill confirmed.

The old man threw down the reins and hopped nimbly from the combine. He hitched up his suspenders and looked steadily at Bill.

"Nope," he said at last. "No resemblance at all, far as I can see. Still, who else would come out here and use that name? When's the last time you saw your grandpa?"

"Two hours ago," Bill said. "In a dream."

"*Scheisse!*" Yoder took off his straw hat and beat it on his thigh, raising a cloud of wheat chaff. "Well, I reckon we'd best go back to the house. I've got a story to tell, and you need to hear it. The rest of you seem to have hands and feet, so I'd be obliged if you'd help me bring the team back to the barn. Don't suppose I'll be get getting any more work done out here today."

He went back to the combine, unhitched the horses and threw the reins to Nellie, Shockdog, Bill and Stan. Stan looked at the huge horse's nostrils towering over him, flinched, and tossed the reins to Ooze. The farmer clucked to the horses and began stumping back toward the barn. The big beasts followed placidly.

Bill followed along, idly scratching a horse's ear. They were about the same size as his.

"Momma said Grandpa was killed by a farm machine," Bill said. "His last words were..."

"Keep that *gottverdammt* thing away from me," Yoder recited. The old man's rheumy eyes bored up into Bill's belt buckle. "I remember it all these years later. Not that he lets me forget. Every year on the anniversary of his death, that *jagoff* sends me a dream." He eyed Bill. "I should have known you'd show up on the same day."

Nellie's eyes went wide. "He died today? I didn't see that on the plate," she said. "It's foodless fate!"

The farmer cocked his head at her, then shot a glance at Bill. "Why did you bring the crazy woman?" he asked.

"She ain't crazy," Bill said amiably. "She just acts that way. She's got mystical powers. She sees things other people don't. Like the beauty in me."

"I'll bet," the farmer said. "Well, she's for sure not getting anywhere near the hemp factory."

"You have a hemp factory?" Shockdog asked with interest.

"For making rope, sonny," Yoder said. "Not for smokin'. Much. We use rope on a farm."

He raised his eyebrows quizzically and appeared ready to accent the remark with more tobacco juice, but then apparently decided not to waste it. "Where was I?"

"My Grandpa," Bill said as the party trudged out of the field onto the gravel and approached the barn. "Can you tell me what really happened with Grandpa? The family could never figure out what he was doing here."

The farmer spat out a plug of tobacco that had the size and consistency of a fresh cow turd. "My boy, do you really want to know this? T'ain't pleasant."

"I need to know," Bill insisted. "Grandpa might have kicked me a lot but he always kicked me in the right direction."

"God knows how," the old man mumbled under his breath. "All right, then. Youngster, you should know that your *groossdaadi* was not a stranger to these parts. He came one springtime during the planting, and fell in love with our whoopie pie."

"Who's she? He had a girlfriend? I didn't think he was that interested in women. He kicked me in the face when I looked at one." Bill sighed with nostalgia.

The geezer gave him a funny look.

"A whoopie pie is a pie," he said "Just as the name says." He spoke slowly, as if talking to a six-year-old. People did that a lot, Bill noticed. "Anyway, he struck an acquaintance with a few of the better cooks in town. I don't know how a skinny fella could put away so many. Course, that was after his shift in the hemp factory. He was on probation for something and we could use the cheap labor."

"Don't you have enough Amish people around here?" Shockdog asked.

"Believe it or not, sonny, there are some jobs we won't do. You can get arthritis in the wrist."

Burn Ward shook his own wrist in empathy.

"It's pretty much all handwork. We don't hold with new-fangled stuff," the farmer said. "They've even got computers to spank your babies! 'Taint natural."

They reached the barn and the farmer led the horses to their stalls. He got a brush and began to groom them.

"Anyway, we got to know Adolf pretty well," the farmer said. "And normally, you always knew where he was, by the smell. Like a bucket of bad headcheese."

"That was Grandpa," Bill said with a smile.

"The night he died, the wind was at my back. I was in the field about midnight with that combine. The moon was up but I just didn't see him in the wheat."

"This is wheat?" Nellie asked. "It comes up to my chest. Where I grew up, wheat was only two or three feet high."

Yoder puffed out his chest. "Every heard of corn-wheat hybrids?"

"No," Nellie admitted. "I didn't think you could cross them."

"That's what the fella from the agricultural cooperative said," Yoder said. "But we put him up in the hemp barn, and after a few months by Goshen if he didn't do it!" Yoder chuckled and spat tobacco juice. "It grows up to your shoulder and the wheat berries are as big as your thumb. I sell it to those fancy New York restaurants." He puffed out his cheeks. "Some of those DuPont and Monsanto slickers came snooping around once but I ran them off. Got about forty acres now."

He turned back to Bill. "So anyway, your grandpa was in the crop. Turns out he got a boot caught in a furrow." Yoder sighed and shook his head. His beard waggled. "Ran right over him. Chipped the blade and spooked the horses."

He finished currying the animals.

"We got the police and they picked up all the bits and that was that. Wrecked a full bin of corn-wheat, too."

"What was he doing out in the field?" Bill asked.

"There are rumors. Are you sure you want to hear 'em? They don't paint a pretty picture."

"If it's short of murder, I can live with it," Bill said. "Or, well, not more than one murder, I mean."

"Well," Yoder said, and took off his hat and held it in both hands. "The rumor was that he was a smuggler."

Bill guffawed. "That was his day job," he said. "We all knew that."

The farmer glared at him. "The rumor is he was smuggling people *here,* illegal Asians."

"Whatever for?" Nellie asked.

"To learn how to work in our pneumatic factories so they could churn out fake Amish furniture and undercut us," the farmer said. "Bitin' the hand that fed him all those whoopie pies. Word is they were gonna dismantle the machinery from one of our factories and take it away on a truck but those Asian fellas got spooked and ran off. Your granddad must have gone into the field to chase 'em. Everybody got away but him."

"Well,' Bill said. "He was a big dreamer with big dreams."

"He was a big schemer who wound up in tiny pieces," the farmer said. "I think you English call that ironic."

Bill looked forlorn. "All I ever saw was his boot. And it's gone now."

"There, there, lover," Nellie said. "Grandpa's got it in Heaven."

"Heaven?" the farmer looked up sharply. "You think?"

"Well," Bill admitted. "I just saw him in the field. I don't where he goes when he's not delivering cryptic messages."

"I can guess," the farmer said sourly. "But you're guests. So, sure, Heaven it is." He stopped for a moment, then snapped his fingers. "Wait, did you say a boot?"

"No," Stan said. "We're not Canadian."

"Not *about*," Yoder said, pronouncing it the Canadian way. "Did you have some brain-swelling disease when you were a boy?"

"No!" Stan said.

"Well, you might try to get one now," the farmer snapped. "You need a bigger brain. I said a *boot.* That you wear. And the reason I said that is because after we finished the harvesting, I found his other boot in the field. I kept it in case the police came back, then forgot about it. I think I still have it in here someplace."

The farmer thought hard for a moment, his hand on his chin, then he clamped his straw hat firmly back on his head, turned and climbed an old ladder to the hayloft. He bent over, half of him disappearing between the bales, and rummaged. Loose straw showered Bill.

"Ah hah!" Yoder exclaimed.

Something dark sailed out of the loft and thumped Bill in the head.

"Watch out below!" Yoder yelled.

Bill picked up the item, and beamed.

It was an old cracked boot. Bill turned it over. Carved into the sole was the blurred word "*Evil.*"

Bill hugged it to his chest.

The farmer climbed down off the ladder.

"I'd be careful," he told Bill. "You don't want to know what might be in there."

Bill shook it. Two stunned field mice fell out. Bill scooped them up and gave them to Nellie. She tapped both of them on the chest until they started breathing and scampered away.

Bill looked at Nellie tenderly. Tears pooled in his eyes, decided they wanted to relocate, and streamed down his cheeks until his beard was soggy.

"It is Grandpa's," he said. "I got the imprint on my..."

"I know, lover," Nellie broke in. "So this is why your Grandpa sent you here."

"Reckon so," the farmer said. "Maybe now he'll stop bothering me. Tell you what, folks. In his honor, come up to the house. We can all have some whoopie pie."

"Whoopie!" Stan said.

"That was hilarious," Shockdog said.

"Yep, first time I heard that," the farmer agreed, and shook his head.

They followed the farmer to the house, wiped their feet on a mat that said "Wilkommen."

"Mrs. Yoder," the farmer called. "We have guests." He led them to a dining room table.

"How many?" a woman called from the kitchen.

The farmer eyed Bill.

"Say a dozen," he said. "There's one youngster counts for five or six."

There was a clatter and a mountainous woman appeared, balancing three plates on each arm, each stacked with mounds of whoopie pies. Two more plates were balanced between her paunch and her gingham apron. She turned sideways and squeezed through the four-foot-wide kitchen doorway. A couple of band members rose to help her.

"Back off, I've got this," Mrs. Yoder said sharply.

"Mrs. Yoder has been doing this for forty-five years," the farmer said with pride. "I think she's got the hang of it. Of course when she was younger she couldn't carry as many plates."

Mrs. Yoder set them down. Heads disappeared behind the stacks.

Bill leered at dark chocolate hemispheres, like half-pound cheeseburgers with frosting swelling between them.

"Hands in your laps!" Mrs. Yoder commanded. Hands slapped Levis.

Mrs. Yoder beamed at them through her bifocals.

"I just whipped these up this morning," Mrs. Yoder said. "Guess I won't have to eat them all myself." She pointed at the stacks with plump fingers. "So, those are pumpkin. These are jam filled, and there's cinnamon, cream cheese, currant, chocolate pistachio, oh, and that crumbly stack that looks like oatmeal? That's an experiment."

"What is it?" Stan asked.

"After you eat some, we'll know," Mrs. Yoder said. "I smudged my glasses while I was cooking it so I'm not sure. Dig in, now. I'll bring coffee." She vanished into the kitchen.

Bill was the first to attack the stacks. He grabbed two pies in each hand, stuffed them all into his mouth. A waterfall of frosting cascaded down his beard. He moaned.

"Ohhh," he crowed, spraying crumbs. "I'm in Junkyard Heaven!"

"He means that as a good thing," Nellie explained to Yoder. She daintily picked up a cream cheese pie with two fingers, took a bite, then dug in, somehow still managing to look like a lady.

Mr. Yoder watched Bill.

"You're a hearty eater like your *grossdaadi* but without the sound effects," the farmer said. "He sure was appreciative." He shuddered and muttered: "Hope we don't have to fumigate the place like with your grandpa."

Mrs. Yoder shoved back through the door with an enormous jug of coffee and a fistful of mugs. She backed to the doorway and stood watching her guests eat and drink the way a zookeeper eyes a pack of jackals after throwing them a carcass - with satisfaction and just a hint of disgust.

"Well," Mr. Yoder said when the sound of grunts and smacking lips had subsided to a low roar. He hooked his thumbs under his suspenders and snapped them to get everyone's attention, then turned to his wife. "Well, that was a fine snack, Mrs. Yoder. I reckon these young folks are pretty content, right?"

Everybody nodded and there was a round of thank-yous. Mrs. Yoder beamed. The farmer turned to Bill.

"You get enough, big fella?"

For answer, Bill combed chocolate and raspberry frosting from his beard, licked his fingers and nodded. The farmer nodded back.

"Good manners are always appreciated. Yours are, too," he said. He eyed the group. "So, you're slopped and ready to go. Where're you goin'?"

"New York," Stan said.

"New Jersey for us," Nellie said.

"Why?" Yoder said. "Got a sick relative?"

"It's a long story," Nellie said.

"New Jersey man gave my Momma a diner but she blew up and now it's mine if I make it to the court on time," Bill said.

Yoder waggled one eyebrow, then the other.

"Yep," he said. "That was an epic. Must be nearin' bedtime already, what with that long gab." He turned to Nellie. "Your man sure knows how to spin a tale."

"There's a lot more," she protested.

"Not that I care about," Yoder said. "Some of us have to work for a living." He leaned over and tapped Bill's arm.

"So you're on your way to get a diner. That's good. A man should have a goal in life. When I was young I went on R*umspringa*. Had a fine time for a year avoiding responsibilities. But I needed to decide if I wanted to be that person or do something meaningful. I realized I was being asked at seventeen to lay out my whole life. I had no guidance but I had to make the choice."

"What decided you?" Bill said.

Yoder looked reflective. "Time comes, sonny, when not choosing is a choice," he said.

"I don't understand," Stan said.

"He knocked me up," Mrs. Yoder said.

Yoder looked at her fondly. "We got eight kids now," the farmer said. "Reckon I made the right choice."

He looked at Bill. "I guess you choosin' the diner means you're following your heart."

"Ain't his heart, old man," Stan said, remembering the Night of the Rocking Trailer.

Yoder snorted. "Throw a cow in there and you'd almost be an Amish comedian," he said. He slapped a rough hand on the table. "Well, I'll tell you what, folks. It's been a long time since we've had so many brats under our roof. 'Twasn't awful." He looked at his wife, who nodded. "So if you feel like stayin' the night, you're welcome."

"That's very kind," Nellie said. Stan and the others nodded.

"Well, then," Yoder said. "That's settled. Now who wants supper?"

At that moment, a bullet blew out a window and smacked into a pile of whoopie pies. Filling exploded everywhere. Chairs overturned and bodies hit the floor in panic. Stan flailed in the sweet, sticky goo.

"Not again!" Nellie swore.

Yoder raised his smeared face and blinked. He began cursing in German, switched to English and barked, "Get the hell out of here. You've overstayed your welcome!"

Mrs. Yoder opened her mouth to chastise him but before she could speak, a voice from outside called, "Sorry. Accident. My sniper stepped in a cow turd. Bill, come on out."

It was a voice Bill could never forget. It belonged to the man who had destroyed his bike. The voice of Mr. Angel.

"You're trapped," Mr. Angel called in a reasonable voice. "Give up. We just want to hold you for a couple of days. Forget about the diner, I'll buy you a damn hamburger."

Nellie saw Bill's muscles tense and crawled over to him. Urgently, she stroked his shoulder like someone trying to calm a snorting bull.

"Keep down," she said repeatedly. "This is forebrain time, lover."

Bill trembled but he stayed down.

Shockdog cautiously inched up to the bottom of the shattered window and peeked out.

"Three of them," he whispered. "With guns."

"Obviously," Yoder said.

Stan looked at Yoder. "I guess we're gonna need the posse."

"What?" said Yoder, pulling broken glass out of his beard as he hugged the floor. "Are you on crack? What in the name of Jehoshaphat are you talking about?"

"Like in that old movie. Harrison Ford is this detective and he hides with the Amish people, and they all get shotguns and pitchforks to defend him from the bad guys."

"I don't watch movies," the old man groused. "I'm Amish. Besides, Kelly McGillis showed her boobs in that movie. Mrs. Yoder hasn't shown me hers in twenty-five years."

"Only twenty-four," Mrs. Yoder corrected. She had thrown herself flat in the doorway. "And if you're not polite to our guests, you'll be waiting another twenty-four."

She flicked filling from her spectacles and said "I'm going back in the kitchen. You menfolk handle this." She heaved herself around and scooted back through the door.

Yoder watched her go. "Got a rump like a hippo," he said appreciatively. "Now you all, get gone!"

"Wait, so you guys aren't sworn to defend guests?" Stan asked.

"Whoopie pics are as far as we go," Yoder said. "Get the hell out of the house."

"I'm waiting," Mr. Angel called. "If Bill isn't out here in, oh, three minutes, we'll burn the house. On the other hand, if Bill comes out, everybody goes free and happy. Oh, and now it's two minutes."

Nellie said: "Mr. Yoder, sorry to have caused all this trouble."

"The man said two minutes," Yoder said, his hands over his head. "Are you deaf? Move them clodhoppers out of my house!"

Nellie touched Bill on the arm. "We givin' up?"

Bill thought about it.

"One minute," Mr. Angel called. "This is a Timex. It doesn't lie."

"No," Bill said. "We run."

"Good," Nellie said.

They rose to a crouch, looked over at the others on the floor.

"You coming?" Bill asked.

Stan shook his head. "Sorry, man, but this isn't our fight. I like you but I can't risk the band. Can't fight guns with guitars. "

Nellie smiled at him. "I know. As soon as we're gone, they'll let you out."

"We'll go back to the bus," Stan said. "We'll wait. If you make it, we'll be there."

"Less chatter, more clatter," Yoder said.

"Gentlemen," Mr. Angel called again. "And whoever else is in there. I understand this is not your fight. Escort yourselves out. You will not be harmed. All we want is Bill."

"Nellie?" Stan queried.

"Don't even think about it, Stan."

Bill grabbed the boot off the table and he and Nellie hurled themselves through the kitchen door. Mrs. Yoder was standing at the big wood-burning stove, rolling pastry and seemingly unconcerned.

"Goodbye, Mrs. Yoder," Bill said. "Thanks for your hospitality."

"Leaving so soon?" she asked politely.

"Yeah," Bill said. "Folks are trying to kill us again."

"Take a whoopie pie," she said. She took a platter from a counter and threw back the gingham cloth covering it.

Bill grabbed four pies. Nellie took one.

"These were really good," she said. "Do you have the recipe?"

"Google it," Mrs. Yoder said. "Time's up. Out the door with you now before Mr. Yoder throws another fit. Shoo!"

And then she cupped her mouth and yelled: "Yoder! Tell 'em they're gone!"

From the dining room, they heard Yoder yelling: "Don't shoot! They're coming out the back door! Go get 'em!"

"Son of a bitch!" Bill said.

He ripped open the door, and he and Nellie sprinted like terrified wildebeests into the wheat field.

Mr. Angel stood on a slight rise a few dozen yards from the front door. Next to him was the sniper, Torres, who looked shame-faced. Mr. Angel glared at him sourly. That cow-turd shot had cost them surprise. He didn't have enough men to go crashing through the door when at least one of his quarry - the fat bitch - had a gun.

So now, they would negotiate. But Mr. Angel always kept an ace in the hole.

He lifted his walkie-talkie. "Jimmy, they're coming."

"I see 'em," a voice responded. "Just came out the back door."

"Got a shot?"

The walkie-talkie crackled. "No. They're already in the field."

Mr. Angel sighed. "Okay," he said. "I'm coming over."

The front door opened. Mr. Angel instantly raised his Glock instantly and leveled it on the figure. Torres pointed the rifle.

The man in the door was skinny, half Bill's breadth. His hands were up and he was frantically waving a soiled white napkin.

"We're all coming out," Ooze called. "All we want to do is go home."

"Advance," Mr. Angel called. "Keep your hands up."

Behind Ooze, Stan and the rest of the band trooped out and climbed the slope.

"Bill's gone!" Stan repeated needlessly. "He and Nellie took off out the back door."

"I know," Mr. Angel said. "Who's still in the house? I heard another voice."

"Oh, that's Yoder, the farmer. He and his wife are inside. She's cooking. Wouldn't leave her stove. And he won't leave her."

"But you left?"

"Yes, sir," Stan said. "We're just a rock band."

Mr. Angel laughed. "And I should just let you go, and trust that you won't call the cops?"

Stan shrugged, hard to do with his hands up.

"Like I told Bill, it's not our fight. Besides, I don't know who you are. I don't think I could identify you."

Mr. Angel thought. "I doubt that you could. What did you say your band was named?"

"SNAR."

"SNAR?"

"Yeah, in capital letters."

"Good. Now I know who to kill if you get any ideas. Bands make easy targets."

"Yeah," Stan said. "I like Bill - I mean, I *don't* like Bill," he added hastily, eyeing the guns. "He's not in the band."

"I'm wasting my time talking to you," Mr. Angel said. "Is that your bus?"

"The SNARmobile," Stan said with a touch of pride.

"Whatever." Mr. Angel turned to the rifleman. "Take these gentlemen to the Crapmobile. Make sure they board. Then watch them until we get done here."

"Let's go," Torres said. "You can put your hands down. Slowly."

The band trooped toward the bus. Torres followed, holding his weapon on them almost casually.

Mr. Angel took a last glance at them, and then moved around the house toward the back field.

He caught up with Jimmy, who was standing at the edge of the field. The grain rose to his shoulders and rippled like a golden curtain in the breeze.

"That's where I last saw them," Jimmy said, pointing. "Lost 'em. They must be crawling. But they have to come out somewhere. Those two are behemoths. Eventually we'll see them."

"I wouldn't count on it," Mr. Angel said. "First rule of war is to know your battlefield, and we don't."

"But if they stand up or clear the field, they're easy targets," Jimmy argued.

"And if they hole up until dark, we might lose them," Mr. Angel replied. He sighed. "I'm going in. You go back to that rise next to the farmhouse so you can scan the whole field and make sure they don't double back. You'll see my head, so you guide me. Call her Hippo and him Elephant," He thrust his face close to Jimmy's. "And if you get a shot, take it. Don't let them get the drop on me."

Jimmy nodded and sprinted off. Mr. Angel plunged into the field.

Bill and Nellie lay on their bellies. The wheat stalks rustled around them. The earth beneath them was warm and dry. They hugged it so closely that the clumps of dirt seemed like boulders. From away and above, they heard a voice call out: "I see you."

Nellie's blood ran cold.

But then the voice added: "Can't see them, though. The breeze is making everything move. Wait!" It paused. "Could be something at two o'clock, twenty yards."

Not far off to their left, the sheaves of wheat thrashed.

Nellie rolled over, pulled her gun from between her breasts and waited.

Mr. Angel pushed through the stalks, thrusting them aside with his hand and the muzzle of his gun. He wasn't trying to be quiet. He knew his quarry had at least one weapon but he doubted they would use it without having eyes on target. Mr. Angel counted on speed making up for noise. In the worst case, they would hear him and run off. If he flushed them, Jimmy would see them from the hill. Besides, his loafers were getting dirty and the wheat chaff made the back of his neck itch. The sooner he was out of nature, the better he liked it.

He paused and listened keenly but heard only the breeze-blown wheat. He stifled a sneeze.

Something erupted in front of him like a black demon. Without conscious thought, Mr. Angel fired. The Glock roared three times, tearing at the wheat in front of him.

Two crows dropped at his feet. A few black feathers drifted down.

Mr. Angel cursed.

"You got it!" Jimmy said excitedly. "You hit something!"

"They were goddamned crows!" Mr. Angel shouted.

"No! No!" Jimmy called back. "Ahead of them. I saw something come up when you shot and then fall down!"

"So, bigger than a crow?" Mr. Angel shouted.

"How big do crows grow?"

Mr. Angel cursed and resisted the urge to unload the rest of the Glock's clip at Jimmy.

"Get me moving!" he shouted. "Now!"

"All right! All right!" Jimmy called. "It went down on your three, no more than ten yards ahead."

Mr. Angel was off like a shot, stumbling through the wheat with his gun forging ahead like the nose of an eager foxhound. He ignored the stalks slapping his face.

"Movement!" Jimmy yelled, his voice childish with excitement. "Definite contact! Maybe Elephant!"

"Where?" Mr. Angel roared.

"Your two, five yards," Jimmy called. "No, your four, six yards. Oh, shit, now it's your six at three yards."

Mr. Angel stopped and whirled.

"Make up your mind!" he called. But then he heard it. Something big and heavy and panting was smashing it way through the wheat five yards to his right.

Mr. Angel caught a glimpse of something like a bulking black shadow as it parted the wheat. The sun glinted on a gun barrel.

Mr. Angel and the looming shape opened fire at the same instant. Mr. Angel was suddenly deafened by the blast and time slowed. He watched as a long-barreled gun spun up from the figure, arcing lazily above the wheat and falling away as the body behind it slowly crashed to the earth.

Mr. Angel stopped firing and became aware that he was on the ground, too. His Glock was empty. Without thought he pulled another clip from his coat pocket and jammed it home.

He rolled to his feet in a single motion but before he could fire again, he heard Jimmy call.

"It's Hippo! Hippo is down! Right there! Right in front of you! Er, twelve o'clock!" His voice warbled as if he were jumping and down.

Mr. Angel crouched and rushed forward, parting the wheat. In front of him, the sheaves were torn to shreds at chest level.

The bitch was on the ground in front of him, face down. One hand was outstretched. She wasn't moving. Mr. Angel cautiously moved forward, gun still leveled on her back.

Nellie groaned theatrically.

Mr. Angel smiled.

"Give me a reason," he said to Nellie. "Please, give me a reason. It would be a pleasure to shoot you."

Slowly, painfully, Nellie rolled onto her side. She propped her head on her hand and looked boldly into Mr. Angel's eyes.

She winked.

"Hey, big boy," she said, and tossed her hair.

At that instant, something hard and heavy thunked Mr. Angel on the side of his head. As he blacked out, Mr. Angel heard Jimmy shout: "Elephant rising!"

Bill picked up the boot and shook out the rocks but Nellie whispered urgently: "Get down! There's a guy on the hill. He can see you!"

Bill dropped. A split-second later, a burst of assault rifle fire ripped the air above him.

"Boss!" Jimmy called. "Where are you?"

"He's down!" Nellie called. "And we got him. Put down your weapon!"

"Why?" Jimmy asked, then added oddly: *"Awwwp!"*

From up the hill, Nellie heard the harsh click of a shotgun being cocked.

Then she heard Mr. Yoder call out: "Ohhh-kay, English, put your hands to the sky or you get another pie!"

Mr. Angel woke with a pounding in his head that made his ears feel as if they were taped to an expanding balloon. He made himself snap to alertness. He was tied to a chair. He was in his boxer shorts. He looked around. His men were also tied to chairs and were wearing only their shorts. Torres looked both glum and embarrassed. He wore pink mesh briefs. Mr. Angel wished he had not seen that.

"Oh, you're awake," said a voice like the squeaky hinge on a barn door.

A pipsqueak of a farmer was leveling a shotgun at him from a corner of the room. "How you feeling?"

"Bad," Mr. Angel said.

"Probably," agreed Mr. Yoder. "But don't worry, the police will be out here shortly."

Mr. Angel looked blearily at him.

"Who are you people?" he asked.

"We live here," Yoder said.

"How do you know Bill?"

"Don't," Yoder said conversationally. "Just met him today."

"Today?" Mr. Angel asked, astonished. "You mean you decided to risk your life for a stranger?"

"Well, I did run over his granddaddy," Yoder said. "Long story."

First the roadblock and now this, Mr. Angel thought, shaking his sore head. *How does he do it? He's either a tactical genius or the luckiest bastard that ever lived.* Mr. Angel's professional pride ached worse than his head. He moaned.

"You don't sound too good," Yoder said thoughtfully. He turned his face and yelled into the kitchen, "Mrs. Yoder!"

There came stomping and clattering. Something heavy shook the floor and Mrs. Yoder barged through the door. Her hands were full.

Yoder turned back to Angel. "Now, then, before we finish this, you have to answer a question," he said. "Chocolate or pumpkin?"

They returned to the SNARmobile, arms loaded with towering stacks of whoopie pies. At the door, Stan turned and faced Bill and Nellie.

"Well, this was great guys. I'm sorry, but it's too dangerous to have you keep riding with us. Gonna get a really great song out of this, though. How do you like "Shootout at the Amish corral?"

"Edgy," said Shockdog.

Stan put down his pies and reached out his arms to hug Nellie.

"Take care of yourselves," he said. "See you again, Nellie. That was one hell of a SNARFEST, huh?"

He tried to pull back but Nellie's arms locked. Stan grunted.

"You're ditching us?" she asked sweetly in his ear.

"Uuurgh," Stan said. Nellie let go and he stepped back, putting one boot into a pumpkin whoopie pie and swearing.

"Look," he said, rubbing a rib. "This guys-trying-to-kill-us thing, we didn't sign up for that. We're a death-metal band, not a *dead* metal band. For fuck's sake, do you not understand that we just barely escaped with our lives back there?"

"*We* escaped," Nellie said. "You surrendered."

"It was a strategic retreat!" Stan yelled. "We came back."

"And now you're thinking of *strategically* being a pussy," Nellie said.

"That's not fair," Stan said. "You weren't straight with us. We signed up for a joyride, not a suicide run. It's not just the band I'm worried about. We have to think about more than ourselves. All the SNARLIES would be lost and lonely without us. We give life meaning for our fans."

"Fine," Nellie said. "Guess I can't blame you."

"Fine," Stan said. "We'll leave you money for a Greyhound or a taxi or something." He turned to Bill. "No hard feelings, huh?"

"You took us this far," Bill said.

Stan reached out a hand and clasped Bill's forearm. Bill grabbed his and they stood there for a moment, teeth clenched and veins bulging. At last they let go.

"See you 'round," Stan said. He picked up the mashed pies and climbed into the bus. The other band members trooped inside.

Then a phone rang. It was a harsh tone but with a syrupy melody, like someone strangling Tinker Bell. Nobody answered it.

The bus loading stopped.

"That's "Chainsaw Angel," Ooze said.

"Chainsaw Angel," Burn Ward repeated with awe.

"Shockdog," Stan said, his voice trembling with surprise and fear. "That's your phone. *The* phone."

Shockdog seemed stunned, then shook himself and pulled a phone from his pocket.

"Probably just another robocall," he said, but his hand shook as he answered it.

"SNAR Productions," he said in a strangely stilted voice.

"That's our business phone," Stan told Nellie in a whisper. "It's the number our agent uses. And he *never* calls."

Shockdog hadn't said a word but as he listened, his jaw dropped inch by inch.

"I see, Bruce," he said. "I'll get back to you, Bruce." Whoever was on the other end must have hung up but Shockdog's ear remained glued to the cellphone. It took long seconds before he appeared to notice that and put away the phone.

"Fuck me with a French poodle," he said.

"What?" Stan asked nervously.

Shockdog swallowed and licked his lips. "It's them," he said, jerking his head at Bill and Nellie.

"Yeah, what? Don't go spastic on me again, Shockdog."

"They're magic," he said at last.

"What the hell are you saying?"

"That rescue at SNARFEST. It went viral. A hundred thousand hits on the SNARpage. We got links to *everywhere.* And Bruce wants us in New York in three days to do the 'Sunrise!' show."

Stan stood stunned. "Well, fuck me," he said at last.

"With a French poodle," Shockdog acknowledged.

Ooze twitched and looked up at the sky as if he expected something to fall on them.

"TV news got it. And ...." Shockdog stopped as if overwhelmed. "The record companies are calling. There's a *bidding war*."

"For us?" Stan asked in a voice like a castrated hamster.

"I know," Shockdog said. "But there's a catch." He looked at Bill and Nellie again. "They have to be part of the show."

Opening his arms, Stan turned to Bill and Nellie, and said, "How would you like to arrive in style at the courthouse? Cause *I* was thinkin' nothing says class and style like arriving someplace in the SNARmobile."

"Stan," Nellie said. "You just threw us out remember? We'd rather walk to New Jersey."

"You don't mean that. See, a band is like a family. And you and Bill are part of our family."

"This is how you treat family?"

"Yeah, we're a big, fucked up family, but we're family."

"We're a family without nuns," Disciple added. "We'd be a perfect family if somebody's sister was a nun."

Everyone ignored him. Nellie looked at Bill, who nodded.

"We'll do your stupid show," Nellie said. "But you better get us to the courthouse on time or I'll turn *you* into a nun."

"Great, great, let's roll," Stan said.

Ooze, Burn Ward and Disciple didn't move. Their heads were down, eyes looking at the ground as if they were mesmerized by ants foraging at their feet.

""Everybody on the bus! We're moving out now! Mush!" Stan said.

They still didn't move.

Without lifting his head, Ooze finally said, "Doing the 'Sunrise!' show would be selling out."

The others nodded agreement.

Stan looked as if he'd been doused with ice water and plugged into an amplifier. He held up his hands and gave Shockdog a "what the hell?" look.

Shockdog came up, turned his back to the band and said quietly to Stan, "Hey, you've been preaching this 'rock rebel' stuff for years. Now you're doing a one-eighty."

"I never thought we'd get a real record deal before."

"Well, you made the problem, Stan. I can't fix it." He clapped Stan on the shoulder and went back to stand with the others.

The squirrel of panic scampered across Stan's face, followed by the pit bull of determination.

Putting his hands behind his back, Stan began to walk slowly from band member to band member, making firm and reassuring eye contact. He touched one or two on the shoulders but that seemed to make them nervous so finally he just stopped, clenched a manly fist and pressed it against his chest like a statue he'd once seen at Caesar's Palace. He wished he was wearing a toga. Maybe the next gig ....

He cleared his throat.

"Guys," he said. "We're a band that lives *real*. No sound overlays, no backing vocals, no bullshit. Ever. We live only for the music and the fans ... especially the, you know, female ones. We don't give a shit about money, or making a living or selling ourselves out to sleep in a soft bed. We don't compromise."

There were uncertain sounds of agreement.

"And there is a time for that," Stan added, then paused and placed his hands behind his back again. "But *this* is not that time."

The drummer glanced at the bassist. "Where are you going with this, Stan? You just told us we weren't going with these guys." Disciple nodded at Bill and Nellie.

"I did, but then I realized something. We're SNAR. We spit at danger. Hell, we *crap* on danger. We hold danger down and we piss in danger's eye. Cause we're SNARRRRRRR!" Then he started chanting: "SNAR! SNAR! SNAR!" But it got progressively weaker as it became clear that nobody else was joining in.

"I'm getting on the fuckin' bus," Ooze said.

"Wait!" Stan shouted. "Look, I know it's dangerous. But Bill's a big target. With luck, they'll go for him and we can ...."

He stopped suddenly short as he caught Nellie's withering glare.

"Fuck this," Disciple said. "My uncle's gonna get me a job as a truck driver."

"Then kiss your band days goodbye," Stan said sharply. "Because musicians aren't truckers."

"There was Johnny Cash," Burn Ward said.

"Johnny Cash was not a trucker."

"Then what about that guy in the '70s who did 'Convoy?"

Stan stamped his foot. "A, that's not music. That's Muzak. And B, that guy was not a trucker. He just sang about truckers. You know why? Because he was busy lying in a five-star Vegas hotel, getting 24-hour blow jobs from six gorgeous women of different colors. And huffing the largest, most expensive line of cocaine you have ever seen. You see, *that's* the difference between a trucker and a rocker."

"I didn't join this band to be a sellout," Burn Ward said.

"That's right! That's ab-so-fuckin'-lutely fuckin' right," Stan said. "But let me ask you this. Was Bob Dylan a sellout? Was Vanilla Ice a sellout? - you know, when he was somebody, I mean. Is Katy Perry a sellout? No! Because making money *isn't selling out!* It's a way to *keep* from selling out. What do I mean?" he added before they could object. "I mean this: Fuck the money. Money is just a means to the end. Greenbacks, SNARbacks."

"When *I* joined," Ooze said. "You said we were gonna live on the edge of society. Be rebels."

"Oh, and we have," Stan said. "We've shared cheap hotel rooms, funky dives, bad pot and foul women. And that's all cool. But you gotta grow up. We're all pushing thirty."

"So what?"

"So have you ever seen a rocker over thirty?"

"Hell, yeah. Mick Jagger ...."

Stan cut him off.

"Who is 70-bazillion years old and has a dollar for every fucking year. I meant, have you ever seen a broke rocker over thirty? I have. They're just old guys wandering the streets with blurry tattoos and hair extensions under ball caps and the only music they make is when they fart. So what am I saying?"

"You gotta be rich to keep the music flowin'," Shockdog cut in.

"That's right!" Stan said. "Just 'cause you've made it, doesn't mean you've lost it."

"It would be cool to have a hot record," Ooze acknowledged.

"And a hotel room without bed bugs," Disciple admitted.

"Exactly. And if keeping it real means a hit record or two, we'll suffer through it. So let's get on that bus and go to New York." He turned to Nellie and Bill, and for a moment it looked like there was a tear in his eye. Then he blew his nose on his sleeve. "God, that was good. I even choked myself up."

"Let's roll!" he shouted. "But first, Shockdog, pass the hat for gas money."

On the edge of the Sproul State Forest, Disciple pointed out a window. "Shit," he said. "They have got some ugly horses."

Stan looked out the window. Enormous humped beasts with shaggy heads glared at the bus from fenced fields.

"Those are buffaloes, doofus," Stan said. "There's a sign for a restaurant up ahead that sells buffalo burgers."

"Wow, burgers on the hoof?" Disciple said. "That is too cool to miss. Let's stop for some food."

A mile further on, the SNARmobile turned off into the parking lot of a large building that resembled a log cabin with hyperthyroidism. A sign painted in branding-iron letters read: "Big Bill's: Where the Buffalo Roam - On Your Plate!"

Inside, everything seemed to be made of buffalo hide or bones. Big shaggy heads on the walls tracked them with glassy eyes. Furry robes and scrimshaw with handwritten price tags were stacked on tables. Nellie eyed a sleeveless buffalo leather vest embroidered with dragons but caught the price and reluctantly let it go.

A stringy man in a bolo tie led them to a table.

"Are you Buffalo Bill?" Stan asked.

"Ho ho," the man said. "First time I ever heard that, sonny. You're a card."

"Well, you look old enough," Stan said defensively.

"This old man'll kick your ass back to Los Angeles or whatever fairyland you're from," the man said.

Nellie looked over and saw that Bill had a tear in his eye.

"What is it, lover?"

"He reminds me of my grandpa," Bill said, sniffling. "Sir, lead us to the buffalo burgers."

The man took them to a long wooden table artfully scratched and blackened.

He handed each of them a menu.

"Special today is fresh Rocky Mountain oysters."

"How many on a plate?" Stan asked.

The man eyed him. "Two, unless the buffalo's a freak," he said. "How many would you get if I oystered you?"

"Uh, I think we'll probably just go with the buffalo burgers all around," Shockdog said.

"Triple for me," Bill said. "And beer."

"Goes without sayin'," the man said. "Leticia'll be 'round in a second to take your orders. Enjoy."

Halfway through the first pitcher, Shockdog got up to pee. In the back, next to an alcove that led to the bathrooms was a long glass display case. It was filled with buffalo jaws and teeth, some of them yellowed with age. A few sported labels that said things like "Cherokee, 1921" and "Brutus, 1964."

A sign above the case read: "Bison Biters. Custom dental appliances." An arrow pointed to the bathroom alcove.

Shockdog went through. Opposite the bathrooms was a room cluttered with what appeared to be dental equipment. A man was sitting at a desk with his feet up, smoking a cigarette. A nameplate on the desk read: "Buford."

"Hey," Shockdog said. "Is that your first or last name?"

"Neither," the man said. "It's not my desk. Enjoyin' your burger?"

"Yeah, man, it's delicious. Fresh."

"You got that right," Not-Buford said. "First one?"

"Yeah but not my last."

"Where you from?" Not-Buford asked.

"St. Louis. You from around here?"

"Nope. I'm from Colorado. Rodeo'd during my college days. Went east to make my fortune and wound up wrangling these stinkin' buffalo."

His long nose twitched.

"Beats wrestlin' alligators in Florida, I guess, but I gotta shower three times a day."

"What's this room for?" Shockdog asked.

"Bison Biters," Not-Buford said. "You illiterate? There's a sign."

"No," Shockdog said. "I meant, what are Bison Biters?"

Not-Buford flicked ash from his cigarette. "All natural replacement dentition for those with large oral needs. Made from the incisors of grass-fed, free-range American buffalo. We're talkin' *Bison bison* - prairie bison, not your wood fellas."

"No way," Shockdog said. "Who buys them?"

"Well," the man said thoughtfully. "We do a lot of business with Ruminants."

"You put false teeth in cows?" Shockdog asked a bit queasily.

"People," Not-Buford said sharply. "You know, body modders. Some folks like to look like tigers or cats or whatnot, so they get stripy tattoos and whisker implants, so on."

"Yeah, I've seen 'em," Shockdog said.

"Well, Ruminants want to look like cows."

"Cows?" Shockdog asked.

"Or gazelles, buffalo, wildebeests, like that. They get tattoos to make them look like heifers, contact lenses to get those big ol' brown eyes. And some go the whole hog and get the teeth."

"That is...bizarre," Shockdog said. "And I know bizarre. I mean, I get wanting to be a predator, but ...." He shook his head in confusion.

Not-Buford shrugged. "Diff'rent strokes. "

Shockdog rubbed his mouth and said: "Aren't they too big for a human jaw?"

"Mostly," Not-Buford agreed. "That's sort of the idea." He paused. "Your big friend out there, though. Fella like that could wear 'em no problem." He winked to show he was joshing.

But Shockdog got a thoughtful look on his face and snapped his fingers.

"TV smile," he said. "Hell, yeah." He turned to Not-Buford. "Be back in a second."

He returned with Bill.

"I want teeth," Bill said. "My woman thinks I need a happy face for when I get to court."

"I can do you in an hour," Not-Buford said. "Have a seat or three." He stood up, crushed out his cigarette, picked up a rifle and a pair of channel-lock pliers.

"Excuse me," he said, and walked out into the alcove and through a back door. Bill and Shockdog heard bellowing, a shot, something heavy falling.

An hour later, Bill emerged with a new full set of teeth, and a pamphlet on oral hygiene.

Wuu held up the index card, waving it in the air to dry. He'd spent two hours looking for the right card but Staples and Walgreens didn't have any prepackaged metallic gold ones. In the end, he'd been forced to buy a package of unlined plain ones and some sparkly gold paint. He wanted the card to glitter like his impending victory.

Wuu blew on the card, then wiped a tiny dot of spittle off it and rubbed a blob of glitter on his jeans. He looked at the wall of his Lair. A huge corkboard was glued in place and spiked to it with push-pins were dozens of pink, yellow and blue cards arranged in elaborate patterns. The pink ones, for threats, ended with one marked "Bill the Biker." Wuu took his special Sharpie, uncapped it and held it like a sword. With quick, hard slashes, he drew a black X through the name. He smiled grimly.

At the very bottom right was a space for the Card of Triumph. Wuu wanted to tack it up now, but he restrained himself. After the court hearing, he would hold a special ceremony just for him and Keeza. He would webcast the ceremony.

True, he hadn't heard from Mr. Angel and there was just one day before the court hearing. But no news is good news not to hear, Wuu thought.

Conquerors were optimistic, he added to himself. Genghis Khan probably wasn't a depressive.

There were so many things to do. There were the mundane tasks, of course, such as dusting his LoveDoll© heads. Gloating was in there, of course, but that would come a little later. Right now, perhaps, was the time to choose his court clothes. He wanted to look impressive before the judge - not that he had any doubt about the outcome but because it would mark his first public appearance as a victor.

Wuu bit his lip thoughtfully and went to his closet. He pulled out his gray Blofeld jacket, held up the hangar skeptically, then reached for his other Blofeld jacket, which was dark blue. There also was his old high school suit, and the fish tie. So many decisions! Maybe a good cardigan, the one his mom gave him. It was threatening. Or did he want to be *more* threatening?

His pleasant musings were interrupted by the gong of his cellphone.

"Hello?" Wuu answered. "Oh, Mr. Angel."

He listened silently for a second, his face impassive.

"I see," Wuu said. "No, I'm not bailing you out." He cut the call and sat absolutely still for nearly a minute. Finally, he noticed the gold card in his hand. He'd gripped it so hard the glitter had smudged around his thumb. Carefully, he unstuck it and placed it on the desk. Wuu glared at the wall of index cards and his face darkened. He reached up to the pink card with the black X on it over Bill's name. With a snarl, he ripped it from the wall, tore it up and tossed it into the air. Pieces of Bill fell into his hair.

Breathing heavily, Wuu opened his desk drawer. He pulled a new pink card from a pack. He uncapped the Sharpie and with trembling fingers wrote: "Bill." Then he added: "The Bastard Biker."

"Minions!" Wuu spat out the word. It was becoming his favorite curse.

CHAPTER TWELVE

State Route 495, Manhattan, New York

The SNARmobile rolled through the Lincoln Tunnel and plunged into the heart of Manhattan like a poison arrow into a pig - as Stan put it. The rising sun gilded the harried dog-walkers and caffeinated joggers along 38th Street. The SNARmobile turned up Madison Avenue but then got lost amid the towers around Rockefeller Center.

Nobody seemed to mind. The band members, amped on the taste of the Big Apple, craned their necks out the bus windows.

"Jesus, that's a lot of taxis," Disciple said.

"Man," Burn Ward said. "It's glorious. What a shitload of ... stuff!"

"You never been?" Ooze asked.

"Once," the guitarist said. "For a bachelor party. Wound up in Times Square. I remember looking up at all the signs and thinking it was, like, a whole universe of neon. And then I looked down and somebody had stolen my wallet."

"Profound," Shockdog said with a sneer.

"I lost fifteen bucks!"

"Wow," Shockdog said. "You're a survivor."

"Oooh, a Banana Republic!" Stan said, pulling his cellphone from his pocket. "Selfie!"

Nellie and Bill enveloped the rear seat.

"So this is what hell looks like," Nellie said, her eyes bright. "That's what my parents always said. They said it was full of crack-smokers and secular humanists. I wanna find some of those Satanic shrines they talked about, like Bloomingdale's. Have they got underwear at Tiffany's? I would love to put some diamonds on these beauties," she hefted her breasts. "Would you like to see that?" she said throatily.

She chuckled and took his arm.

"And now I'm gonna be on TV!" she said. "What if my parents see me? Here, in the Temple of Beelzebub." She guffawed.

"You know," she continued. "I never told you this but I was real religious when I was growing up. Church on Sunday be damned, it was church every day and all day Sunday. I knew the Bible by heart. I didn't watch "The Flintstones" because my parents said it preached evolution. Hell, you know what, lover? I was in an abusive relationship with God. It felt like He had his thumb on the back of my head." A shadow of pain crossed her face. Then she grinned.

"And then, salvation arrived. On the very day I turned sixteen - the very day! - I heard the sound of a million angels clearing their holy throats." She closed her eyes in memory. "I looked out my bedroom window, and I saw a man in black riding a tricked-out Harley. I don't remember anything about him but the *bike* - oh my Lord. And right then and there, I was converted by the miracle of chrome and thunder."

She opened her eyes, which were shining.

Bill looked like he'd shrunk in the rain. His shoulders were hunched and his beard touched his belt buckle. He looked like a cross between King Kong and a lawn gnome.

Nellie felt a prickle of annoyance.

"What's wrong, lover?" she asked. "Bad burrito? You look like somebody kicked you in the crotch. You better not let anybody do that but me."

She smiled. Bill said nothing - loudly.

"Oh, for..." Nellie stopped herself from informing Bill of her aggravation in the usual obscene terms. Clearly something was bothering him. *If it's that goddamn bike again,* she thought. But all she said was: "Really sweetie, what's wrong?"

"Nothing," Bill said.

"Nothing," Nellie scoffed. "You look like you're about to shit a roll of barbed wire."

"Just don't like attention," Bill admitted. "Or buildings, much. People."

"People?" Nellie asked.

"And more people. And fucking stoplights."

Nellie sighed.

"Is it really bad?" she asked.

Bill nodded morosely but said, "Nope."

"All right," Nellie said with a sigh. "Let's look at it like this. If we were in a doctor's office, would this feel like a wear-this-paper-gown, ass-showing anxiety?"

"Worse," Bill admitted.

"Hmmm. Prostate exam?"

"Worse."

"Big needle drawing your blood?"

Bill shivered and shrank further. "Jesus, no, not that bad!" he said.

"Okay, got it," Nellie said. "Well, lover, I understand. But when we get through all of this, we're back on the road. No eyes on you but mine." She leaned over and put her mouth close to his ear. "And lips." She darted a tongue into the hairy orifice.

Bill gave a grunt like a rutting wildebeest and for a moment his face cleared. His ear twitched and he put a huge arm around Nellie's shoulders. But his eyes remained hooded.

I have got to screw this man out of his funk and soon, Nellie thought. They would need to find a large restroom at the studio. Or a supply closet. Or maybe an empty soundstage.

She was still considering the prospects when the SNARmobile was flagged into the parking structure of Dingo Studios. A huge photo banner over the main gate showed a chirpy woman, an Amazon and a jolly middle-aged man. It read: "Sunrise! Start your morning with Mary Jo, Yooneeka and Jake."

The SNARmobile was guided into a guest spot next to a freight elevator. Roadies appeared from nowhere and began unloading the instruments.

"Wow!" Stan said in awe as guitars, amplifiers and other gear vanished into the brawny wave of arms. "They aren't dropping shit!"

"That's 'cause they're professionals. They're actually paid," Shockdog said. "Look, that little guy's carrying my tambourine."

One man held up a long stick with what appeared to be a shrunken head on it. "Where does this go?" he asked.

"That's the mallet for the gong," Shockdog said.

"Is that real hair?"

"Yeah, my sister's. She had leukemia. I got her a cool scarf." The man took it away, holding it at arm's length.

A little woman with thick designer glasses and an electronic clipboard approached. "Hi, I'm Amy," she said. She looked Nellie and Bill up and down. "Did you bring any other clothes?"

"No," Nellie said sharply. "Why?"

"Ummm, nothing," Amy said quickly. "It's just...ummm...that the camera lights are hot and I wouldn't want that leather thing to shrink." Nellie gave her a look that the President probably gives to annoying interns. Amy seemed to retreat into her clipboard.

"Never mind," Amy said with a nervous smile. "So, you have about an hour before they finish the first segment. You'll start the second segment. How long do you need to get into costume? Is one dresser each okay?"

"Why, what are we storing?" Disciple asked.

"No, moron," Stan said. "A dresser is a person that helps us get dressed."

"Cool!"

Disciple looked at Amy. "Our platform Orc boots are so big we have to tie each other's. It'll go real fast now. Uh, are they chicks?" he added hopefully.

"They're professionals," Amy said, and realized instantly it was a mistake.

"Jesus! Pros!" Disciple said. "This place rocks!!"

"She doesn't mean hookers," Stan said under his breath.

"Oh. Oh, shit, well...all right," Disciple said. "I just thought, hell it's New York, you know?" He shrugged.

"Sooooo!" Amy said, desperately glancing at her watch and tapping it with malice aforethought. "Anything else?"

"Yeah," Shockdog said. "We'll need time to check the stage setup and do a run-through."

"It's a live outdoor set and the audience is already there," Amy said. "I'm afraid there's no time for a warm-up." She smiled. "But I heard you guys really know how to improvise." She tittered. It made her seem like a nun caught telling a naughty joke.

"Yeah, okay," Stan said. "Shockdog, go after those guys and handle the setup, then join us in costume."

Shockdog saluted and followed the departing line of instruments.

Amy led the others into the elevator and then through a warren of hallways to the makeup room, which was a spaceship full of chrome, light and mirrors. The air was full of hairspray and perfume.

"Sunrise!" blared from wall monitors. Bill, Nellie and the band were seated in a long row facing a wall of mirrors bordered by high-wattage light bulbs. Tables were cluttered with blow dryers, tissues and archeological piles of cosmetics, combs, ointments, gels and sprays.

Nellie primped and chattered as she was dabbed, brushed and styled.

Bill scowled and was silent. The makeup artist cursed as he broke two combs in Bill's beard.

"Practice your smile, lover," Nellie said reassuringly. Bill did and the makeup man passed out. "Never mind," Nellie said as the man was hauled away.

He was replaced by a grizzled veteran. She had four-color hair, blurry tattoos on her wrinkled arms and skull earrings that dangled from drooping ear lobes.

"Hey, honey, love those choppers," she said in a voice from a gravel quarry. "Yours?"

"Buffalo's," Bill said.

"Awesome," she said. "I used to work in a morgue. Then I did Keith Richards on tour." She patted his shoulder. "Nothin' scares me, honey. Now here comes the blush. Don't cringe."

The door opened and two men came in, escorting a wheelchair. The man in it was stiffly erect and unmoving. His eyes were open. He looked stern and confident - and mummified.

"Hey," Stan said. "That's Jake, the guy on the banner outside. Not so smiley, though."

"Yeah," said the woman powdering Stan's forehead. "He had a polo accident last month. His horse hit a taxi on Fifth Avenue. He's brain dead. But as long as he can breathe on his own, they keep him. Something about discrimination lawsuits. Besides, his Q Score is still off the charts."

Jake was wheeled over to a mirror and an entire crew descended on him, powdering, polishing and adjusting hidden electrodes. A man with a head-mounted microphone stood behind him, fussing with a handheld device. Jake's mouth twitched, then he beamed. His eyes blinked rapidly. The man adjusted something and the blinking slowed. The man spoke into the mike.

Jake's mouth opened.

"So, Mister President, how would say you're doing so far?" Jake said. "Mister President...Mister President..."

The controller tweaked something. The voice became deeper, resonant, confidential.

"Okay," the controller said. "We got it. He's on after these guys. Wheel him out."

The crew wheeled Jake out of the room.

"He looks better on camera," Nellie said.

"Who doesn't?" somebody said.

When they were finished, a page led Bill and Nellie to the green room, which had leather sofas, flowers and tables full of magazines and ashtrays. It was air-conditioned to a mausoleum-like chill.

"Can I get you folks anything?" the page asked brightly. "Latte? Cappuccino?"

"Beer," Bill said grumpily. "And 'ludes."

"Let's see," the page said, thinking. "We've got Xanax, clonazepam, and I think some decent weed. I can ask the stage guys if they have any 'ludes."

"Naw," Bill said. "Just beer, then."

"Belgian, German, Czech or Mexican?"

"American," Bill said.

"Craft, microbrewed or private label?"

"Are we still talking about beer?" Bill asked. "Just normal, piss-colored beer."

"Five-Oh-Eight? Finback? Brooklyn Pour?"

"Look," Bill said, and his eyebrows twitched menacingly. "I'm a quart low."

"He's not real happy to be here, sonny," Nellie said. "Don't make him angry. We don't want to scrape you off these fancy chandeliers. Just get him something generic and lots of it."

"Right-o," the page said and vanished so quickly he left a breeze.

Nellie hoped a beer or two would pull Bill out of his mood. He hated attention and now she saw how he handled it. Bill either tried to disappear - despite his size - or vanished behind his own impenetrable emotional wall.

She glanced at the big clock on the wall. There was just enough time for a quickie.

But before she could pull Bill into the crapper, the page returned. He swiftly put a six-pack of Dos Equis on the table.

"Mexico is technically North America," he said nervously. "It's all I could find. Sorry." He retreated under Bill's stormy gaze.

Bill pulled a bottle, cracked the top with a thumb and downed it in a single gulp. Two more followed. It didn't seem to take the edge off Bill's mood. He didn't even belch, Nellie noted with concern.

The door opened and the band clumped in, in full costume. They filled the couches with wings, snouts and shoulder armor. Stan, wearing his best mutant head, borrowed a drumstick and pushed it into his beak to scratch his nose.

They were barely settled when Mary Jo breezed in. There was no other word for it. She carried a cloud of perfume and energy. Her hair had a life of its own. Things gleamed when her smile struck them as if they were shining for their lives. Mary Jo seemed permanently breathless.

"Hi, everybody!" she said with take-no-prisoners cheeriness. "It's great to see you all!"

Her chestnut eyes caught each and every one in the room for exactly half a second. Her eyelashes would have batted had they not been concreted with stage mascara. She clattered into the room on Empire State heels, went over to Nellie and put a manicured hand on her shoulder.

"I love your outfit!" she said, glancing coyly at Nellie's vest, which barely contained her enormous cleavage. "Leather is almost back. Did makeup manage to ..." She patted her own chest. "They have to powder things to tone down the reflection."

She waited with an air of sincere curiosity.

"They powdered 'em," Nellie said, nodding her head.

"Great!" Mary Jo said. "The camera tends to white out everything, which is a shame, isn't it? That's showbiz!"

Her laugh was tinkly with just a trace of horsey snort behind it to cut the sweetness. It was like the exhaust of a rhinestone-covered tractor. Or a sugar-coated unicorn. Or a gold-dusted Clydesdale.

Mary Jo turned to Bill, who had stood up when she entered. Her eyes widened.

"Mr. Butcher, I have to say that I've seen the cell phone videos of your rescue and you are a true hero, down to your boots."

She put a hand on his forearm, and flipped her hair. It was viciously fetching.

Nellie's nostrils dilated.

Suddenly, Mary Jo straightened and was all sweet authority.

"Okay, folks," she said, addressing the room. "We're on pretty soon and I just wanted to run down how it will go out there. First of all, the band will already be onstage and ready to go. Bill, Nellie, you'll walk out and we'll direct you where to stand. Who's Stan?"

"Satan," Stan said loudly from a corner.

"Sorry, Satan. You'll join us, too. I'll do my intro, then they'll roll clips of the rescue, and then I'll ask all three of you a few questions. No hardballs, I promise. Just answer as briefly as you can, and remember to smile if that's appropriate. After that, Satan, you'll move upstage and join the band. You can intro your song and then we'll let you play us into the commercial."

"Sounds great," Stan said.

She smiled. "Could I just add that you will be on national television, and there's a three-second delay in the broadcast. If any of the lyrics to your song are inappropriate, we'll bleep them out. Too many bleeps and we'll just cut away early and you'll have lost a chance to share your genius with the world. Which is why I hope you weren't thinking of playing "Pygmy Babies from Hell."

Her smile seemed to grow pearly shark teeth.

"But that's our theme song," Ooze said in a small voice.

"It's okay," Stan said quickly. "No problem."

"Great," Mary Jo said, clapping her manicured hands together. "Well, that's it, then. And remember, have fun out there. This is *your* moment!" She touched a button nestled inconspicuously in her ear. "Frank, they're ready to go. I'm coming out now." She cast one more glance at Bill, which took its time traveling up to his face, and breezed out. Light and a substantial amount of air went with her, leaving everyone in the room stunned as if they'd just survived a hurricane.

"Jesus," Shockdog said in the dazed silence. "It's like being hit in the face with a solid gold sledgehammer." He clenched his tambourine.

"I'm scared of her but I want to fuck her," Disciple said. "She's like nun porn."

For a beat, everybody turned and looked at Disciple.

"All *riiiight!*" Stan said finally. "We're gonna show the world what we've got! No pressure but this is the biggest thing we've done since that beer commercial in Saigon!"

"I am going to kill that bitch on camera," Nellie said tightly.

Stan turned sharply. "Don't blow this for us, please, Nellie?"

Nellie smiled. "Sweetness and light," she promised.

A red light went on over the door, there was a knock and Amy entered, wearing a headset.

"All right, folks, you're about to go on," she said. "Follow me, please. Remember, when you get out there, there'll be lots of lights and cameras and a whole lot of people and they'll be *right in your face.*"

Bill turned a shade of concrete. Nellie gripped his hand.

"Don't let it get to you," Amy said. "The thing to do is to concentrate on Mary Jo."

"I can do that," Disciple volunteered. "Parts of her, anyway."

"Mostly the plastic parts," Nellie said.

"Here we go, then," Amy said. "SNAR guys, you gentlemen follow me first and go straight to the band setup, except for Stan."

"Satan," Stan said.

"Right. Anyway, Satan, you and Bill and Nellie will follow the band. I'll stop you at the door and then signal you when Mary Jo's ready for the interview. Then you just walk straight out and wait. Got it?"

They nodded.

"And have fun out there," she said.

"So we've been told. Repeatedly," Nellie said.

"It's showbiz," Amy said. "You've gotta be cheerful on camera or we lose ratings." She added darkly: "Mary Jo won't like it if you lose ratings."

There was a sudden chill in the air as the room emptied.

Bill and Nellie heard the roar as they approached. Nellie thought of gladiators entering the Coliseum. Bill kept his head down and stomped forward, breathing out beer fumes. Nellie tightened her grip on his hand and straightened her shoulders.

We're not the gladiators, she thought firmly to herself. *We're the lions.*

From speakers, they heard Mary Jo introducing a video clip of the SNARFEST debacle. It was met with oohs and ahhs from the crowd. Then they heard, echoing from the speakers inside and out of the building: "And now, we're going to meet those amazing people. Welcome, please, William Butcher and Nellie Florentino!"

"Okay," Amy said. "You're on."

They walked out into the "Sunrise!" plaza. It was cool, still partly in shadow, although by noon it would be warm and humid like the rest of the city. The block was walled by skyscrapers and pulsing with people - a sea of faces. The band was in place on a raised stage at one end. People packed right to the edges. Not SNAR fans, apparently. Many seemed to be coeds on vacation, holding cell phones or signs declaring things like "Omaha loves Mary Jo."

A narrow lane had been created in front of the stage, the audience held back by unobtrusive, jacketed security guards and red, waist-high banners with the "Sunrise!" logo. The crowd gasped as Bill lumbered in. Mary Jo was waiting, standing directly below Stan and holding a microphone like a cheerleader's baton.

She beckoned them over. Bill trudged as if he were going to a firing squad. Nellie kept her chin up.

"Bill, Nellie," Mary Jo said. "Welcome. We've all just seen your astonishing experience. Before we hear from you, though, Stan..." She turned to face him.

"Satan," Stan said tightly.

"Stan," Mary Jo said firmly. "Tell us what was *supposed* to happen." Her eyes glinted with a *don't-fuck-with-me* warning for him alone.

"Well, " Stan said, cowed. "Every year we have a music festival, SNARFEST, outside of St. Louis. It's a sort of gift to our loyal fans. *Go, SNARLIES!*"

He raised a gauntleted fist. A few hoarse shouts and cries erupted from fans at the fringes of the crowd but they were quickly choked off as the burly security guards tackled, hog-tied and dragged them away.

Stan dropped his fist.

"Um, so," he said. "The finale is where we raise this giant SNARPIG balloon - that's our mascot - and it eats a maiden..."

Mary Jo cut him off.

"That's fascinating!" She made a U-turn and pushed the microphone under Nellie's chins. "So Nellie, *you* were the maiden." She paused for a pregnant beat. "*Amazing!*"

Then Mary Jo turned straight into the camera. Her voice became confidential. Her eyes darkened with concern.

"But something went badly wrong. Badly. *Very* badly." The audience followed her. She turned back to Nellie.

"Nellie Florentino, what do you remember about that night?"

"What I remember most was the sound," Nellie said. "There was this roaring and I couldn't tell if it was the water or the crowd. And I couldn't breathe. Everything was going dark," she paused, making the crowd wait.

You're not the only one who knows how to play folks, sister, Nellie thought.

The crowd , hushed, held its collective breath. Nellie let the silence stretch for a heartbeat.

"...And then I saw my Bill," Nellie said quietly. "He was climbing. And that's the last thing I remember. Until I woke in his arms."

There was a massive sound as two thousand pairs of lungs released their air. Then, a weird sound filled the plaza - an echoing, reverberating *"Awwwww!"*

Mary Jo milked it for almost a full second, let it die away, and then turned to Bill's towering figure. She looked up with sincerity in her eyes.

"Bill, it must have been terrifying to see your girlfriend in danger. What was going through your mind?"

Bill thought about it.

"I thought it was fucked up." The crowd skipped a beat, then hooted and laughed with delight. Coeds around the stage shrieked with laughter and snapped photos of Bill's ass. Mary Jo's smile froze and for a moment she looked like Jake. But she recovered quickly. She turned to Nellie, whose face had developed a polite smirk.

"Nellie, when you look at this video, does it shock you to know how close to death you were?"

"Well, *Mary Jo*," Nellie said, emphasizing her name, and smiled thinly as the host's smile twitched. "I really did wonder if I would make it." She chuckled. "I also asked myself: 'How in the world could I have agreed to do such a completely *stupid* thing?" The audience laughed. "You know that feeling, Mary Jo?"

"I think we all do, Nellie," Mary Jo said, and her laugh was so tinkly Nellie felt like someone had smashed her in the face with a cut-crystal vase.

Mary Jo's smile was predatory.

"But luckily, you had Bill."

Despite the tightly confined space, Mary Jo somehow seemed to turn her back on Nellie and sidle closer to Bill; her breasts nearly touched his belt buckle. Nellie flared but she was off-camera by then.

"Bill," Mary Jo said, with an extra portion of breathiness and adulation. "Just watching that video made me wish *I* was in that cage." She put a manicured hand on his chest. "Every woman wants a hero, and you are one. Isn't he folks?"

The crowd broke into rapturous applause.

"I'll put her in a cage," Nellie said but she was off-mike. Mary Jo glanced over at her and lifted her chin in triumph. Nellie wished she had a straight-razor. She ached to carve "bitch" into Mary Jo's forehead.

Bill, though, seemed to relax. Nellie cursed silently. Obviously, all the blood had left his head. And if he wasn't thinking, he wasn't scared.

"Naw, it wasn't a big deal," Bill said, and his voice was almost conversational.

No big deal! You saved my life, you jerk! Nellie hoped Bill would smile at Mary Jo and scare the shit out of the tramp.

Mary Jo was just ramping up.

"You mean you've done this before?" she asked, plastering the sentence with awe.

"Well, not in water," Bill replied. "But it's about the third time we've been nearly dead in the past two days. People have been trying to *kill* us."

That made the crowd murmur in confusion. Mary Jo suddenly put a hand to her ear.

Nellie smiled grimly. *Bet you didn't expect that, bitch,* she thought. She'd bet somebody was screaming in Mary Jo's ear to get the camera off that weirdo. Nellie's smile became genuine and almost warm. Her Bill always surprised people. He was never what they wanted him to be. She almost could feel sorry for Mary Jo. The plastic bitch had thought she was in charge.

Mary Jo took her hand away from her ear and deftly turned away from Bill toward the puzzled audience.

"Well, on that note, *Stan*, I believe you have a song for us." She turned around and looked hard at Stan, who had donned his mutant head and was waiting for the cue. He took the stage microphone from its stand, stomped a clawed boot on the stage, and broke into the first wailing notes of "Dragon with a Maiden's Heart."

Off-camera finally, Mary Jo eyed Nellie with venom and respect. Nellie pushed over to Bill and hugged him.

"You were great!" she said.

"You were!" Mary Jo said. "But we have to move on now. The band will play us into commercial. Thanks for coming all this way. Bill, look me up anytime. Bye!"

She touched them each with a single glossy red nail in benediction and dismissal, grinned especially hard at Nellie, then turned and moved off to greet fans.

Bill let out a breath. Nellie let out a curse. Amy came out to take them back. Heads in the crowd were bobbing in time to the music as SNAR laid waste to the three-chord tune. Notes shrieked through the amplifiers like wailing ghosts.

From the far end of the plaza, something was happening.

The crowd broke apart, pressing away from the center and swarming towards the sides, creating an empty lane surrounded by boiling chaos. Yells and screams echoed along the back of the block, heard only faintly above the music.

The waves of disorder surged towards the stage, a gap appearing like magic in the center as bodies flung themselves away from it and against the building walls.

Down that clearing raced an apparition from Hell. A black horse galloped towards the stage, its eyes rolling wildly and its muzzle white with foam. A red-eyed orc clung to the reins with one clawed hand. With the other, it whirled a huge black mace over its deformed head.

Nellie saw that the horse was barreling down on Mary Jo, who stood rooted in shock in front of the crowd barrier.

"Oh crap!" Nellie said with disgust. She leaped at Mary Jo, knocked her out of the way of the flashing hooves and body-slammed her to the ground.

Bill was right behind her. Frowning, he stepped forward and swung a fist with all his weight behind it. It clocked the horse squarely between the eyes. The animal went cross-eyed and dropped like a sack of rocks.

With a shriek, the orc soared over the horse and slammed into Stan, dropping him. Both collapsed in a heap. The mace tumbled through the air wildly and smacked into the drum set, sending Disciple sprawling in a discordant clang of cymbals. Shockdog, his gong mallet held like a war club, raced forward and bashed the orc in the head.

In front of the stage, Nellie rolled herself off the flattened Mary Jo.

"Am I hurt?" the host asked weakly.

"Not bad," Nellie said. "Your forehead's grazed."

"Really? I can't feel anything. I must be in shock."

"No, it's the Botox." She pressed a knee on Mary Jo's chest. "Stay put until it's safe."

Stan was wrestling with the dazed orc. He planted a knee on his chest. The others came up and took both arms, pinioning him. Shockdog hovered over him, the mallet raised threateningly.

Security guards struggled to reach the stage but most were too busy controlling the frantic crowd. Several also were trying to pull the downed horse away by tugging at the saddle. Under the saddle, a blanket was stamped with the letters "NYPD."

"Cynthia! Cynthia!" the orc screamed.

"Oh shit," Stan said. He took his knee away, reached over and tore off the man's costume head.

"Hey, it's crazy Roger," Shockdog said.

"You took my life from me!" said Rog, struggling.

"You never had much of one," Shockdog said, perplexed. "What do you mean?"

"Cynthia left me!" Rog cried, his eyes darting madly. "Because you banned me for life! I wanted to humiliate you. I wanted you to cower like the...cowering thing you are. On TV. So Cynthia could see what a ... cowerer you are."

Stan rolled his eyes and grunted an obscenity that echoed eerily through the beaked jaws of his mask.

"Well, Rog, you fucked that up, too," Shockdog said, not unkindly. "Just validates the decision to ban you."

"What do we do now?" Stan said. "He messed up our big moment."

"Maybe not," Shockdog said. He gave Stan a look that said *follow my lead.*

Shockdog knelt down and put his head close to Rog.

"Listen, Rog," he said quietly. "You look like a dork right now in front of Cynthia. But I think I have a deal for both of us. Might even help you get your girlfriend back."

"I don't believe you! You're evil!"

"I'm evil? You just ran down about a hundred people."

"I never rode a horse before," Rog said. "I just grabbed one when that cop went for coffee."

"Yeah, whatever," Shockdog said. "The plan is this. We want to make people believe this was just a big hoax - you know, part of the show. Big scare, not so many broken bones."

"Right," Stan broke in, looking at Shockdog. "So how about this? If you just shut the fuck up and play like we planned this, everybody will have a big laugh and Cynthia will see that I've forgiven you. In fact, I really have. You can even have your old job back."

"You lie!" Rog said. "Why would you do that?"

Stan snorted through his beak.

"Well, I've been thinking about this for a long time. I know you blame me for what happened, and I'm truly sorry. So if you go along with the act, we can bury the hatchet. And I promise I'll help you get Cynthia back. You just have to *chill*, okay? There's a lot of eyes on us."

Rog glared at Stan. Hope and hate battled in his eyes.

"I don't believe you," he said again. "You will?"

"Oh, yeah," Stan said. "You're not such a bad guy, Rog, even if you did piss in my Red Bull. I never meant to hurt you. In fact, I was ... jealous of you. Cynthia doesn't know what she gave up. But you and I, we can show her."

He turned to the band members holding Rog. "Let him go," he told them. He faced Rog again.

"So how about it, *SNARRIOR*. Friends?" He held out a clawed hand. Rog eyed it with mistrust, but then reached out and grabbed it and struggled weakly to his feet. The effort made him dizzy. He rubbed his head where Shockdog had pounded him. His eyes were unfocused.

Stan stepped back a couple of feet as if giving him room.

A couple of security guards, having finally cleared an area around the stage, began to move in but Stan held up a warning hand and they stopped, hovering at the edges, unsure what to do next.

Sirens could be heard in the distance, moving closer.

"Easy," Stan said to Rog. "You look wobbly. You okay?"

"I think so," Rog said, weaving. "Feel sick."

"Aww," Stan said sympathetically. "I think somebody needs a hug." He began to raise his arms and Rog came forward, automatically aping the gesture.

Suddenly, Stan put his hands up in a warding gesture and fell back with a shriek.

At the same instant, Shockdog surreptitiously tripped Rog, who stumbled. Lunging forward, he grabbed Stan to steady himself.

"Help! Help! Get him off!" Stan shouted, and then collapsed theatrically, not moving. Shockdog pushed Rog away and knelt beside Stan, putting a hand on his chest.

"He's not breathing!" He began to pump his chest.

Just then, police forced their way through the crowd, bolted over the unconscious horse and swarmed Rog, who managed to raise one hand in confusion before he was Tasered. He jerked and fell to the ground next to Stan, who opened one eye, winked, and rose slowly to his feet, shaking his head.

"I'm all right," he said loudly. The remaining fragments of the crowd applauded wildly.

Stan staggered to the microphone, which had remained miraculously upright. "This man is mentally ill," he said, pointing to Rog's spasming body. "He's been stalking us. We had a restraining order. Thank God the NYPD was here. Gentleman, we owe your our lives. And a song." He added: "Here's a personal favorite. We call it: 'Cynthia's Mouth.'"

"I want you dead!" Rog burbled, foaming and spitting as he was hauled to his feet and dragged away. Stan smiled at him through the jaws of the SNAR mask. It was not a pleasant smile.

"What song is that, Stan?" Shockdog whispered.

"Just do 'Death Bunny Boogie," Stan said with his hand over the mike. "I'll improvise the lyrics."

A few feet away, Nellie took her knee off Mary Jo's chest and said sweetly: "You can get up now. I think it's safe."

The host, who'd been struggling to get up for minutes, scrambled to her feet, gasping and desperately trying to pat her exploded hairdo into place.

"Was that really called for?" she asked Nellie angrily.

"Saving your life? Probably not," Nellie said. "But I'm just that kind of girl. Not the kind who shoves her tits in the face of somebody else's man."

"I don't know what you're talking about," the host said.

"I know you don't," Nellie said. "It's just reflex with you. But we don't all get to have any toy we want. The song's about over. Better get back on camera, bright eyes."

Mary Jo gave her an impenetrable look, then flipped her hair and hobbled toward the stage.

Wuu shut his phone in disgust. Once again, relying on minions had failed him. As usual, he would have to do it himself. Thoughtfully, he stood up and went to his cabinet. He opened it and gazed at his finger collection.

"It's time to finish this," he said.

CHAPTER THIRTEEN

State Route 495, New Jersey

Crossing the New Jersey state line, SNAR celebrated with a Costco haul: refrigerator-sized bags of Doritos, cases of Coca-Cola and crates of warm Kirkland Signature beer.

"We got two hit songs in two days – and it's the same song!" Stan crowed around a mouthful of habanero chips. "'Cynthia's Mouth' is bootlegged all over the damned Internet."

"The agent wants us to record it next week," Shockdog said.

"Wait, can't Stan just redo the lyrics?" Disciple asked. "It's just 'Dragon with a Maiden's Heart.' It's the same music! Just do a vocal overlay."

"Naww. It's gotta be orchestral," Shockdog said. "I'm thinking a string section, maybe New York Philharmonic..."

"And a children's choir," Disciple added. "Castrati."

"We'll save that for the video," Shockdog said. "In the meantime, we're going to Hackensack!"

In the corner with Bill, Nellie pushed away the remains of her roadhouse chili and stared dolefully at the plate.

"I wish food lied sometimes," she said.

The SNARmobile pulled up in front of the Bergen County Courthouse, a dignified old stone building in a surprisingly clean block that included City Hall and a medical center.

"Well," Stan said, gulping a final handful of chips and wiping the nacho cheese on his jeans. "Nellie, Bill, here we are. It's been a trip."

"Death or glory, rags to riches," Shockdog added.

Nellie and Bill stood and made their way to the front of the bus, shaking hands and giving high-fives to the band members.

"Wait," Stan said, holding up a hand as they reached the front. He reached behind the driver's seat and hauled out two tote bags. Each bore the "Sunrise!" logo and images of the Holy Trinity of Mary Jo, Yooneeka and Jake.

"We got you a little something," Stan said, and presented one to Bill. He opened it and rummaged inside. It contained a Costco twelve-pack of toothbrushes, a four-pack of Sensodyne toothpaste, bundles of athletic socks and XXL underwear and an industrial variety pack of condoms.

Stan smirked and the band laughed. Bill grunted.

Bill reached behind him, pulled his grandpa's boot out of his belt and dropped it in the bag.

"Now I got everything," he said.

"And this one's for you, Nellie," Stan said. He handed over the other bag. Somebody had scrawled devil's horns on Mary Jo's face and blackened several teeth.

Nellie beamed and reached into the bag, then gave a puzzled frown.

She pulled out a gigantic black satin bra. The front was embroidered with two rhinestone SNARPIGs.

"Oh my Lord," Nellie said.

"Disciple did it," Stan said.

"On the bus," the drummer said. "I have a needlepoint addiction."

"I just thought you were working on a costume piece," Nellie said.

"Naw, I got it at a transvestite clothing store when we stopped for our first pee break," Disciple said. "It was Stan's idea."

"Stan," Nellie asked. "How did you know where to find a ...? Never mind." She held the bra across her chest and posed for Bill. "Like it, lover?"

Bill grunted but Nellie knew it was a grunt of love because his teeth almost showed.

"How did get you the size?" Nellie asked Stan.

"My cheeks remembered," Stan said, and patted his face with a leer, glanced at Bill and quickly crossed his arms defensively across his chest.

"Oh, yes." Nellie blushed.

"Anyway, that's to commemorate ... you know... stuff," Stan said.

"Almost dying, and like that," Nellie said ruefully.

"Yeah, like that," Stan said a little uncomfortably. "Well, hey, enough of that. You guys have to get going. Bill, permission to hug your girlfriend goodbye?"

"She hugs you, Stan. Watch the hands."

"Noted." Stan let Nellie crush him to her bosom. His hands twitched but remained at his side.

"You're an asshole, Stan," Nellie whispered to him. "And a great guy." She leaned back. "We'll see y'all again," she said out loud.

"Three cheers for Bill and Nellie!" Shockdog shouted, and the band cheered them off the bus.

Nellie waved as the SNARmobile choked and sputtered and finally chugged away in a cloud of diesel fumes.

Bill and Nellie turned to the courthouse. But then Bill's head jerked up. He stopped and stood, as if sniffing the air. Nellie looked at him, puzzled.

"What?" she asked.

"You hear that?" Bill asked.

"I don't hear anything," Nellie said.

Bill looked both confused and hopeful. Nellie did not like that look.

From far up the street she faintly caught a rumbling sound. She looked at Bill in understanding.

"Harleys," she said. "Sweetest sound in the world." She took his arm. "Must be a good omen."

She tugged him a little towards the steps but Bill stood rooted.

Nellie frowned, nettled. She tugged him a little harder.

The rumbling got louder, started to distinguish itself into a chorus of distinct engines. And then she heard it, wafting over the sound of the motors: "Big Bad Moon."

"Oh fuck me with a French poodle," she swore.

Around the corner came the PRIKs. They approached slowly. They looked battered, road-weary and were covered with dust.

Reggie led them toward the courthouse. They pulled up in a ragged cluster and halted.

"Gentlemen, stop your engines," Reggie said, raising his arm. Nellie noticed that the seam of one shoulder was ripped open. The engines coughed into silence.

Reggie dismounted. Nellie saw that there was new duct tape holding his speaker to the handlebars and his chrome helmet was cracked.

Reggie limped up to Bill.

"Good to see you, Bill," Reggie said. He took off a glove and held out a hand.

Nellie stepped between them.

"Reggie," she said. "What are you doing here?"

Reggie dropped his hand.

"Well, we all just wanted to wish you well," he said. He stroked his moustache. Nellie noticed that half of it was missing.

"Really," Nellie said. "So you kicked my man out of your little posse and then you just happened to show up in the neighborhood - two thousand miles away?"

She made a blubbery noise of contempt. There was a lot of spit in it.

Reggie stepped back.

"Naw, truth is, we came to *get* you, Bill. Not like a threat!" Reggie added hastily. "Get you in a *good* way. We just thought we were a little hasty when we parted."

"You were cruel," Bill said. "You didn't have the decency to beat me up. That hurt."

"Yeah," Reggie said, nodding. "You know, Bill, it takes a big man to admit when a mistake's been made." He swept an arm towards the seated gang. "And they really messed up."

"So you're *going* to beat me up?" Bill asked. "Make it official?" His eyes gleamed with hope.

"No!" Reggie said, and attempted one of his patented smiles but his lips were too swollen and it came out grotesque.

"Bill," Reggie said. "I'm allowing you back in the club. On behalf of the entire gang, we say now, and for all eternity: You are a PRIK."

He reached into his jacket pocket and pulled out a handful of patches. He held them out to Bill.

Bill shivered. Nellie put a hand on his trembling arm.

"Wait," she said. Ignoring Reggie, she stepped over to Little Weenie. He tried to look up at her face but the Arctic ledge of her breasts blocked his view. He squinted in her shadow.

"All right," she said. "What's this really about?"

"I told you," Reggie began but Nellie whipped around savagely and gave him a stare that would have cold-cocked a rabid badger. She turned back to Little Weenie.

"Well?" she said.

Little Weenie rubbed his bald head in chagrin.

"We got chased out of Phoenix," he said. "Once word got out that Bill wasn't with us, we were dogmeat. He's the only one who could fight."

"I thought you didn't go to New Jersey," Nellie said.

"Well, we don't plan on staying long," Little Weenie said with a nervous glance around. "But we had to risk it. We need Bill."

"The Pink Slashers took our Red Devil gig," somebody said.

"Your what?" Nellie asked.

"We ran fireworks," Reggie explained. "See, there are some counties that frown on them. So there's a market."

"You smuggle fireworks?" Nellie asked.

"It's not smuggling," Reggie said defensively. "We got a safety officer - had a safety officer."

"One-thumb," Little Weenie said. He brushed away a tear.

"Anyway," Reggie added. "The Slashers stole our fireworks. And we want you to help us get them back."

The other club members nodded their heads. Some raised their fists and looked expectantly at Bill.

"Come back to Phoenix with us and help us regain our kingdom," Reggie said.

"He's got a new kingdom," Nellie said. "Just up those steps."

"Bill, we need you, man," Reggie said. "I'm not ashamed to say it. We need you - and we miss you."

Reggie waved the patches. He held out a patch that was larger than the others, gaudy and trimmed with gold thread.

"If you come back, you won't be at the back of the pack anymore," he wheedled.

The patch glinted in the sunlight.

"You'll ride right behind me." He gave a dramatic pause and then added: "As our new Sergeant-at-Arms! Hip-hip..."

"Hooray!" came the ragged shout.

"Bill?" Nellie turned to her man and saw naked hunger on his face. If he'd been a dog, she thought, his tail would be up and quivering. She looked at the gang. And if *they* were dogs, they'd all be dancing in a circle and sniffing Bill's butt, she thought with disgust. Her hand strayed to her cleavage before she remembered that she'd lost the gun in the Amish field. Her instinct was to make a crotch-crushing emotional display. But then she drew a breath. She was a woman of action but this was a time, she knew, to be still.

She stepped back, squeezed Bill's hand and then let it go.

"Lover," she said quietly. "Do what you gotta do."

Bill opened his mouth to speak. But at that moment, a sound they must been ignoring earlier suddenly came clear.

It was the sound of motorcycles - Harleys - and they were coming fast.

Reggie's nostrils flared and seemed to quiver. His puffy lips curled into a sneer and his nose twitched.

Around the corner roared another motorcycle club. There were at least two dozen members. Their leader wore a bronze-colored helmet.

With savage speed, before the PRIKs could do more than stare, they were encircled by chrome and gunning engines. The air was filled with the smell of burnt oil.

The pack leader bumped Reggie's bike and stopped. From a speaker taped to the handlebars came the sound of "Bat Out of Hell" but it was scratchy, as if Meatloaf was singing with strep throat. The leader raised a black-gloved fist and the engines died. Everybody glared at everybody.

A growl erupted from Reggie's throat. "DIKKs," he said, and his half-mustache quivered with rage.

"*Reggie*, we heard you'd come," said the other man, whom Nellie now noticed had a striking resemblance to Reggie, except he had a scraggly soul patch instead of a scraggly mustache.

"We're not staying, Nigel," Reggie said.

"Doesn't matter. You broke the sacred treaty. *You passed Omaha*. Blood must spill. Vengeance must be taken. You always were the asshole in the family, Reg."

"Family?" Nellie asked. She looked from one to the other. "Oh my God. There's two of you?"

"Half-brothers," Reggie said. "But I got the badass half and he got the pussy half."

Nigel started forward until he was inches from Reggie's face.

"Don't use the P-word!" he shrieked. "Mom said not to."

"Well mom isn't here, Nigel, so shut your piehole and tell your little demony horde to back off."

"Make me!" Nigel said, and clenched both fists with the thumbs inside.

"Don't think I won't!" Reggie squeaked, his bruises purpling. "Mom hated me more, because I always kicked your ass. I was the kick-asser. *You* were the kick-ass-ee. and you still are."

"Yeah, right, that's why I got the right speaker from the car and you got stuck with the left," Nigel said.

"The right one was busted, that's why you got it."

"And now I'm gonna bust yours," Nigel said. "I need a matching pair." He stuck out his jaw.

"You need a pair, all right," Reggie said. "All right, let's settle this. On three."

"OK, bro, it's beat-down time."

"I hope you got enough left in your half of the trust fund for a new set of teeth," Reggie said.

"Speak for yourself, pretty boy," Nigel replied.

The rest of the two gangs rolled their eyes.

"Reg," Little Weenie said. "There's a parking meter lady coming up the street. We gotta get movin'."

"Yeah," Reggie replied. He stuffed the patches back in his pocket. "All right, brother, you heard the man. It's go time! What number were we on?"

"I was gonna say one," Nigel said.

"All right, one," Reggie said.

"No," Nigel replied. "*I* get to say one."

"Why? You started the fight. I get choice of weapons. Numbers."

"Well, isn't that just like you all over. Still selfish."

"And watch the nose. I got hit there two days ago."

"I'm not surprised, with your people skills," Nigel said.

"Oh for God's sake," Nellie shouted. "Just hit each other! One, two, three, go!"

They glared at each other, and reluctantly raised their fists, curving them in like boxers from a previous century. They made little back-and-forth scuttling movements but neither one struck.

Nellie, cursing silently as the meter maid bore down on them, stalked forward, grabbed both men by their jacket collars and slammed them together.

Both made squeaky protests and then began punching. The blows made tiny slapping sounds but did no appreciable damage. Nigel reached up and slapped Reggie's helmet and then the fight began to look like two parochial schoolgirls in a playground tizzy.

The meter maid gaped, shook her head, and said, "Fellas, take it somewhere else or I'll get someone to impound your bikes. It's a no-parking zone."

"Looks like it's not much of a fighting zone, either," somebody quipped.

"I'll handle this, ma'am," Little Weenie said.

He got off his bike and with two quick pushes separated Reggie and Nigel. They stood panting and glaring at each other. Little Weenie squinted thoughtfully at them.

"I've thought about this for a while, Reg," he said. "But until just this moment I didn't want to say it out loud. You're nothing but an idiot."

"That's what I said," Nigel said.

"Well, you're one, too," said a bald-headed DIKK. "Beats me why the hell we've been following you, Nigel. Just 'cause you have a trust fund and own the clubhouse. I am right ashamed of this display."

"Hell, I'm ashamed I was ever taking orders from this knucklehead," Little Weenie said. "And I think it's about time I stopped." He stepped forward. "PRIKs, I hereby call for a vote on removing Reggie as our leader."

"Seconded,'" three voices chimed up.

"All in favor, let's hear those engines," Little Weenie said.

The motorcycles roared to life. It was a unanimous cacophony.

"Wait!" Reggie said, thunderstruck. "I own the junkyard. And if you demote me, I will sell it," he grinned painfully but triumphantly. With his puffy, purple lips and ripped clothes, he looked like a homeless clown.

"You'd do that to us?" Little Weenie said. "That's low, Reg, even for you. That's blackmail."

"I'll *do* it," Reggie warned.

"Well," Little Weenie said, and rubbed his head. "You know what, Reg? You just made a direct threat to the property and well-being of the club. And according to the by-laws, that's grounds for expulsion."

"You wouldn't dare," Reggie tried to sneer again but his lips had had too much action.

"All in favor of expelling Reg, our former leader and current jerk-off - engines!" Little Weenie said.

The roar reverberated through the street. The meter maid put her hands over her ears.

"It's done," Little Weenie said. "I'd pull your colors but this kind and patient lady wants us to move."

"You can't do this!" Reggie screamed, spitting with rage.

"Yeah, there's rules," Nigel said.

"You're right," Little Weenie said. "I forgot the most important part of the ceremony." His fist snapped out and hit Reggie squarely in the nose. Reggie made a smushy sound, staggered back, and fell on his ass.

"Wish you'd done that to me," Bill said.

Little Weenie's DIKK counterpart dismounted and strode over to Nigel.

"I think it's time for you to quit gracefully, Nige," he said. "I'm pretty sure we're all pretty sick of you, too."

Nigel put a hand protectively over his nose.

"I'll go quietly," he said.

"Pussy!" Reggie burbled through his bleeding nose.

"Shut up!" Nigel screamed, but he backed away and got on his bike.

The bald DIKK stood face to face with Little Weenie.

"Brother, that was fine. Seems a PRIK and a DIKK want pretty much the same thing. You guys staying in New Jersey?"

"Well," Little Weenie said. "We're from Phoenix but we got our asses kicked there."

"Yeah, we get ours kicked here all the time," the DIKK nodded. "Maybe if we teamed up, we wouldn't get kicked so much." He grinned, a gap-toothed smile. "Phoenix's got a lot of sun, I hear."

"'bout three hundred days a year."

"Well, none of us has any real ties here, now that we lost our clubhouse." He raised his voice. "Whataya say, DIKKs? Partner up and head for Phoenix? Beer, booty and maybe a brawl or two we can actually win?"

"Seconded," a dozen voices said.

"Mount up!" both men said at once.

But then Little Weenie said: "Wait!" He walked over to Reggie, who had crawled under a tree. He leaned down and pulled the patches from Reggie's jacket pocket. Then he reached out and tore off Reggie's leader irons. Reggie seemed too stunned and miserable to protest.

Little Weenie straightened, went to Bill, and held out the patches and medals.

"Bill," he said. "This club's gonna need a new leader. I think you'd do fine. How 'bout it?"

Bill didn't take them. He looked at Nellie and sighed.

"What time is it?" he asked at last.

"Time?" Little Weenie asked.

Bill nodded.

Little Weenie, looking puzzled, pulled a big silver pocket watch on a chain from his vest. "Ten minutes to ten," he said.

Bill looked at the four dozen bikes, the bearded and jacketed men, the downcast Nigel and at Reggie, who was divoting the grass with his butt. It was a long glance, one that seemed to stretch for an eternity. Then he sighed again.

"Gotta go," he said. He took Nellie's hand, picked up the "Sunrise!" shopping bag, and began to walk up the courthouse steps.

Halfway up, Bill stopped and called over his shoulder to Little Weenie.

"The PRIKKs and DIKKs could do worse than to have you for a leader," he said. "See you later - Giant Weenie."

Then Bill and Nellie walked through the doors of the courthouse to their destiny.

"Sir, why are you trying to bring a boot into the building?"

The security guard was glaring at Bill. He and Nellie had left their shopping bags outside, ordering Reggie to guard them, and now stood in front of the metal detector.

Bill held the boot protectively.

"It was my granddaddy's."

Several more guards moved closer.

"Sir, you cannot bring that into the courthouse."

"Can you hold it for me?"

"No, sir. You'll have to leave it outside."

"It's evidence," Nellie said.

"Of what? Foot odor? You suing Dr. Scholl's?"

The other guards chuckled.

Bill bristled.

"Listen, donut-sucker..." he began but Nellie quickly stepped in front of him.

"Sir, it really is a keepsake," Nellie said, dripping womanly sentiment. "Didn't you ever have a...a teddy bear or something that you didn't want to give up?"

"I had a Rottweiler," the guard said. "And I wouldn't take that into a courtroom, either. Come on, now. There's people behind you."

He gestured at a line forming behind them.

Bill, gnashing his teeth, took a step forward and raised the boot, waving it. Suddenly the guards surrounded them. Their hands hovered over their holsters. One was saying something urgently into a shoulder-mounted radio.

"Sir," the guard in front of Bill said slowly, moving his lips thickly for emphasis as if talking to a demented gorilla. "Put the boot *down.*"

"Make me, *authority figure*!" Bill's glower turned his eyebrows into a ledge over his eyes.

The guard's hand clutched the handle of his weapon.

"Son, you have five seconds to take that boot outside or we *will* take you down."

"You're holding up the line," grumbled someone at the back of the queue.

"Bill," Nellie said. "Give me the boot. I'll wait outside with it."

"No, I need you in there." He looked embarrassed. "I don't want to do this alone."

Nellie thought about it.

"Let's kill two birds with one stone," she said.

She turned to the guards and half-raised her hands.

"I'm going to sit down on this table here."

Carefully, eyeing the guards, she pushed aside some gray plastic trays, plopped down on the table, lifted one leg, tugged off a boot and stuck out her foot.

Bill was suddenly nervous.

"But the other one didn't fit."

"The boot works both ways," Nellie said. "Before, you weren't sure. But you're sure now, right?"

"Right ...."

"Go ahead, then. Love transforms."

Bill knelt on one knee in front of her, slowly took the boot and held the top open with both hands. Nellie was wearing a thick woolen sock. Slowly, she peeled it off. Underneath was another sock, made of pale lace. Nellie blushed. Bill's nose hairs twitched. The guards looked at each other and took a step back.

Daintily, Nellie dipped her toe into the boot. It was like watching a fat gopher squeeze into a hole.

It touched the bottom of her calf and stuck. Nellie raised her head, looked Bill full in the face, and shoved with all her might. Her grunt echoed off the marble walls of the hallway.

The foot swelled the sides of the boot and the leather creaked. Nellie's foot bulged the boot like a meal making its way through a python.

And then, suddenly, her foot was in. Nellie stood and stamped her heel firmly.

Bill looked up at her with astonished eyes. The rest of the world fell away.

"Why did this one fit?" he asked.

"You know why," Nellie said.

"Because ... because it was meant to!"

"Yep. Plus, your granddaddy had different-sized feet. Probably his kickin' boot." Nellie admired the boot, stamped it a little more. Dirt fell from the sole. Nellie lifted her foot to look at the bottom and squinted at the carved letters.

"Huh," she said. "Sweetie, what did you say the letters were on this boot?" She traced their grooves with a finger.

"E-V-I-L," Bill recited. "Evil."

Nellie's angel-pink fingernail picked away the last crust of dirt from a groove.

"No," she said, with wonder. "Not E-V-I-L. It's E-V-*O*-L."

Bill's eyes went wide. He imagined Grandpa kicking him with the boot, and visualized the imprint on his ass.

"L-O-V-E," Bill said.

Nellie reached down and held out both hands to Bill, who was still on his knee. He took her hands and rose. Suddenly she felt all of her 350 pounds lofted into the air as Bill picked her up and whirled her around. He gently lowered her to her feet.

Nellie looked at the guards.

"It's my boot, right?" she asked.

"Yes, ma'am," one said. He was smiling.

She took her old boot and tossed it in a trash can, then strode through the metal detector with her head held high as a queen's.

They entered Room 211. It was clad in functional wood paneling. Fluorescent lights glared from the high ceiling. Clerks and bailiffs were in place at their desks, glancing at computer screens and rifling through paperwork. The judge's bench was empty. A barrier separated the bench, counsel tables and court bureaucracy from the spectator seats.

A huddle of dark-suited lawyers stood chatting in front of the barrier. Nellie's eye was caught by a thin, intense-looking Asian man. He wore a voluminous leather trench coat and was haranguing his lawyer, a short-haired woman who looked pained. The man looked up as Nellie and Bill entered the room, glared, and stuffed his right hand into his coat pocket.

A balding man in a dark suit, holding a thick leather binder, spotted Bill entering and stopped chatting to a clerk. He glanced over the tops of his gold-rimmed spectacles, then walked over and held out a hand.

"William Butcher?" he asked, craning his head to meet Bill's eyes.

"Bill," Bill said. He engulfed the hand.

"I'm Philip Thibideaux. Phil. I represent Mr. Cho's estate." He looked at Bill approvingly. "So you're Lynette's son. A pleasure. Your momma was a hell of a woman."

"You knew momma?" Bill asked.

"Very well. Professionally. No one was more of a pro than your mom. She was well known around my, er, these parts. That must have been nearly thirty years ago. Nobody knew her last name but she had "Lynette" tattooed on her ... she had a memorable tattoo."

The lawyer sighed. "I was in law school then. I didn't realize she was my client's beneficiary until he tracked her down and had me amend his will and trust. So, you're representing her interests?"

"I *am* the interest," Bill said sadly. "She died two days ago."

"Oh, my lord," Thibideaux said, and took off his glasses, pulled a silk handkerchief and polished them thoughtfully. "I'm so sorry. May I ask how she died?"

"Pie explosion," Bill said.

The lawyer nodded and put his spectacles back on.

"That was her all over," he said.

"That's what we heard," Nellie replied.

"Well, it's a shame," the lawyer said. "My sympathies. Well, as the only child, that makes you the heir. I'll have to notify the judge but it shouldn't affect the hearing if you have the documentation. I *hope* we can get this done today. Probably can. Judge Nardini has been on my case to settle for six months now. He won't give us any more extensions. Did she die at home?"

"Yeah," Bill said.

"Okay," the lawyer said. "Give me a moment. Let me call my office. If I get the coroner's office down there to confirm her death, I think that will satisfy His Honor, that cranky bastard."

He whipped out his cell phone with authority and stepped outside the court room, returning a few moments later.

"All right, we're set there, I think. Now, do you have the document?"

"You mean the Christmas card?" Bill asked.

"That's it," Thibideaux said.

Bill reached into his vest pocket and took out a wrinkled, water-stained hunk of paper. He handed it to Thibideaux, who took it with trepidation and scanned it quickly. He nodded.

"It's a little worse for wear but it's legible and it looks right. I can make out the signature," he said with a professional smile. "Let's hope the judge agrees." He placed it carefully in the binder.

"Take your seats," a bailiff called out.

"You two sit here with me in the front row until we get called," Thibideaux said. "Then we'll all walk to the counsel table."

They sat. The other lawyers in the scrum at the barrier also took seats in the front rows. The thin Asian man plopped down at the very end of the row.

"Silence in the court," the bailiff called.

The bustle ceased.

"All rise for the Honorable Judge Anthony Nardini," the bailiff called.

A moment later, a stoop-shouldered, hook-nosed man in a black robe came out of the door and strode up the steps to the bench.

"Take your seats and come to order," the bailiff said.

"First case, counsel approach the bench," the judge said without ceremony.

"Wuu versus Cho estate," the bailiff called.

Thibideaux, Nellie and Bill stood. The intense Asian man leapt to his feet, nearly knocking down his attorney, who scowled and tightened her grip on a folder bulging with papers.

Both lawyers grabbed the handles of stuffed rolling cases and wheeled them through the gate. Bill and Nellie followed. The Asian man cut in front of Nellie, brushing her with his flapping trench coat. A sneer was on his thin lips. She decided to hate him on sight. It wasn't even a hard choice.

The lawyers placed their papers on twin tables but remained standing.

"Are we finally ready to proceed?" Nardini asked. He turned a gimlet eye on the attorneys.

"I am, Your Honor," Thibideaux said.

"Yes, your honor," the woman said.

"Very well, let's proceed."

Wuu leaned in, put a hand on his attorney's arm and whispered in her ear.

"No," she said harshly. "We're done with that." The whispering grew frantic. The lawyer shook her head.

The judge gave her a withering glare.

"Is there a problem, Ms. Zuckerberg?"

"Your Honor, my client wishes me to ask - yet again - that you consider his argument that his uncle was *non compos mentis* when he amended his will and trust." She looked uncomfortable.

Nardini gave a judgely snort.

"Yet again, no. Please advise your client that in this court, as in baseball, three strikes and you're out. Now I have a full docket and you are wasting my time. *Do not waste my time.* Am I clear, Ms. Zuckerberg?"

"Crystal, Your Honor. Sorry," she said.

She glared at Wuu and muttered something under her breath. Wuu shook his head but remained silent.

"Okay," the judge said. "That leaves the matter of proving a connection between Mister Cho and ..." he squinted at his computer screen. "Lynette Windflower."

"Who?" Bill muttered. "I thought we were Butchers. I never heard her use that name."

"Shhh," Thibideaux said. "Your mother had a lot of names, apparently. We all used to call her..."

"Mister Thibideaux," the judge called sharply. "If you want to chat with your clients, just tell me and we'll all go down to Howard Johnson's and have coffee and pancakes. You will address the bench and only the bench. In fact, if anyone here says anything to anybody except me, I will be very - and I stress this - *very* displeased."

A handful of people waiting their turn in the spectator seats shook visibly.

"I apologize, Your Honor..." Thibideaux began.

"Don't," the judge said. "Now, do you have the document?"

"I do."

"Oh, goody. Let me see it."

Thibideaux took the Christmas card from his leather binder, passed it to the bailiff, who walked it to the judge. Nardini grimaced at the sad-looking paper and motioned the bailiff to put it on his desk. He bent his head until his nose almost touched it. After a moment, he looked up.

"Counselor, are you prepared to state that this is Mister Cho's signature?"

"I am, Your Honor."

Ms. Zuckerberg raised a hand.

"Objection, Your Honor. Question of provenance. We haven't seen this document and may wish to challenge it."

Nardini sighed.

"Approach the bench," he said.

"Yes!" Wuu stage-whispered and thrust a clenched fist in the air.

Zuckerberg and Thibideaux both walked to the bench. Zuckerberg examined the card. For several minutes, the lawyers traded urgent whispers. The judge shook his head repeatedly and glared at Zuckerberg, who seemed to be remonstrating but finally shook her head as well.

"Okay," Nardini said at last.

The lawyers returned to their tables. The judge looked up.

"Counsel for Mister Wuu has wisely decided against challenging the authenticity of the document, so it will now be submitted into evidence." The judge straightened up and picked up the gavel.

"Having reviewed the evidence and considered the facts pertaining to the case of Wuu v. Cho Estate, I hereby find that the last will and testament of Wu Tsien Cho, as amended on the date specified, including all dispositions, is legal and valid."

Wuu jumped and hissed like an angry gecko.

"I further find," the judge continued, "That the trust created by Mr. Cho and administered by his estate is valid and lawful in all its particulars. I reject the challenges to both with prejudice." He smacked the gavel firmly and a wooden clack echoed through the courtroom.

Nellie gave Bill a bone-creaking hug and an enormous slobbery kiss. Thibideaux put out a hand. Bill engulfed it.

"Well, congratulations, Mister Butcher," he said. "You and I still have a little paperwork to deal with - proving you're the sole heir and such - but I'm confident you've got yourself a diner."

"What do I do with it?" Bill asked.

"That's really not my decision," Thibideaux said, smiling. "I'd recommend first off that you find yourself a good attorney and a good accountant and go over the books."

Bill looked down on the lawyer, nodding.

"Not a reader," Bill said. "You want to be my lawyer?"

Thibideaux beamed. "I would be happy to serve in that capacity."

"So," Bill said. "As my lawyer, I will ask: What the hell do I do now?"

Thibideaux took off his gold-rimmed spectacles and buffed them.

"Well, I'm still handling the Cho estate, so I'm not officially your counsel. But unofficially - hell, Mister Butcher, it's your diner. Go get a hamburger."

At the other table, Wuu was shaking with rage. His thin shoulders danced up and down under his trench coat like two weasels struggling for air. His face contorted in a rictus of shock. Then, he willed himself to calmness and turned to his lawyer.

"So," he said brightly. "When can we start the appeal?"

"Mr. Wuu," Zuckerberg said. "I'll be honest. I would take your money but you really don't have any grounds to fight this. You wouldn't have a snowball's chance. I advise you to get used to buying your own dinners. And by the way, if you don't pay me what you owe, you'll be back in court and I won't be on your side."

She held out a hand but Wuu ignored it.

Stuck up little bastard, the attorney thought but kept her professional face as she walked out of court.

With an odd smile, Wuu walked over to Bill.

"Well played, Mr. Butcher. You won it fair and square." He held out a hand. "No hard feelings?"

Bill, with Nellie still hanging to his neck, reached out and enveloped Wuu's hand in his. He felt a sharp prick, pulled back, and saw a welling spot of blood on his palm.

"What the fuck?" he said.

Wuu danced back, raising his hand. A sixth finger was dangling, exposing a tube tipped with a wicked-looking needle. He made a five-fingered fist and shook it, the fake finger flopping.

"Ha ha!" He chortled. "Bwah hah hah hah!"

Bill felt dizzy. Suddenly, there were two Wuus in front of him.

The twins capered from foot to foot, overcoats flapping like bats' wings.

"You thought you won?" Wuu shouted. "*Not!* Nobody wins against Wuu!"

"Honey?" Nellie's voice seemed to come from far away. The world seemed to be weaving, like a bike with a blown tire. Bill's vision narrowed as if he were looking at the world from the wrong end of a telescope.

"Help?" he said, and stopped breathing.

The last thing he saw was a pile of bailiffs tackling Wuu, who screamed gleefully: "I am invincible!"

Actually, that was the second-to-last thing Bill saw. The world tilted up, there was an enormous crash and the floor shook. Bill found himself looking up at the courtroom lights, like vanishing stars.

The *last* last thing he saw was a bailiff's fat worried face, with a bristly mustache, leaning in to French kiss him.

CHAPTER FOURTEEN

Joe's American Syrup & Fries Diner, New Jersey Turnpike

Apollo Martinez manhandled the rig into the diner parking lot. Those hitchhikers had recommended Joe's, and so he'd picked up a short-haul contract from Pittsburgh. It looked closed, though; there were no other rigs in the lot. Still, as long as he was here ....

Martinez stretched a kink out of his stiff back, climbed down from the cab and walked to the door.

It was closed, all right. A uniformed security guard stood out front, playing with a walkie-talkie.

"Hey, amigo," Apollo said. "I thought this place never closed."

The guard, a middle-aged man with greased but receding hair and thick shoes, frowned.

"You mean you didn't hear?"

"Hear what? I've been on the road."

"The place is shut down indefinitely. Some accountant guy that worked here went crazy."

"Oh shit," Apollo said. "Don't tell me he shot all the customers."

"No, no," the guard said. "But he got arrested. I heard he stabbed somebody in court. Killed him right in front of a judge."

"*Hijole!* That's some twisted shit."

The guard looked smug. "That ain't the half of it," he said confidentially.

"Yeah?"

"Yeah. The cops went all over this place. Didn't ask me a thing. No respect for fellow law enforcement. So I didn't volunteer nothin.'"

"Damn straight," Martinez said. "You gotta demand respect."

"I see you are a gentleman of perception," the guard said. "Like Yoda."

"So what didn't you volunteer? Is it ... a drug stash?"

The guard scoffed.

"Naw. Weirder. Much, much weirder shit." He looked at his walkie-talkie, which was squawking mindlessly, and turned it off.

"Keep a secret, *compadre?"*

"I don't even tell myself shit."

"Follow me." He produced a key on a ring attached to a long retractable chain, and unlocked the front door.

Inside, only a few security lights picked out the cavernous room. The guard walked a few steps forward and then opened a door on the left that said "Employees only."

Martinez followed. The guard snapped on some lights and led him down a short corridor, then opened another door that said "Stockroom."

Inside was Wuu's desk, partitioned by a small barrier from piles of mops, wringer buckets, floor polishers, and shelves of goods.

"This was his office," the guard said.

"The accountant?"

"Yeah, guess he liked to keep an eye on the merchandise."

The office area had been searched. Papers had been rifled, there were empty file drawers and boxes on the floor and smudges of fingerprint powder all over the desk.

"This is where he worked," the guard said.

"The fruitcake?"

"Yep. The cops went it over it pretty good. Too bad they didn't know about ...." He paused for dramatic effect, "The *other* room."

"The other room? Where? I don't see no door."

The guard chuckled. "That's 'cause you didn't need to take a dump on the graveyard shift and run out of toilet paper." He pointed to a shelf stocked floor to ceiling with huge bulk packages of toilet paper.

The guard grabbed the shelf and heaved. The shelf rolled sideways on hidden casters. Behind it was a door.

When the door opened Martinez's eyes jolted as wide as if he'd swallowed a bottle of amphetamines. When the guard switched on the inside light, Martinez realized the row of female heads facing him from the shelf weren't real.

"Pretty freaky, huh?"

"Why would a dude collect doll heads?"

The guard knelt and pulled what looked like a corpse bag from under the bed. He pulled down the zipper in the middle. Inside was a headless, naked, life-sized female doll.

"Want to pop one of the heads on it and play with it?" the guard asked.

Martinez took a step back to make sure the door hadn't closed behind him.

"I'm just funnin' you," the guard said.

Martinez felt a wave of claustrophobia.

The guard stood and pushed the bag back under the bed.

"Check these out," the guard said and opened the cabinet with Wuu's finger collection. "I don't even want to know where these came from."

Martinez felt queasy and looked away to see the cork bulletin board covered with multi-colored index cards arranged precisely, each held in place with pushpins in every corner. Suddenly, he heard a rustling noise behind him and nearly jumped out of his skin. He spun around and saw the terrarium. On top of it was one of the freaky doll heads from Wuu's collection. Inside, Wuu's lizard was standing on its hind legs, clawing at the glass side in a vain attempt to get free.

"Ahh," Martinez said.

"His name is Killer Boo Boo," the guard said. "His name's on his collar. I think he likes you."

"Yeah, you think so?"

"First time the thing ever moved when I was in here. Not that I've been in here more than once or twice," the guard said, looking uncomfortable.

"Damn, that's a cute one," Martinez said. "And I do get lonely on the road."

"Oh, really? She's my favorite too. I'm partial to redheads, myself," the guard said. Her name's Sinead, from Ireland."

"I was talking about Killer Boo Boo," Martinez said.

"Oh, the lizard," the guard said.

He pointed at it and said: "Er, ah, maybe you'd like to take that thing with you? It kinda creeps me out. Just kinda stares. Besides, it'll just starve with nobody here to feed it."

Martinez pulled out of the diner parking lot with his belly still empty but his heart full. Killer Boo Boo was a stupid name for the fine little amigo who now sat comfortably sunning himself on the dashboard. He'd have to think up a new name. Something with a country Western flavor. Cause, damn, he could tell the lizard was going to enjoy his music collection. Inspiration struck. He had it. He'd call him Eddie Dead after Eddie Rabbitt and The Grateful Dead. Or maybe Grateful Rabbitt. Or best yet, Eddie Dead the Grateful Rabbitt.

Sure enough as they drove along, Eddie Dead the Grateful Rabbitt voiced no complaints about the music and even bobbed his head to the beat. He was a lizard with class, Martinez thought. He knew that before too many miles Eddie would know all the lyrics and be singing along with him.

CHAPTER FIFTEEN

Hackensack University Medical Center, New Jersey

Bill opened his eyes to see Nellie asleep on a chair that sagged under her weight. Her red hair fell like a waterfall over her face. She snored like a tranquilized rhino. A line of drool traced her chin like a stream of moonlight.

"I had the weirdest dream," Bill said. "I was on the road, on my bike. But it had a dragon's head. And I kept eating the bugs that flew into my teeth. They were ... delicious. Then I licked my goggles with my tongue."

Before Bill continued, the doctor came in, checked the machines, shone a light in Bill's eyes and inspected his hand.

The doctor frowned and said, "Mr. Butcher, I'm an unhappy man. I bet the ward nurse fifty dollars that you'd die on my shift." He shook his head. "I was sure I had it this time. Do you know where you are?"

"Hospital. You?"

"Yes, well done," the doctor said. "I have to tell you that you are a bit of a minor miracle. You were poisoned. The dosage you received was enough to kill six men - or a mastodon, if they weren't already extinct. You must have a liver like a polar bear. Did you know that polar bear livers contain so much Vitamin A that they are actually toxic to people? How do I know that?" He shrugged. "Lost a bet."

He tapped Bill's chest. "You seem to have shaken off the effects, your breathing is normal, and there's no sign of serious organ damage. I am, frankly, amazed."

He took a breath, straightened up and patted Bill's shoulder.

"Here's my medical advice. Go out and wrestle a crocodile. Parachute off the Matterhorn. Kick a Mafia don in the groin. Do anything and everything you want to do, because son, you have beaten the odds. You are as close to invincible as I'm ever likely to see."

He looked over at Nellie.

"Girlfriend?"

"Fiancée," she snapped.

"Good," the doctor said, and winked. "Give him lots of kids. Humanity can use those genes." He strode out, yelling: "Florence! Come and get your blood money!"

Just before sunset, Thibideaux pulled his Mercedes into the parking lot of the diner between a bright red Peterbilt and a dusty Mack truck with a bulldozer chained to its bed. When Bill squeezed out of the Mercedes and stood up, his head came even with the caterpillar treads.

A winking trucker in neon towered three stories high over the parking lot. Instead of hair, he had red flames. Carnival light painted itself on their faces like garish war paint.

Bill had left the hospital early. He'd actually been scheduled for discharge the next day but had decided he was ready for something more enticing than sponge baths and pats of bland food on plastic plates. Nellie had called up the lawyer, who had graciously offered to take them for dinner.

The parking lot was as long as a football field. Two dozen trucks were lined up at various bays, some getting washes, others oil changes.

Bill, Nellie and Thibideaux went up to the diner door. It was the revolving kind flanked by two huge windows. Fixed to the windows were gigantic versions of mud flaps - the kind with chrome silhouettes of women in seductive poses.

One by one, they squeezed through the door and were met by a blast of frigid air and a continuous soundtrack of road-themed songs. Then they were in Wonderland.

The dining area was enormous, like a bush league baseball stadium. The ceiling was painted to look like the sky, with trucker angels rising to Heaven, some blowing air horns. They seemed to be circling a full-sized big-rig, gleaming midnight black with painted flames that hung overhead and looked about to plunge onto the salad bar. Some walls looked like desert scenes, complete with stuffed buzzards; others had miniature versions of the Brooklyn Bridge, the Grand Canyon and so on, next to genuine roadway signs. Dark gray and black carpeting led between booths, with broken white and yellow lanes down the center to imitate highways, and turn lanes leading to tables that looked like hollowed out truck cabs - complete with smokestacks that belched steam. Above them, crystal chandeliers in the shape of semis threw a glintering light. One portion of the place was just for counter service. It had a motorcycle theme; the stools had leather bike seats and the countertop gleamed with lacquered art of skulls, chopped Harleys and other frills.

Some tables were double-sized to accommodate Fred Flintstone-sized guests - of which there were a surprising number. Waiters and waitresses rushed around with enormous plates of food, somehow managing to avoid collisions. The waitresses wore jeans, work boots and midriff-baring construction vests with "slow" "caution" and "speed bumps ahead" printed on them.

In the center of the diner, shining on a revolving pedestal surrounded by a low glass wall and gleaming in its own spotlight, was a custom-crafted softail Harley with hand-tooled leather seat. Its gas tank was painted in pink diamond enamel. The pedestal slowly rotated.

Bill's eyes watered and his breath caught.

"She's beautiful," he whispered.

"She sure is," Nellie said, and suddenly her hand was in his. Callus met callus.

As Thibideaux led Bill and Nellie to the bike, Bill's eyes went wider.

"That's Luscious Lynette," Thibideaux said with pride. "Named after your momma. Mr. Cho always wanted her to see it but she never came back."

"Anyone ridden her?" Bill asked.

Thibideaux did a double-take.

"We mean the bike!" Nellie said.

"Mr. Cho never did but he told me it was ready to ride in case she ever came. He never took her off the pedestal but he had a mechanic come in regularly and change the oil, inflate the tires, and so on. She's yours now," the lawyer added with a wink. "And she's ready to roll. Somebody needs to make her roar."

"Luscious Lynette," Bill said thoughtfully. "She is a beaut. But I don't know. It wouldn't feel right, somehow, to be ridin' my momma."

Nellie slapped him on the back of the head. Twice.

"That's a family heirloom," she said. "And a damn fine bike. Your momma would want you on that, and me behind. Think of it this way: your momma will always be supporting you. And I'll have your back."

"Still," Bill said. "I'll give her a new name." He crushed Nellie in a hug that made her leather corset creak.

"Nasty Nellie," he said and grinned.

Nellie leaned close, then gripped both of his ears painfully. "Seriously?" she said.

"No?" he said.

"No. It ain't cute. It's insulting."

"Uh, Naughty Nellie?"

She twisted one ear like a throttle. Bill grunted.

"Naked Nellie?" The other ear turned forty-five degrees.

"Jesus. *Men.* Think harder," she said.

"That hurts."

"Like my feelings."

Bill thought of all the N-words he knew but none of them seemed appropriate for a lady.

"What's your middle name?" he croaked.

"I'll give you a hint. I am a princess. You are my consort, and that is our steed. Work with that."

"Does it have to rhyme?"

"It must have poetry, like our love," Nellie said, twisting harder.

"Nellie's Belly?" Bill said. "I love your belly."

"I will twist these right off," Nellie said. "I've done it before." She was really getting angry.

"How about 'Noble Nellie?'" Thibideaux suggested.

The grip loosened. Nellie gave a flirty glance at the lawyer and tossed her hair. "I can tell you're a married man."

"Twenty-five years total. Five times but this last one's my soul mate."

"Yes, it takes a woman to bring out the poetry in a man's soul. I'm still training this one." Bill tugged on both ears to make sure they were still attached. "But I love him anyway."

"I was gonna say noble," Bill said.

"Lawyers are quick with words. But I knew it was in your heart."

"Let me show you the rest of the place," Thibideaux said.

There were TV rooms and internet chat rooms. Buffet tables offered dishes from a dozen different countries. Signs pointed the way to a barbershop, massage therapist and even an emergency dentist.

At last, the dazed couple were allowed to eat. They chose to sit at the counter.

"Order anything you like, folks," Thibideaux said jovially. "It's on the house. *Your* house, so I guess you *are* paying for it. Enjoy."

Bill was hungry but he heeded his doctor's orders and started light.

"I'll have the five-pound Dump Truck Lasagna, Eighteen-Wheel omelet and the White Line Sundae. Bring the sundae first," he added.

The lawyer turned a little green.

"And keep the beer coming," Bill added.

"May I recommend the Tank?" The counterman asked.

"Which is ...?"

"Tankard of whatever you want."

"Something dark, dank and destructive," Bill said. The counterman nodded.

Nellie had the Italian Blasta Paint-Stripper Con Carne, which was a bright red chili and came with a side of firecracker jalapenos. She dumped the jalapenos into the chili.

"I'll have a tuna melt with soy cheese," Thibideaux said. Now it was Nellie's turn to turn green.

Behind them, a sinister figure dressed in black to the eyes stepped through the revolving door, moving with the practiced stealth of a panther. He was followed by a nearly-identical figure, then another, and another. Finally, a mob of dark-clad figures clogged the entrance, balancing pigeon-toed and squinting uneasily into the cavernous eatery.

"Table for twenty?" asked Sheila, the hostess.

"No," said one of the men, and leaned uncomfortably lose. "Do not draw attention to us," he whispered. "We are one with the darkness." The figure raised two fingers, pointed them at his eyes, and then at hers. "We are watching you but you are not watching us."

"Oooooookay," Sheila said, and was glad her shift ended in ten minutes. *Fratboys,* she thought.

A busboy came by, holding a tray of dirty dishes and stopped.

"Hey, *amigos,*" he said. "Haven't seen you around for a while. You know your friend got busted, right? And there's a new owner so I don't know if you'll get the VIP room for your little ninja meetings anymore. We're kinda full tonight."

"Ah, a new master," whispered the head ninja, who wore a black silk headscarf with Japanese characters stitched in purple. Underneath, in parentheses, it read: "Clyde". He looked around him at the others, who nodded stealthily and tapped their iron-shod toes three times in unison.

Clyde reached into the breast of his polyester *gi.*

He drew out an envelope on which was written in purple ink: "Open only in case of emergency. Wuu." He stealthily slit it open and drew out the letter. He scanned it for an instant and then both letter and envelope vanished into his pocket.

"Brothers," Clyde whispered "And Maxine. Our comrade Wuu has invoked his free assault. He says we must - quote – 'humiliate, desecrate and annihilate' his enemy. That is our mission tonight."

"Who is this enemy?" muttered the black-hooded mob, which jostled suddenly as a trucker squeezed through the entrance and bumped one.

The ninjas shuffled out of the way.

"It is the new owner," Clyde said. "The *usurper.*"

"The new guy?" the busboy asked. "He's over there eating. You should go ask him about the room. He seems okay."

"We will go then," Clyde whispered, and the deadly troop flowed fluidly as black oil into the restaurant and rolled like a wave toward Bill's broad back.

He seemed to get larger as they approached.

Silently they surrounded him except for the occasional grunt when one iron-shod toe trod on another.

Clyde made a soft whistle as he took in Bill's enormous girth and involuntarily took a step back. But then, he squared his shoulders and put a hand to the hilt of his concealed *katana.* He moved easily into the pigeon-toed fighting stance of his clan.

"Turn and face your doom," Clyde proclaimed in a stage whisper.

Bill said nothing but continued to shovel lasagna.

"Turn and face us, honored enemy," Clyde repeated, a little louder.

"Fuck off," Bill said.

"Bill," Nellie said. "You can't be treating customers like that."

"Naw, I know these guys," said the counterman, who'd moved in to watch the show. "Wuu let 'em in on Thursdays. Can't really call them customers. They never pay."

Bill put down his fork and rotated slowly on the stool. He sighed.

"Wuu? You friends of that asshole?"

"We are his avengers," Clyde said in a harsher whisper. "He has invoked the one free assault given to non-premium members. He has called for your death."

"Actually, he wants your humiliation and desecration first," Clyde added. "I'm not sure about the desecration bit. Not sure exactly what that means. Or, really, the humiliation part, either. But the Iron Pigeon Drop Fighting Stance Secret Society of the Greater Tri-State Area does know death."

The lawyer rolled his eyes.

"Mr. Butcher, if I may interrupt," Thibideaux said. "I knew Mr. Wuu. This seems like something he would do. But I'd like to remind you that the property you may damage if you fight them will be your own. May I suggest that you simply call security and have them escorted out."

Bill glanced over at Nellie, who nodded and then looked down at Clyde.

"Normally my procedure would be to put your face through the ceiling and use you for a piñata. However, my woman has reminded me that I am now a man of property and maturity. So instead I will offer you all free cheeseburgers and then we can part on friendly terms and I can finish my goddamn lasagna." He turned back to his meal.

Some of the ninja began to talk over the proposition. Clyde shushed them.

"Can't do it," he said, almost apologetically. "It's in the charter." With a snake-quick motion, he drew his gleaming katana and raised it over his head. He went into the Half-Horse Pigeon-Toed stance that would lend both power and finesse to the killing stroke.

Without turning, Bill elbowed him in the solar plexus. Clyde dropped like a sack of rocks.

The ninjas gasped.

"Retreat!" a ninja bleated in a loudish whisper. They grabbed Clyde by the ankles and dragged him gasping back to the revolving door.

"Like your style, Boss-man," the counterman said, and wiped up spattered lasagna.

Clyde returned to full consciousness as his head banged through the revolving door. In the parking lot, he staggered to his feet and stood unsteadily. He leaned against a semi, wheezing and clutching his chest. Somebody handed him the sword but he batted it away.

"So, our enemy is resourceful," he croaked in a Brooklyn-inflected voice before recovering himself and switching to a whisper. "A frontal assault obviously was a poor tactic. We are ninja, after all. In the enemy's territory, we must use ...."

He paused.

"Stealth?" somebody suggested.

"Subtlety?" another said.

"Subterfuge?" a third asked.

"No, caution," Clyde said. "Our first attack has failed. But now we know his tactics. We know how he thinks. But that means he also knows how *we* think. So we must unthink and then rethink. As the ninja code says, we must improvise, adapt and overcome."

"I think that's that Marines," a voice whispered.

"They stole it from ninjas," Clyde spat. "Now, look around you. What can we use to regain the element of surprise?"

Back at the counter, Nellie's eyes gleamed as she watched her man casually annihilating his food.

"Sweetie," she said. "That was just elegant."

"I hope that guy won't sue," the lawyer said.

"Naw, that was just an accident," Nellie said, winking Thibideaux.

"Ah," the lawyer said. "Well, we're insured for that."

Bill returned to his food, ignoring the steadily rising sounds outside of muffled shouts and thuds, a diesel roar and finally, an odd, robotic clanking. For the first time in a long time, he felt good just sitting still.

Through the speakers, a plaintive voice was singing about a trailer for rent and rooms to let, fifty cents.

Then the side of the building caved in.

Everything shook. Cinderblocks tumbled and the air was full of plaster dust. The dim light got even dimmer. A dozen feet of the building had been reduced to broken concrete, bent rebar, shattered glass and torn drywall. A gust of hot, highway-scented air blew in. Part of the ceiling above the broken wall came down - heaven falling as the painted acoustic tiles rained on booths. People scattered. Food flew.

Bill looked over.

A bulldozer had crashed through the building and halted, growling in the dining room.

Behind the controls was a ninja.

The snorting machine clanked backward and twenty more ninjas poured through the hole, leaping and hopping over the wreckage like lethal crickets.

Emergency lights snapped on and made lurid slashes of blinding light that only picked out swirling haze. Red warning lights blinked like bloody eyes. Behind the rise and fall of warning sirens could faintly be heard the chorus to "Highway to Hell." Truckers and waitresses stumbled towards exits, some bleeding from superficial shrapnel wounds. In moments most of the room was empty.

Then Bill heard a sound that chilled his soul. Nellie was screaming.

He looked over. Her face was covered in red and she was clawing at her eyes.

"Princess!" he bellowed and caught her face in his hands. She looked hideously wounded, moaning and screaming.

"Goddamn chili!" she roared. "It's in my eyes!" She writhed in pain. Thinking quickly, Bill grabbed his stein of beer and splashed it on her. The red cleared, leaving her sticky and puffy-eyed.

"Are you OK?" he asked. "Please be all right!"

She wiped her streaming nose and nodded. "I'm all right," she said. "This chili stings like hell. Plaster chunk or something hit me in the head and I did a face plant."

But Bill couldn't stop looking at her streaked face as he inhaled the pungent smell of cement dust, diesel and chili. He saw her hurt, bleeding. He saw her gone, leaving a super-sized hole in his life. He flexed his hands, and the knuckles cracked like exploding M-80s. Veins stood out on his neck and his new teeth clamped together with a sound like tectonic plates grinding.

His huge nostrils snuffed gouts of cindery air. Something like a frown that went bone-deep cut his brow. From somewhere below his heart came a sound Nellie hadn't heard before. And in fact, it was a sound nobody had ever heard who was still breathing.

Bill was pissed.

The noise that finally escaped from his throat could be heard over the roar of the bulldozer, the yells of the patrons. It boiled up and singed the shiny buttocks of the trucker angels on the ceiling, blew a hole through the miasma of dust, and stopped the ninjas in their tracks.

Then Bill jumped to his feet, put both hands around a counter seat, and tore it free.

"Stay here," he said to Nellie and the lawyer.

Raising the stool like a chrome club, Bill strode forward to meet his enemies.

The ninjas moved like prowling ants, deathly silent except for the occasional curse as one fell over an overturned table. They converged on Bill.

Bill came forward like a freight train. He was met by a hail of throwing stars that flashed through the air with deadly menace. Bill threw up an arm and eight buried themselves in his forearm. He tore them off with his teeth, not breaking stride.

He slammed into the knot of attackers like a charging rhino. The cluster broke into flying forms like spray thrown up by a breaching whale. Bodies tumbled, crashed into tables and lay tangled in wreckage like broken marionettes. Other ninjas flipped or tumbled more or less gracefully and landed on their feet, ready to advance again. Bill scythed with the bar stool, flinging them a half-dozen yards until they crashed in heaps like dead crows dropping from a tree.

Someone kicked Bill in the crotch but he was a bar fighter. He scraped one bootheel down a ninja's shin and stomped hard on the foot. Something gave with an ugly crack.

Someone holding a pair of *tsais* leaped feet-first, straight for his face. It was like a bad anime cartoon.

Bill clubbed the man down in flight like a downed Frisbee. Then he grabbed him by one foot, and whirled the limp body around before letting him fly a half-dozen feet into a convenient wall. The ninja hit an electrical panel, which gave way. The ninja and the panel fell to the floor, leaving a tangle of sparking electrical wires.

But more came. A swarm of ninjas pulled swords, knives, chains, nunchuks. They swarmed Bill, slashing and screaming.

He swept the bar stool in a vicious arc, clearing a fighting space and colliding with somebody's ribs. There was a sickening crack and a ninja was on the floor, moaning. The other attackers scrambled back, putting a foot of distance between Bill and them.

Another half-dozen stumbled in to the melee, trying to jab, thrust and pound him.

"Not all at once, you morons," someone finally yelled. The ninjas stopped. Fingers began pointing. "And don't stop to choose!" the voice said in exasperation. "Nearest first! *Eee-yah*!"

"Eee-yah!" came the reply, and five pigeon-toed killers moved in on Bill from all sides.

A fist tipped with razor-sharp claws raked Bill's shoulder, slashing through the tough leather jacket but catching on the studs. Nunchuks punished his ribs, a knife rang as it struck his belt buckle.

Fists and feet rained bruising blows. A steel-toed foot caught him behind the right knee. For an instance his leg went numb and Bill crashed to his knees. But he threw out an arm, grabbed the foot and twisted. The ninja went down with a girlish shriek, jerking and slapping at Bill.

"Maxine!" somebody shouted.

Bill roared and dragged the ninja along the floor in a sweeping arc that caught two other attackers and tumbled them. A few seconds later pins and needles erupted as feeling came back into his leg. Bill lurched to his feet and a length of chain crashed against his neck, snaked around. The ninja pulled but Bill tore the chain away. His left fist came down like the hammer of God, dropping the attacker. Another dove for him but Bill put out a hand and clamped him by the throat. The ninja pedaled in mid-air like Wiley E. Coyote, until Bill slammed him to the ground. As an afterthought, he back-handed a pudgy ninja who was pounding his side with nunchuks.

The others scuttled back but Bill managed to punch two of them. They went down and didn't get back up.

A ninja gripping a katana with both hands danced forward. He made a wicked slash at Bill's throat but seemed confused about whether Bill actually had a neck since his head seemed to grow right out of his massive shoulders. The cut scythed off part of Bill's beard and left a long, bloody furrow under Bill's jaw. Bill plowed forward. The ninja leapt back and aimed with a desperate cut at the side of Bill's head. The blade struck and sliced off a piece of Bill's ear. Bill's eyes went red.

The ninja squeaked.

Bill slammed him with one shoulder. The sword went flying, and so did the man, through a convenient plate-glass window.

Then came one of those weird pauses in combat where everyone seems to stop and catch their breaths. Grunts, moans and wheezes rose like ground fog in the silence. And so did a weird sound - a snakelike hissing.

Nellie, who had been watching Bill work with shining eyes until he vanished in the haze and scrum of flying bodies, suddenly sniffed. The chili had cleared her sinuses to almost superhuman sensitivity. She could practically taste the cloud, denser than air, as it slowly poured from somewhere deep at the other end of the dining room.

Her guts churned.

Gas.

Somebody or something must have cut through a gas line and the plume was rolling towards the counter.

Behind that counter was a kitchen full of hot gas grills with open flames.

"Shit!" she yelled. "Bill, Bill!"

She looked desperately for him but could see nothing except for an occasional flying body. Putting aside her womanly dignity, she put her hands to her mouth and shouted "William Butcher! Get out! They hit a fucking gas line! There's gas!"

"Hey, that's what we should have had," a ninja panted. "Knockout gas! Next meeting I'm gonna make a motion ... *Whuhhhh.*" Bill clubbed him to the ground before he could finish. Some part of Bill's forebrain heard the warning but his lizard brain was already in fight-or-flight mode - well, fight mode, anyway - and wasn't inclined to switch to run-and-hide. He drove his elbow into a groin and his bleeding knuckles into a masked face and ignored the rest of the world and the sinister hiss.

Nellie had no more time. She'd done all she could but it was too dangerous.

Thibideaux had been watching the carnage, shell-shocked, his tuna melt forgotten.

"What's that smell?" he asked suddenly. "It smells like burning latex love dolls. Don't ask me how I know that."

In a single motion Nellie grabbed him in a bear hug and flipped them both over the counter. They landed with a bruising jolt that took all the breath out of her and for a split-second she simply lay in a jungle of broken plates garnished with lasagna and chili.

The staff, unbelievably, had continued to grill and fry and chop, clanging pots and clonking crockery. They were so focused on their work that they had ignored the warning sirens.

They did look up, though, when an enormous woman dragging a dazed man in a suit under her arm bowled into the kitchen.

"Gas leak!" she shouted, panting. "Everybody run! Now! Now!"

Everyone looked up. Stopped and stared. Did nothing.

"Now!" Nellie said in a booming voice. "Run! *Peligroso! Vamanos!*" She plunged through the kitchen's narrow aisle, her hips scraping pots and pans off the stoves. Workers scrambled out of her way.

Only then did the panic begin.

A dozen people in paper chef's hats, white smocks and checked pants raced behind her, smashed through the loading door, tumbled out, and ran for their lives. They were halfway across the back lot when all hell broke loose.

The gas finally reached the grills, or perhaps the sparking electrical panel. There was a boom and an immense blast seemed to blow the roof off the building and drop it back. A stupendous, fiery demon hand punched Bill in the chest and blew him thirty feet. Then something that felt very much like the entire diner fell on him.

His vision and his mind went black.

The next thing Bill knew he was lying in darkness. He couldn't move. His lungs were choked with crap. He hacked and spat. Something warm and gooey splattered on his cheek.

With enormous effort, Bill opened his eyes. He was face up, which explained why he'd wound up spitting into his own face. Bikers in general never counted gravity as a friend. Groggily, Bill saw that something like an enormous chrome robot face was leaning over him. No, it had him in its jaws and its big headlight eyes were staring down at him with the dispassionate, heartless gaze of the cat with a rat under its paws.

On its brow were the glittering letters MACK.

No, wait, Bill thought. Those *were* headlights. His head was clearing, and he understood. The truck on the ceiling had come down on him and was now on his chest.

Bill was stuck under tons of steel.

"Nellie!" he tried to yell but couldn't catch his breath. He hoped nothing too important was broken.

It was an embarrassing way to die. So Bill decided he wouldn't. He concentrated. His own body had plowed a furrow through the wreckage in its flight, creating a shallow trench. The front of the truck had landed on him but he was wedged in the trench so that only its bumper had actually hit him. Most of him was trapped but Bill found that his right hand was free and, surprisingly, he was still gripping the bar stool. He held it up, jammed the seat part under the truck bumper, placed the bottom against the floor and pulled. The stool wedged itself but then stopped at a sharp angle. The truck didn't move. Bill gave another pull. The stool moved another inch. The truck groaned and shifted. The bumper dropped another half-inch onto his chest.

Bill stopped.

The truck stopped moving.

Bill coughed, caught a breath that wouldn't have filled a kiddie balloon. He let go of the stool, flexed his fingers, then grabbed it again and pulled sharply. His bicep bulged so high that some smart developer could have built condos with panoramic views on it. Tendons in his arm stood out like bridge cables.

The stool protested, bent. But the bumper was jacked up, and up. A final tug, and the stool held the truck up. Bill felt the weight on his chest ease. He gulped air like pilsner. Then, gingerly, he began to worm his way free.

He dragged himself out using his arms and began to get to his feet but red hot pain slashed through him and his right leg buckled.

Bill collapsed onto the rubble, black stars fizzing at the edge of his consciousness. He looked down and saw a splintered chunk of wood had gored him; six inches of the jagged end protruded from the side of his thigh. It had gone all the way through him. If he pulled it out, Bill knew he would bleed to death.

He tried to move the leg and nearly blacked out again. When he could see again, he looked around. Singed ninjas staggered or were being dragged through broken glass and rubble. A dozen fires roared here and there like demon candles. A few shreds of roof girder and scraps of walls were virtually all that remained. It looked like Armageddon with a trucking theme.

Far in the distance, he thought he heard police and fire sirens. But closer in, he heard something else.

Clanking.

The bulldozer rolled back into the shattered diner and came to a stop in a clash of gears. Its toothed shovel slammed to the ground.

"Pigeon Masters!" Clyde shouted through the open cab door above the grumbling engine. "The enemy is defeated. We are victorious! Let us vanish, silent but deadly, into the darkness."

This was met with groans and whimpers that Clyde apparently took for agreement.

He raised a fist in triumph.

"It is done!" he yelled.

"Fuck you if it is," someone shouted.

The ninja looked around in confusion. He leaned forward, squinting at the rubble, and finally saw Bill. He had stumbled to his feet. He was covered in white dust and bleeding cuts. His beard and hair were so caked that he looked like a wounded yeti.

But through the pallor, his eyes were red with rage.

Behind his mask, Clyde's brown eyes bulged like a throttled canary's.

He shrieked in fury, slammed the cab door shut. He pounded one steel-shod foot on the gas pedal and let out the clutch. The dozer jerked forward with a diesel roar that sounded like the war cry of a cornered bear.

Bill roared out his own challenge.

The dozer bore down on Bill, its shovel leering like the maw of an angry dinosaur. Its tank-like treads gouged the rubble and threw up grit. It crawled forward at just six miles per hour but in the confined space it was brutal and terrifying. Thirty-thousand pounds of metal filled one side of the diner from the broken walls to the smashed tables. Bill, dragging his maimed right leg, limped forward to meet it.

He came up to the beast. The ninja worked the levers and the front shovel rose high in the air with a furious hiss of pneumatic pistons, then crashed down. Bill couldn't move fast enough to avoid it completely. One tooth caught him a glancing blow on his shoulder, spinning him around. He fell sideways as the shovel slammed into the ground with a shuddering impact six inches from his head.

The dozer's shovel rose again and slammed down once more but Bill had rolled out of the way. Again, he managed to get to his feet, although he hunched over and balanced on his good leg, barely able to keep his balance. Gore pulsed from his wounded thigh with each heartbeat.

The bulldozer's engine surged. Gears clashed and the huge machine crunched forward over the rubble. Unable to outmaneuver it, Bill retreated, backing towards the wreckage of the fallen Mack truck.

The dozer followed, the driver in no hurry. At the lip of the trench, Bill suddenly stopped, doubled over in pain. Then he straightened, raised his head, and bellowed: "Come on, you fuck! Let's finish this!"

Clyde, his eyes glowing with the intensity of a rabid raccoon, slammed at the controls. The shovel gouged up a ton of rubble and raised for a third time. Bill put his back to the Mack and waited defiantly. He looked up and bared his teeth at the deadly load hanging over him.

Clyde hauled on a lever. The shovel rose to its highest level, looming over the top of the dozer like a threatening fist.

Clyde shrieked in triumph and slammed the lever forward to drop the shovel onto his trapped quarry.

The shovel dropped - and then jerked to a halt. Clyde craned his neck and looked up through the safety cage. The shovel dribbled showers of rubble. Its teeth were snagged in the massive chains that had supported the fallen Mack.

Clyde swore and threw the dozer into reverse. The brute machine moved but the chains held fast and the dozer roared and twisted, like a dog thrashing furiously on the end of a leash.

Clyde threw the dozer forward again. It tilted on a wedge of uneven rubble, and Bill saw the left tread leave the ground. He watched six inches of empty space grow under the tread as it gouged at empty air.

Bill's long-buried nerd brain - and the part of him that knew the innate balance of things from years of riding a bike - saw the canted, clumsy monster and knew that it was dangerously unstable. If the idiot at the controls kept pushing it forward instead of backing off, and the chains held, then its own immense weight would make it teeter. And then all it might need is a little push...

Bill limped forward and put both hands under the left shovel arm. He took a ragged breath that made his bruised ribs scream, and pushed up with all his might.

The dozer's left tread lifted three more inches. Bill strained to his limit, forcing it up another inch – and another. Then some balance point was reached and the tread suddenly lurched three feet into the air.

The dozer rolled like a breaching whale but it didn't topple. For a moment the chains held it in place. The dozer, its tons of metal balanced on a knife edge, swayed like a punch-drunk fighter.

The chains snapped.

Bill hurled himself back as the dozer keeled over sideways. It slammed to the ground with a bone-jarring vibration. The right tread, still moving, forced the fallen shovel along the floor in an arc, gouging a five-foot-wide swath in the debris before it finally jammed. The straining transmission ground broken teeth.

Clyde, his black mask askew, dragged himself from the wrecked cab with his one good hand and slid down the slanting wall of metal. An instant later, something hot met something flammable in the guts of the dying monster.

There was a tiny cough, a hiss and then the entire machine exploded in a ball of fire.

Bill, his face demonic from the flames, laughed as he watched Clyde, his robe smoldering, scurry away like a singed rat.

The burning dozer ignited plastic and other wreckage and suddenly the diner began filling with black oily smoke. It smeared Bill's sight and finally doused his rage. He remembered the world again.

And his world was Nellie.

He turned around, looking for her but all he could see was swirling clouds of darkness.

"Nellie!" he screamed.

There was no answer but the roar of flames.

Bill put his arms out and began to struggle forward blindly. It was a bad move. He stumbled over the debris. His bad leg was clawed by vicious pieces of debris. Something hard and metallic smacked him in the forehead and he reeled. He stumbled, something sharp caught him at the knees, and he fell.

He clawed his way to his feet again, coughing. He was wrapped in a suffocating blanket of smoke.

"Nellie!" he yelled again, and that unleashed a storm of hacking. Spitting black phlegm, Bill wrenched himself forward, blinded, trying to get out of the cloud. He vaguely heard the sound of distant sirens.

The roar of flames became louder and he felt heat slap one side of his face.

"Nellie!" he tried to shout again but all that came out was a racking series of coughs. He wept black tears.

Bill's head began to swim. Each breath was a searing lungful of ashes. He wasn't getting enough oxygen, and he couldn't fight his way out of the rubble. His leg was a burning log that barely kept him upright.

With confusion and wonder, Bill felt the rise of a new emotion.

Panic.

He moved jerkily, wildly swinging his hands around him like a drowning swimmer. His leg finally collapsed and he went down hard. His face slammed into broken concrete.

He lay there, his head pounding. Panic turned into shame. He had won the fight, and now he was stupidly going to die anyway. He tried to whisper Nellie's name but could only manage a few black bubbles.

He couldn't even die with her name on his lips. Just drool. It was shitty.

His consciousness dimmed and sound dimmed with it.

Bill closed his gritty eyes.

And then he heard the roar of a motorcycle. He opened his eyes.

A headlight beam stabbed through the darkness.

"Bill!" someone shouted. "Lover! Where are you? Move it, dumbass!"

Nellie's voice was afraid and peeved, an odd combination. Bill gasped, spat black drool, and began clawing his way over the wreckage towards the light.

A shape emerged from the roiling smoke. To Bill, it was a religious vision.

It was Nellie, astride a gleaming motorcycle. She looked like a Valkyrie, riding forward to take his soul to Valhalla.

Well, at least someplace other than this shithole of a diner, Bill thought.

Nellie leaned over the handlebars and the bike glided forward, weaving skillfully through the rubble. It stopped six inches from his head. He looked up at Nellie.

"Am I dead?" he asked.

"No, lover. And I'm not either, but that could change real fast, so hop on."

She reached out a hand. Bill grabbed it and hauled himself to his feet. He touched the handlebars but Nellie shook her head and slapped the seat behind her.

Bill goggled.

"You want me to be in the bitch seat?" he asked, then collapsed in a fit of coughing.

"The *Queen* seat," Nellie corrected him. "And you can't drive with that thing in your leg. You can't get over the seat."

"Good point," Bill said, and collapsed sideways onto the back of the bike. His feet dragged on one side and his head and arms on the other as Nellie wheeled the bike around, spotted a gap in the broken wall, and throttled up. The bike bounced through the opening into the star-lit parking lot and pulled up under the disbelieving eyes of the neon trucker.

Bill looked around, dazed. A handful of semi-trailers lay on their sides, knocked over by the explosions. Bill looked at the building. The entire second story was gone. Smoke and flames poured into the summer sky. An endless stream of fire engines was pulling up, sirens wailing. Firefighters scrambled out, unrolling hoses, struggling to thread order into the chaos. Police were corralling the milling crowd. Cell phone flashes were popping off like miniature stars. A dozen ambulances were treating scratched and scorched people. Everyone seemed to be rushing somewhere.

Except for Thibideaux.

The lawyer was standing next to his flattened Mercedes. He was shouting into a cell phone. Nellie caught his eye for an instant. He shook his head, grinned ruefully and gave her a thumb's up.

A policewoman came up, glanced at the wrecked building and then back to Nellie.

"You came out of that?" she asked.

"Yep," Nellie said.

"See anyone else alive?"

"Nope," Nellie said.

"You're lucky to be alive yourself," the cop said. "The whole second story collapsed. You'd better move back. Is he hurt?" she pointed to Bill.

"No, I always ride like this," Bill said.

"Shut up," Nellie said.

The policewoman noticed Bill's wound.

"Oh, Jesus," she said and shouted for paramedics.

Two raced up, hauled Bill up with brusque gentleness and helped him hobble to an ambulance.

Nellie drove the bike slowly through the crowd. She passed a man in a security guard's uniform. He was holding what appeared to be a woman's head.

"What the fuck?" Nellie said, and then saw it was a doll's head.

The guard saw her and almost dropped it.

"Shit!" he swore. "I should have taken the redhead."

"Go away, freak!" Nellie said. The man veered away.

Nellie parked the bike next to the ambulance. Bill was laying down with his leg extending out over the back of the ambulance where a paramedic was bandaging Bill's thigh. Another was holding something that, to Nellie, looked like a blood-stained javelin.

"Bill," Nellie said. "Are you okay?"

"Fine," he said.

"Is he?" Nellie asked the paramedic, who was peering at the two-foot-long length of wood.

"Amazingly," the paramedic said. "This missed major arteries. He didn't lose much blood. We'll transport him."

Bill grunted as the other paramedic finished gift-wrapping his thigh.

"What will they do to him at the hospital?" Nellie asked.

"Well," the paramedic said. "They'll need to treat him for possible shock and he may have to stay a few days to make sure he doesn't develop a blood clot. And he'll need stitches. Has he had a tetanus shot?"

"Last year," Bill said. "Got stabbed with a rusty icepick."

"You'll have to tell me about that sometime," Nellie said. "Now lie down. They're gonna take you to the hospital."

"Fuck that," Bill said, and shrugged off the paramedic. "Let's roll."

"You need stitches, Mr. Butcher," the paramedic protested. "And antibiotics."

"Nellie can sew me up," Bill said. "And I got a friend in Tucson who can get me anything I want."

"Lover, this is not a good idea," Nellie said.

"Princess, my whole life hasn't been a good idea," Bill said. "Until I got you, that is. You and the road are the only things that will heal me."

Nellie felt hot tears threatening. She wiped the corners of her eyes with a sooty knuckle.

"You're an idiot, William Lime Butcher," she said.

Bill stood up, wincing as he put weight on his wounded leg. He shook the paramedics' hands. "I'm sure you got other people to treat," he said and pointed to the ravaged diner. "If my lawyer gets this thing rebuilt, come by for lunch." He hobbled over to Nellie.

"I didn't know you could drive," he told her.

"Never said I couldn't," Nellie said. "Just said I didn't."

Bill put a hand on the handlebars. "Mind if I...?" he asked.

She smiled and slid back onto the passenger seat as Bill gingerly mounted.

"I like the back seat,' Nellie said. "If I can put my arms around the right man."

Bill smiled. "Where we headed?"

"Wherever the highway takes us," Nellie said.

Bill smiled a second time, twice in one day, a rare event. His Bison Biters gleamed.

"Those teeth are beautiful," Nellie said. "I love to see 'em."

"Yeah. I got kicked in the face six times back there and not a chip," Bill said. He kicked the bike to life.

"Let's see what this baby can do," Bill said, and twisted the throttle. Noble Nellie rolled onto the highway under the shining moon into the warm, soap-scented night.

They rode like the wind.

EPILOGUE

Wuu found prison life less disturbing than he had expected. He'd begged for solitary but they'd refused. The prison psychologist suggested he might work towards "socialization for personal development" by interacting with other prisoners. Wuu explained that he already knew how to pick locks, set fires and kill people.

Instead, he went to the library, where he found old building codes for New Jersey government structures.

At night, after lights out, he risked the wrath of his cellmates by tapping at the walls with a spoon.

He asked if any of the Iron Pigeon Drop ninjas were being held and found out that they all were.

So in the prison yard, while ducking men with blurry tattoos and no eyebrows, Wuu collected the ninjas, by the simple expedient of performing their secret arm-waving, splay-toed *tai chi* exercises. Some of the bank robbers joined in, too.

"I have a plan," Wuu told them one day. "It turns out that this prison was built in 1933.

"That's important?" one ninja asked, between puffs on a jail cigarette made of toilet paper and pencil shavings.

Wuu gave him a hawk-eyed stare. "It is," he said. "Because they didn't use rebar."

Then, Wuu taught them to dance.

The prison recreation yard officer thought it was a fine idea when Wuu suggested it: A dance performance. He willingly opened up a vast, empty storage room on the second story, where Wuu and his team could practice. Soon, other prisoners wanted to join.

On the day of the performance, the guards herded an audience of hardcases into the room. At Wuu's nod, a guard hit the button on a portable stereo, and one hundred prisoners launched into the moves to Michael Jackson's "Thriller."

They jumped and jerked in perfect syncopation. The audience cheered and stomped. One bruiser pointed at Wuu and shouted: “I love that bitch! I want her!” until a guard Maced him.

The music reached a crescendo. The floor shook. The walls trembled. Cement dust rained down. Wuu’s dancers snapped through shoulder-swaying, foot-thumping motions, sweating, precise with the focus of true would-be ninjas.

Wuu’s cell was directly underneath the room. At the ninjas’ last leap, something cracked, the floor suddenly gave way and all one hundred dancers plunged into it, landing in a heap.

The wall of the cell was crazed with cracks and the barred window was gaping.

Wuu waited for the massed rush that smashed down the concrete. Delicately, he stepped over the grappling, thrusting bodies, and then they were all running to freedom. Wuu’s evil chortle soared ahead of them on the wind.

THE END

The following is from the forthcoming novel, *Bill the Biker—The Rise of Wuu*:

CHAPTER ONE

September 27, 2010

Swamp Gardens Memorial Park and Golf Course, Bitter Poncho Springs, Arizona.

The bride wore white and carried her mother-in-law's ashes.

Nellie Florentino was glad she was wearing gloves because the funeral urn was copper, and it was 106 degrees in the shade. Her palms still felt like barbecued flank steaks, but she was doing her best to proceed at a stately pace to the altar. However, she took the last few steps at a lumbering trot as her gloves began to smoke. The two beaming, cherubic children who were holding up the train of Nellie's dress were dragged for several feet, screaming with terror. Nellie reached the altar, knocked over the flower girl and slammed the urn down with a gasp of relief. She yanked off the scorched gloves, tossed them and blew on her fingers. Her bridesmaids, a half-dozen burly women from the Pink Slashers motorcycle club, rushed forward in a desperate bid to retrieve them. Glynis, the club president, emerged triumphant after a short but furious discussion involving switchblades and motorcycle chains. Nellie waited demurely until the wounded were dragged away, then turned and smiled warmly at her fiancé.

Bill the Biker looked like a stunned yeti, only hairier. He wore a new black leather tuxedo. Nellie had had it tailor-made as a wedding present. The jacket had steel zippers so the arms could be removed. Bill could wear it as a motorcycle vest. The pants replaced the ones that the paramedics had cut off Bill when he was wounded during an epic fight with ninjas at Bill and Nellie's diner. Bill had single-handedly defeated the Iron Pigeon Drop Fighting Ninjas that day, even toppling a bulldozer. The thought of Bill's heroics made Nellie feel warm and sweaty, although she admitted that being wrapped in fifty yards of chiffon probably helped. Still, she had a sudden urge to cut the wedding short and ride Bill like a Harley into paradise.

Bill caught the scent of her excitement. His nostrils dilated, gaping like matching railroad tunnels. His false teeth — tombstones made from genuine bison — gleamed in the harsh sunlight, blinding the entire first row of guests. His long hair, beard and eyebrows had been slicked down with a stiff coating of something like motorcycle clear coat. Nellie thought he looked like seven feet of deliciousness.

Stop it, Nellie warned herself. This wasn't about base desires. This wasn't romance; it was a wedding. Nellie had been fantasizing about her wedding since she was a girl pretending to be a princess. She'd long ago given up the thought that she needed a man to protect her — although Bill had saved her life at least twice — but Nellie still cherished the idea that getting hitched was in some sense a sacred ceremony. So, for at least the next hour, Nellie promised herself that her thoughts would remain as pure as the white dress that covered her from head to toe.

I look like a giant burrito, thought Nellie, who viewed food as sacred and could read the future from leftovers. *I'm a beautiful burrito.* She saw desire in Bill's eyes.

And hallelujah, does my baby look hungry, Nellie thought. Before she could stop herself, the tip of her tongue darted out and made a voluptuous orbit of her lips.

Bill's eyebrows crackled and his huge knuckles cracked as he reached out and took Nellie's hand. Their callouses rubbed enticingly.

For just an instant, Nellie frowned.

Maybe, she thought, *I should have told him ....*

Also by J.R. Waterbear

Bill the Biker

Bill the Biker

Standalone

Killswitch

Hollywood Bodies

About the Author

J.R. Waterbear is the pen name of authors John Pulver and Robert Jablon. They currently collaborate electronically as one lives in California and the other in the south of France. Their award-winning novel, Hollywood Bodies, is a mystery set in the music scene of the 1980s.

Read more at https://johnpulver.com/.

www.ingramcontent.com/pod-product-compliance
Lightning Source LLC
LaVergne TN
LVHW091042080826
845145LV00002B/587

* 9 7 8 1 9 6 4 0 9 4 0 9 0 *